HONOR FROM ASHES

HONOR & DUTY BOOK 3

SAM SCHALL

Copyright © 2016 by Amanda S. Green. Second Edition copyright © 2019 by Amanda S. Green (writing as Sam Schall).

E-book ISBN: 978-1-949901-30-6

Print ISBN: 978-1-949901-31-3

Hunter's Moon Press

Cover art: Spaceship and asteroid field copyright © by Luca Oleastri.

If you enjoyed this novel, please visit Nocturnal-Lives.com for more titles.

To Mom

HONOR FROM ASHES

Honor and duty above all else.

———

Grounded

———

1

"Please have a seat, Colonel. The others will join you shortly."

Before she could reply, the young lieutenant stepped back and the door slid shut. For a moment, Lt. Colonel Ashlyn Shaw stared at the door, her concern growing. It went beyond this unscheduled – and so far unexplained – summons to meet with General Helen Okafor, Commandant of the Fuerconese Marine Corps. It even went beyond the very bad memories she had of this particular conference room. Something was wrong, very wrong. She could feel it all the way down to her bones. She simply didn't know what it might be.

A frown tugged at the corners of her mouth as she looked around. Memories washed over her. Two and a half years ago, she had stood in this very same conference room, still unaware that her life was about to be turned into a living Hell. That day, the JAG officer in charge of prosecuting her and the surviving members of her squad had offered her a *deal*. If she pled guilty to all charges, he would recommend a sentence of twenty-five years – without parole – and would make sure her people served only ten years He assured her it was much better than she would get if she were found guilty of the charges that had been leveled against her. She had refused. How could she plead guilty, how could she ask her people to plead guilty, when they had done nothing wrong? Foolishly, she had believed her beloved Corps would not turn its back on her and her squad mates.

That decision had cost all of them two years in the military penal colony on Tarsus. Two long years when she believed the Corps, her family and her homeworld had turned their backs on her. She knew better now but the hurt and the distrust sometimes returned. She had no doubt it would continue until those responsible for framing her and her squad, not to mention being responsible for the deaths of their squadmates, were tried and found guilty.

But she had to put that behind her.

She *had* put it behind her.

Breathing deeply, she turned and made her way to the table in the center of the room. The only other person present watched her, his expression betraying a mixture of concern and curiosity. Seeing it, she guessed he had more idea why they had been sent for than did she. Unfortunately, that did nothing to reassure her. Experience had taught her bad things came all too often from such meetings.

"Stand easy, Ash," Admiral Richard Collins said before she could brace to attention. "Have a seat."

"Thank you, sir." She sat opposite him and smiled in appreciation as he poured her a mug of coffee the carafe someone had left.

"By any chance do you know what this is all about?"

"That's a negative, sir. I was hoping you could tell me."

She heard the uncertainty in her voice and silently cursed it. No, she cursed the reason for it. The nightmares that had plagued her might be coming with less frequency but they still lurked just beneath the surface of her self-control. They mingled with the ever-present doubt that the last few months had been nothing but a ruse and she would soon find herself back on Tarsus, once again a military prisoner. Intellectually, she knew that to be false but it was hard to put the betrayals of the past behind her.

"I guess we have to wait and see then."

Ashlyn nodded again and produced her datapad. She might have to wait to find out why she'd been sent for but that didn't mean she couldn't work. There were always reports to review or to write and assignments to be made. Even though the Devil Dogs had been groundside for almost a month, it was her job to keep them at combat readiness. Fuercon was at war and that meant they could be shipped out any time or, worse, the capital could once again come under attack.

The door once again slid open. Instantly, Ashlyn and Collins slid their chairs away from the table and stood. As they braced to attention, two others entered. They remained silent as they move to the table. Then, as the door closed and a low hum filled the room, signaling full security block had been put in place, Linden Klingsbury, Secretary of Defense, motioned for everyone to be seated.

"Thank you both for coming." His deep voice might not betray his feelings but his eyes did. Ashlyn saw the worry and something else, anger maybe, reflected in them. "I apologize for not only the early hour but also for the lack of notice in getting you here. I assure you, it was necessary. The last thing General Okafor and I want is for certain parties to start asking questions we aren't ready to answer."

He broke off as a soft tone signaled someone at the door. A moment after the admiral lowered the security screen, the door slid open. The lieutenant who had shown Ash in earlier stepped inside, followed by an ensign carrying a tray with coffee and several covered dishes on it. They quickly served coffee to the newcomers and then topped off Ash's and Collins' mugs. After making sure nothing else was needed, they left the room. Klingsbury reactivated the security screen even as he motioned for everyone to help themselves.

"Admiral, Colonel, what you are about to see and hear cannot leave this room. The only reason you are being read in right now is because this information came to us through your actions as well as the actions of your people. Your last mission gave us a treasure trove of information we are still examining. To be honest, even that isn't reason enough to read you in. However, both of you have started asking questions that show you have started putting two and two together. These questions, while valid, are best left unasked for the moment. It is my hope you will understand before you leave here."

Concern once again growing, Ashlyn reached for her mug. As she did, she thought back to that last mission. They had been lucky, probably luckier than they had any right to expect. For whatever reason, the enemy had moved out of the Cassius System, leaving only a minimal defensive presence. Whether they had been overconfident or there had been another motive, she didn't know and, frankly, she didn't care. That decision had meant First Fleet and the Devil Dogs had been able to liberate the system and rescue the POWs with minimal losses.

None of which explained what the admiral meant.

"Before we get started, I need you to confirm, on record, that none of what you are about to see or hear will leave this room without permission from either myself or General Okafor," Klingsbury continued.

For a moment, neither Collins nor Ashlyn spoke. "A point of clarification, sir," Collins said. "Does this apply to our XOs?"

"It does."

Ash frowned. She did not like keeping her XO in the dark, no matter what the information might be. That was especially true if the information could help the Devil Dogs do their duty. "General, begging your pardon, but that could put our people at a serious disadvantage."

"Ash, I understand your concerns," General Helen Okafor said. "All we are asking is you don't jump to conclusions until you have seen what we have to show you. If, after you have, you still want to discuss reading in your XOs, we will consider it."

Knowing she could ask for nothing more, Ash nodded. "Then, with that proviso, I agree."

"As do I," Collins said.

"Thank you, both of you." Klingsbury punched a code into the console in front of him and the holo display over the table came to life. The Fuerconese flag filled the display. "Admiral Collins, Colonel Shaw, the two of you, along with the men and women under your commands, have served Fuercon and its allies well. This information will help bring an end to the war, hopefully sooner rather than later. But it is not something we can move on just yet. Not without further confirmation of what it appears to represent. However, I believe that once you see this, you will understand its importance and the need for secrecy until we are ready to act.

"Help yourselves to food and then we'll get started. There is a lot for you to see and, unless I miss my guess, there will be even more to discuss," Okafor said.

Ash cast a quick glance at Collins who shrugged. Like it or not, she would just have to wait to find out why she'd been summoned to this off-the-books meeting with the Commandant of the Fuerconese Marine Corps and Secretary of Defense.

———

"Sir, we just entered the outer limits of system detection range," Tactical reported. His dark eyes burned with anticipation as he glanced at his commanding officer before quickly returning his attention to his board.

"Status?"

"No challenge yet, Commander," Comms answered.

"Order the squadron to maintain formation. Start squawking our ID. Don't give them any reason to doubt who we are – yet."

At the rear of the bridge, he sat a bit straighter in his command chair. A smile played at the corners of his mouth and his pale eyes mirrored the almost feral delight of his tactical officer as they neared their target. He watched as his senior bridge crew checked their readings, occasionally comming CIC to confirm a reading. With each moment that passed, they were closer to their goal. His expression reflected his determination to successfully complete their mission or die trying.

Seconds turned into minutes before Comms motioned for quiet. "Incoming message, Commander. We are being challenged."

"Sensor readings?" He stood and moved closer to the holo display of the Cassian System.

"They've hit us with passive scans. Wouldn't have picked them up if we hadn't been looking for them, sir." The dark-haired man kept his head down and his fingers flew across his board as he swiped from one display to another. "No indication that they suspect anything yet. Defense platforms still neutral."

"Sir, they just commed that if we don't respond, they will bring defenses to bear on us," Comms reported.

"Put on your best Fuerconese accent, Comms, and tell them we are having an issue with our short range comms. Then squawk the ID again. Let's see how far they let us come before they realize the trap has been sprung."

"Aye, Commander." He glanced over his shoulder, his expression thoughtful. "Sir, you might want to step back so you don't show on my pickup."

He nodded and moved back to the command chair. As he did, he quickly scanned the bridge, as if making sure nothing that would betray them. Then, when Comms once again signaled for silence, only the normal sounds of a merchant ship making an approach to a friendly port could be heard.

"Approach Control, this is the merchant ship *Dreki*, registered out of Halstrom's Landing. I repeat, the merchant ship *Dreki*, carrying a Halstrom's Landing registration. We were ambushed by privateers in the Radke System and have experienced extensive drive damage. Short range comms have been compromised. Request permission to dock and make repairs."

"*Dreki*, this is System Approach Control. We are unable to confirm ship's status. Resend full registration and crewing as well as damage control reports. I say again, verify ship's registration, crewing and current status."

Frustration flashed across the commander's face and was gone. As he nodded to Comms to do as instructed, the fingers of his right hand entered a series of commands into the console at his right knee.

"CIC reports defense platforms powering up, Commander."

"Tight beam to the squadron. Prepare to break formation and begin the assault."

"No." At the sound of the soft voice, all heads turned to the far end of the bridge.

"No?" The commander's tone, as well as his expression, betrayed his anger at being countermanded.

"No." A tall, thin man stepped forward. Unlike the others, he did not wear the dark blue uniform of the Callusian Navy. His black trousers and white uniform tunic stood in stark contrast to the others. His expression, however, was just as hard as the man currently trying to stare him down. "Commander Dorescu, I would recommend you continue following the battle plan. If you break formation now, you give the enemy time to respond as well as to send word to their allies that they are under attack."

"I will not allow them to bring their defense platforms online."

"I am not saying you should. However, it will take time for them to power up their defenses. That is one reason why our respective commanding officers chose this system as a target. They have become complacent and do not maintain the same level of security as others who are allied with them. But that doesn't mean we can be rash in how we approach them." He waited until Dorescu gave a curt nod. "Comms, respond that you are doing your best to comply but the damage to our systems slows our response time. Add that you have sent for your captain and are working on getting visual comms back up. Tactical, plot firing sequences on those platforms. Let's see if we can keep them from committing to action before we are in place."

"Do it!" Dorescu snapped. "If this blows up in our faces, you will be the first out of the airlock, *Advisor*."

"It won't," He glanced at the holo display, his expression thoughtful. "Comms, signal the squadron to break formation in two minutes. I repeat, break formation in two minutes. Tactical, initiate firing plan ten seconds before formation break."

Both looked to their commander for confirmation. Without a word, Dorescu nodded once.

"Give us a countdown on screen," the advisor ordered.

"System Approach Control is issuing their last warning, sir. They don't sound quite as sure of themselves as they did," Comms reported at the sixty-second mark.

"They will be a great deal less secure shortly," Dorescu grinned. "Their defense platforms?"

"Scanners show they are continuing to power up. Estimate we have two minutes before they are online."

"Sir, CIC reports LACs have scrambled and are an intercept course."

"Prepare to initiate Attack Plan Deimos."

"Attack Plan Deimos, aye, sir."

"Commander, order the squadron to break formation. Launch your LACs and take out the orbital defense platforms. Once that is done, focus on planetary defenses."

That look of frustration crossed Dorescu's face again. Then he nodded curtly. "Do it!"

"Very good, commander." The man smiled, approval and something else reflected in his eyes as he stepped forward to assume his place next to the command chair. "Your people have done well. I am confident our respective governments will reward you and your crew accordingly."

———

"WHAT THE HELL?"

Ashlyn blinked as the lights once again came up. Then, realizing she had spoken aloud, she pressed her lips together so she would say nothing else. At least her exclamation had been almost immediately echoed by Collins. A quick glance told her all she needed to know he was as surprised – and stunned – by what they had seen as was she. That should have reassured her but it didn't. Neither did her hope that it had all been part of an elaborate prank. Unfortunately, she knew neither General Okafor nor Secretary Klingsbury would joke about this.

That left one very big question unanswered. How had they managed to lay their hands on the video?

That was the first question she wanted answered. She had no doubt what they had just seen was a real time recording of the enemy's bridge during the attack on Cassius Prime. While it was the first question needing an answer, it was not the only question. Not by a long shot.

It was not, however, her question to ask. Not unless and until no one else did. So, instead of speaking up, she activated the virtual keyboard in front of her and entered a series of commands. Almost instantly, the small holo display built in for the convenience of the person sitting there came to life. A moment later, the video they had just watched started streaming. She had to be sure.

A few moments later, she stopped the feed. As she studied the image, she fought the urge to curse once again. Instead, she drew a deep breath and wondered if this was why she and Collins had been sent for.

If so, what did it mean?

"Well?" Klingsbury asked. He leaned back in his chair at the head of the table, his expression calm, his eyes alert.

"Has the vid been verified?" Collins asked in return.

"And how did we get it?" The question was out before Ash could stop it.

"To answer your question, Richard, yes, the video has been verified. Rico Santiago and his people have been working on it and other intel non-stop for the last month. They assured us this particular vid is an accurate record of what went on onboard the *Anubis* just prior to and during the attack on Cassius Prime. They found nothing to indicate the feed had been altered in any manner."

Ash studied the Secretary of Defense, her expression thoughtful. One month, he'd said. Approximately the length of time First Fleet and the Devil Dogs had been back in the home system after their last assignment. It could be a coincidence but she doubted it. So what did it mean?

"As for how we obtained the feed, we have you and your people to thank for it," Okafor took up. "It was among the data you recovered on your last mission. From what we've been able to tell so far, the *Anubis* downloaded the ship's logs as well as other data before leaving the system with most of the other ships that had been stationed there. Apparently, the Callusians hadn't expected us to make an attempt to liberate the system."

Ashlyn nodded, her mind racing as she thought back to when she first received orders for the Devil dogs to retake the Cassius System. Now that she thought about it, she had been surprised the operation had been Fuerconese only. At the time, she had decided it was because Fuercon and its allies were still ramping up to full mobilization with the resumption of hostilities with the Callusians. She also remembered from the last war how some of their allies felt it more important to protect their home systems than it was to take the battle to the enemy. Now she wondered if there had been more to it than that.

Much more.

"General, I assume you and the other senior officers have been over this frame by frame." It wasn't a question even if she tried to frame it as such.

"We have."

Ashe typed in a command and, a moment later, the image she had stopped the feed on appeared on the main holo screen.

"I also assume I'm not dreaming or imaging this." She pointed to the image. As she did, she found herself almost hoping they did tell her she had imagined it. That would be much easier to deal with than the alternative.

"Unfortunately, Ash, it is very real." Okafor sounded as worried as she felt. Before Ash could say anything else, Okafor looked at Klingsbury who gave an almost imperceptible nod. "For the moment, let's leave rank and all that behind us. Linden and I want to hear your honest opinions about what you've just seen and how you think we should respond. That includes you, Richard."

"It's simple really," Collins said and there could be no mistaking his anger. "We rally our forces, deal with the Callusians once and for all and then we deal with this betrayal." He jabbed a finger in the direction of the frozen image.

"I wish it were that simple," Klingsbury said.

"If I may?" Ash waited for the others to nod before continuing.

"Assuming there is no subterfuge with regard to the uniform he is wearing, it is clear this *advisor* is a member of the Midlothian Naval Defense Force."

Another nod from both Klingsbury and Okafor.

"From my security briefings, Midlothian has maintained its allied status with Fuercon but has not committed much in the way of material, ordinance or manpower to the war effort as of yet."

"All true but not unexpected. It didn't do all that much in the last war, Ash. Its key importance then was in keeping the trade routes open in that sector of space and making sure our ships were free from attack."

Now Collins nodded, his expression thoughtful. "Do we have an ID on this *advisor*?"

"A tentative one," Okafor said. "Santiago didn't want to search too deeply and risk tipping our hand to the Midlothians in case our suspicions are correct."

Suspicions? Ash almost snorted. She had no suspicions. She knew the Midlothians were involved. But how deeply and to what extent still had to be determined.

"Based on what Rico and his people found, we are reasonably certain the man in the vid is one Commander Bernard Hughes. He was one of their few squadron commanders in the last war who actually engaged the enemy when he had the chance. Afterwards, he fell off the screen and it was assumed he had left the Navy. Obviously, we were wrong," Okafor said.

"It seems safe to assume at least part of the Midlothian Navy is involved." Ash thought for a moment. "I will leave it to Rico and his people to figure out how deep the betrayal runs. I will say this. I think we now know why the Callusians suddenly changed tactics after so long and how they have managed to get their hands on newer ships and weapons."

One question answered and a hell of a lot more suddenly there to take its place.

"I understand why you would prefer us to not ask the questions we've been asking, at least not outside of these walls." Collins' voice turned hard and Ash waited, wondering how the others would answer.

"Yes, but not for the reasons you might think." Klingsbury held up a hand before either Collins or Ash could say anything. "Richard, Ashlyn, we aren't asking you to ignore this. Nor are we asking for any sort of cover up. Far from it, in fact."

Before anything more could be said, Okafor motioned for silence. She listened closely to something coming in over her comm link. Then she glanced at Klingsbury. The look that passed between them was enough to warn Ash that another bombshell of some sort was about to drop.

A moment later, the door slid open. As it did, Okafor came to her feet. "Atten-shun!" she barked.

"Stand easy, everyone," President Derek Harper said as he stepped inside. The door slid shut behind him. "Please, sit."

Habit, born from her years as a Marine as well as growing up with Marine parents, kicked in. Ashlyn sat with her spine ramrod straight, her booted feet flat on the floor. One simply did not slouch in the presence of the President, especially not when he had been instrumental in clearing her and her people of the false charges leveled against them.

"I take it they reacted as we expected?" Harper took his place at the table and shook his head when Okafor lifted the coffee carafe in question.

"Yes, sir," Klingsbury replied. "Admiral Collins had just asked why they were being read into this."

"Then my timing is perfect." He nodded to them, his expression serious. "As I'm sure Linden and Helen assured you, we aren't asking you to forget your suspicions or to quit asking questions. Quite the contrary, in fact. The two of you, along with a few others, have been saying from the beginning – hell, let's be honest. You raised questions during the last war and were ignored. I'm not foolish enough to make the same mistakes my predecessor did. You've asked if there wasn't more to what's been going on than we knew or suspected. The recording you just saw, as well as other material you will be read in on, confirms that there is.

"What I am requesting, as your president, is that you review the materials and then give us your honest opinions of what our next course of action should be. We will meet tomorrow to discuss your recommendations. I'd prefer today, to be honest, but I can't and won't ask you to alter your schedules in any way that might alert anyone that we are on to our so-called allies. That means, I'm afraid, no deviation from your schedules once you leave here."

"We understand, sir," Collins said and Ash nodded in agreement.

"The only others who have been read into this so far are Lt. Colonel Santiago and his team, Brigadier General Shaw and Admiral Tremayne. You may confer with them if need be. We will meet again in the morning to discuss your impressions and recommendations."

"I would request permission to brief our XOs about this, Mr. President," Collins said.

"Not yet, Admiral. We need to make sure we are on the same page before we read anyone else into this," Harper replied.

"For the moment, both First Fleet and the Devil Dogs will remain in the home system. It is being put out to our allies that some of your ships are in for repairs and refitting, Richard. Ashlyn, your excuse is simpler and has the expediency of being the truth. You and your Devil Dogs are here until the trials of Sorkowski, O'Brien and the others are concluded. The reality is that I want our best Marines in-system in case the enemy decides to try to attack here."

"As you wish, sir." She agreed the Devil Dogs were the best to defend the planet's surface in case of attack but she did not look forward to the upcoming trials.

Harper glanced at his wrist unit and grimaced slightly. "It's time to wrap this up before your staffs – and mine – start asking where we are. Richard, Ashlyn, we wouldn't know what we're potentially facing if it weren't for what you and your people did that last mission. Thank you."

With that, he stood and, before they could brace to attention, he was gone. As the door slid shut, Ash blew out a breath. Then she once again turned her attention to the others.

"Everything we have so far is on these." Okafor handed Ash a data chip while Klingsbury gave one to Collins. "These are classified, needless to say."

"Aye, ma'am." Ash's fingers closed over the data chip. She thought for a moment and then reached inside her collar with her unencumbered hand. A moment later she pulled her dog tags over her head. Okafor watched as she carefully slid the data chip into a small notch in one of the tags, embedding it there until she released it. As she slid the dog tags back on, Okafor nodded in approval.

"Dismissed, Colonel. I know you have morning PT scheduled with Alpha Company. Let's not have them wondering why you aren't there." The general's grin told Ash all she needed to know Okafor approved of her doing PT with her Marines.

"Ma'am, Admiral." She braced to attention, executed a perfect about face and left the room.

She had a lot to think about and somehow she had to get through the day without letting on to those who knew her best that there might be anything wrong.

2

"Care to tell me what's been bothering you all day, ma'am?"

Ashlyn looked up from the report she had been reading and frowned slightly to see her executive officer leaning against the doorframe. For one moment, she fought the urge to tell Captain Lucinda Ortega nothing was wrong. Tempting as that might be, she knew better. Ortega had held her tongue through PT as well as the series of briefings that had followed. Then there was the simple fact they had known one another too long for Ortega to fall for the lie. Besides, Ashlyn had been expecting – and dreading, if she were to be honest – the question. More than once during the morning, she had caught her XO watching her, her expression troubled. What surprised her was that it had taken Ortega so long to ask.

"It's just been a long day already, Luce," she hedged. She hoped her friend would let it drop but one look at her former roommate's expression told her the likelihood of that happening was about the same as her suddenly sprouting wings and taking flight.

"Ash, don't give me that."

Ortega moved further into the small office and waited for the door to slide shut behind her. As she did, Ashlyn didn't try to hide her sigh. One thing all her officers knew was that she kept an open door policy. If the door was shut, it meant something serious was taking place behind it. That Ortega now closed the door told her the XO meant to find out what was going on.

"I'm not *giving* you anything." A hint of frustration colored her voice as she motioned Ortega to a seat. "It has been a long day. It started with me not sleeping well and it's gone steadily downhill from there." That much was the truth.

Ortega studied her for a moment, her expression no longer as stubborn as it had been. "The trial?" she asked simply.

Ashlyn nodded. Then she leaned forward, elbows on the desk and her chin resting on her fists. "Let's just say the nightmares are a bit closer to the surface than they have been lately." Which was an understatement. The memories of her time at the Tarsus penal colony, as well as of the farce of a court martial that sent her and the others there, haunted her. The courts martial of those responsible couldn't get there soon enough.

"What does Liu say?"

"He tells me there's nothing to worry about."

A slight smile touched her lips as she remembered her last discussion with Lieutenant Jianyu Liu. The JAG officer had all but rubbed his hands together and licked his lips in anticipation. Over the last few months, Ash had come to realize he hated the corrupt officers who had set her up as much as she did. Liu valued duty and honor almost as much as Ashlyn did. Neither of them doubted that Sorkowski and O'Brien had tarnished both through their actions. The only questions left unanswered were if they had been solely motivated by profit or if they had turned traitor to Fuercon and, after the meeting that morning, Ashlyn couldn't help wondering if that might not be the case.

Not that she could say anything about it to Liu or to anyone else – yet.

"You know he's right. He's built an airtight case against those bastards, Ash." Ortega's eyes flashed and Ashlyn nodded.

"I know but, after what happened the last time, I won't be able to rest easy until the verdicts are read and those sons of bitches are on their way to Tarsus or one of the other penal colonies." Even then, it would take time for her to forgive those who had turned a blind eye to what had happened. At least they were no longer in positions where they could betray her, or anyone else, ever again.

"What's the timeline now?"

Ashlyn didn't smile, not quite. Ortega knew exactly when each of her pre-trail meetings with Liu or one of his co-counsels were scheduled. That was part of her XO's job description. It went beyond that, however. Not only did Ortega go above and beyond when it came to her work as the battalion's XO, she had also been trained as an intelligence officer. So she had more than a passing understanding of what had been done to build the cases against Rear Admiral Alec Sorkowski (ret.) and Major Thomas O'Brien.

Besides, Ortega had been one of those who had worked behind the scenes, risking her own career, in an effort to discover exactly what had happened on that last mission. The information she dug up had been used to help free Ash and the others.

"Nothing's changed, at least not as far as I know. I meet with Liu and his team one last time the first of next week. Their courts martial starts a week after that. If Sorkowski and O'Brien continue to fight the charges against them, Liu said he thinks it will take at least two weeks to present the evidence that's been put together against them. He's told the powers that be that I will not be able to leave the system for at least another month or two." Now she did sigh. As much as she appreciated having time with her family, and especially with her son, Fuercon was at war. The Devil Dogs should not be held dirtside when they were needed on the front lines. "As Liu reminded me last week, even after the cases against Sorkowski and O'Brien are heard, there are at least two other trials he needs me here for. Any others that might follow, he will use my recorded statements and previous testimony."

Ortega nodded. "Does he think there's a chance any of them will plead out?"

"He doesn't seem to think so." She lifted one shoulder in a shrug. "What would they gain by doing so? Liu and his superiors have made it clear they aren't going to deal the charges down. From what they've told me, not to mention what they've told the Commandant and others higher up the chain of command, they want both Sorkowski and O'Brien to serve the maximum terms available– and that is assuming they aren't found guilty of treason. If they are, they will be lucky to avoid the death penalty."

Another nod from Ortega.

"Since you're here, there is a change to my schedule you need to know about. I'll be late coming in tomorrow." Ash did her best to sound apologetic. "I promised Jake I'd take him to school. Besides, I need to talk with his teacher. Mr. Uzun sent a message last night that he's been having some problems with Jake."

"Is he all right?" Ortega's concern for her godson was obvious.

"He's fine." Ashlyn smiled a little ruefully. "My son has decided that he doesn't need to go to school. He would much rather come to work with me and he has made that quite clear to anyone who will listen. He even tried sneaking away from campus when he thought no one was watching."

Now it was Ortega's turn to smile. "I think we all know why."

Ashlyn nodded. As bad as the two years on Tarsus had been for her, in many ways they had been harder on her son. He had been too young to understand why his mother had been taken away and why he couldn't see her or talk to her via comm-link. Since her return, he'd watched her leave twice more. Fortunately, both times had been relatively short missions and she had received leave once home. Now, however, he wanted to be with her as much as he could, even if it meant missing school.

"Not that it helps any."

"I'm sure you will figure it out, Ash."

Ortega might have sounded reassuring but Ashlyn saw the amusement in her eyes. Not that she blamed her friend. At least she could ask her parents to back her up when trying to convince Jake he had to go to school. She just hoped neither of them remembered how she had tried to pull the same thing when she was Davey's age.

"Right." She chuckled softly and then turned serious. "Since we are going to be stuck here for another couple of months, FleetCom has decided the Devil Dogs are to act as system security. We both know how boring that can be. So we need to keep our people on their toes."

Ortega nodded and reached for her data pad. Ashlyn relaxed, relieved her XO had decided not to push any more about why she had been so preoccupied.

"It's not the first time the DDs have been held back, Ash, and certainly won't be the last."

"I know. I don't have to like it though." Another shrug and a slight smile. She knew Ortega understood. "So, how did Bravo Company do on the latest proficiency tests?" She pulled up the training the schedule they had worked out the week before as she waited for Ortega to respond.

"Better but they still aren't near the level they should be." Ortega looked no happier than Ashlyn felt at the XO's response. "To be honest, Ash, I wouldn't want them backing up the crew on any ship I happened to be on right now."

Ashlyn frowned. The response worried her. The Devil Dogs had been in-system a little over a month and, in that time, all the companies, with the exception of Bravo, had managed to maintain or improve their scores. Bravo, on the other hand, had done more than slip. There were any number of explanations, none of which made Ash, as battalion commander, feel better.

Before Ortega could say anything else, Ash motioned for her to wait. For a moment, she considered her options. Then, a slight smile touched her lips as she quickly sent off a message to Admiral Collins. Since he and First Fleet were stuck in-system as well, maybe he would be willing to help her out.

"Ash, what are you up to?"

"Nothing much, just doing what I can to figure out what's going on with Bravo Company." She quickly entered a response to Collins before turning her attention back to her XO. "I've just issued orders for Bravo to report to First Fleet, 103rd BatCruRon by 0600 tomorrow. Once onboard, they are to report to Gunnery Sergeant Andrew Noffsinger. The gunny will be filled in on what I am expecting from Bravo over the next few weeks."

"Care to fill me in?"

"Even if I didn't want to, I'd have to." Ashlyn waited for Ortega to nod in understanding. "You and Adamson are to accompany Bravo but only as monitors. I know Noffsinger by reputation but have never served with him. Admiral Collins trusts him and, from what I remember of conversations with Loco, he does as well. But I want you and MJ there to be my eyes and ears."

"Understood."

"I want to know how they do in the sims as well as in live exercises. Noffsinger and the squadron commander will be informed that I want Bravo put into positions of having to fill in for their Naval counterparts, just as they might be expected to during a real battle." She paused, knowing she didn't need to say the next bit but wanting to make sure there were no misunderstandings. "Push them, Luce. I need to know if the drop in their efficiency and proficiency ratings is because they are simply slacking off or if there is a deeper issue I have to deal with."

"Will you be briefing MJ and me before we leave?"

"Negative. You know what I expect." Now she grinned. "Hell, Luce, you will probably be harder on them than I would and we both know MJ most definitely will be. Just don't let her space any of them simply because they are being idiots."

Not that Adamson would, even if the *idiots* might prefer it. The master sergeant had earned her reputation of being one of the toughest non-coms in the Corps.

"And you?"

Ash knew what her friend meant. She also knew Ortega had every right to ask, both as her XO and as her best friend.

"Even if I didn't fully expect you and MJ to tell Talbot that he is to stick with me while you are with Bravo Company, I know better than to leave my back exposed. He'll fill in for you while you're gone."

Ortega's expression told Ash all she needed to know her guess had been right.

"Luce, I don't like having a shadow, much less a babysitter. However, I'm not quite as trusting as I used to be." She held up a hand to stop her XO from interrupting. "Sorkowski and O'Brien might be in custody but I don't believe for one moment they don't have contacts on the outside. The closer we get to the trial, the more they have to lose. The easiest way to sabotage the case against them is for something to happen to me. I don't plan to let that happen. Why do you think I haven't objected to the extra guards you've put on me? More importantly, why do you think I've increased security around my family?"

Instead of saying anything, Ortega simply nodded once. "Sorry, Ash. I worry. You know that."

Ashlyn nodded. The hardest part of reclaiming her life after being pardoned had been trying to convince her friends and family that she didn't need them constantly trying to protect her. Intellectually, she understood why they felt that need. What she couldn't get them to realize was that she had a hard enough time returning to the life she thought gone without wondering if they knew something she didn't. Maybe now Ortega would take a step back. Ash doubted it, but she could hope.

"And I do appreciate it." Even if she felt smothered at times. Before she could say anything else, her comm signaled an incoming message. As she scanned it, her expression turned hard.

"What?" Ortega's expression matched Ashlyn's as she watched her friend scan the message.

"It seems Captain Krumholtz is questioning my orders, respectfully of course." She all but spat out the words.

"Damn it." Ortega spoke softly but Ash heard her frustration. "I thought we'd dealt with the slackers before our last mission."

"So did I." Ash breathed deeply. She did not need to jump to conclusions. After all, there might be a reason why the captain had concerns about the company's new assignment. She had to remember that. "So let's give him the chance to explain. Tag MJ and tell her to meet us in the armory ASAP. Bravo Company should be there prepping for some range time."

While Ortega did as instructed, Ash stood. This was part of the job of battalion commanding officer she hated. Even so, she knew it was a necessary part.

"She'll meet us there," Ortega said a few moments later.

"Let's go."

Perversely pleased to have something else to think about other than the morning's unexpected briefing, Ashlyn left her office. It was time to remind everyone exactly what the Devil Dogs were all about.

3

Alexander Watchman sat at the far end of the table and listened to the latest report about the renewed hostilities with the Callusians. Outwardly, he looked at concerned and, at the same time, relieved, as the other present for the briefing. Inwardly, he fumed. How could the Fuerconese have taken such a bold step without any of his operatives finding out? Worse, he had someone on Fuercon who was supposed to be in the position to warn him of exactly this sort of thing happening. Their failure to learn what their so-called allies planned was bad enough. Worse was the possibility the operative had chosen not to pass the information along to him.

As much as he wanted to excuse himself and leave the briefing, he couldn't. No one else there would understand his need to find out exactly where the failure in communication had happened. They wouldn't understand because they weren't part of his plan. It went beyond them not being read in. It went far beyond that.

His actions, and the actions of a handful of others strategically placed in the government and military could be seen as treason. The current leadership did not understand the need for Midlothian to cut ties with Fuercon and its other allies. Years of being satisfied with taking what was basically a stance of neutrality in the conflict between the Fuerconese and the Callusians, the government had forgotten that, once the war was decisively finished, their own interests would be impacted. No longer would the Fuerconese need to use their shipping lanes to avoid Callusian-held space. The fact the Fuerconese had moved to retake the Cassius System should have opened the government's eyes. Instead, the Prime Minister and his advisors were heaping praise on their allies for taking such a bold step. They didn't even question why Fuercon had acted alone instead of calling for assistance from any of its allies.

So it was up to him and those like him to keep the conflict alive, no matter what they had to do to accomplish the goal. The financial survival of Midlothian demanded it.

An hour later, he returned to his office. Before his aide could say anything, he said he wasn't to be disturbed. They could discuss any messages that had come in during his absence later. For now, he had work to do.

Secure in his private office, the security screens in place, Midlothian's Intelligence Czar pulled up the latest reports from Fuercon. As he studied them, he frowned slightly. He'd had concerns about their operative there for some time now. In fact, if he were to be honest with himself, he had worried about her from the beginning. He disliked using independent contractors for this sort of work but Evan Moreau had a spotless reputation. She did the job, no matter what it was, and never left any trace back to herself or who employed her. More importantly, he had trained her personally. So he knew what she was capable of.

This time, however, she had disappointed him. From the beginning of the mission, she had seemed off her game. Maybe it had been a mistake to send her back to Fuercon, her homeworld. But she had turned her back on the system long ago, just as it had done to her. Whatever the cause, she had been warned about the consequences of failure.

His frown deepening, he reached for his comm and sent a quick, two-word message. *It's time.*

Ten minutes later, a slim, nondescript man sat across the desk from him. To the casual observer, he looked like any other office drone. Watchman knew better.

"Sir?"

"You need to get to Fuercon as quickly as possible, Martyn." Watchman slid a data disc across the desktop in his direction.

For a moment, the man said nothing. His fingers closed around the small disk before carefully placing it in the left thigh pocket of his trousers. "Does this concern our mutual friend?"

Even in the safety of the office, he didn't name Moreau and Watchman smiled slightly. Martyn Baudin took no chances. That was why, when Watchman retired from field work, he had recommended Baudin as his replacement. When he had become the Intelligence Czar, he'd reached out to Baudin and tapped him as his "special operations advisor". In other words, Baudin did those jobs Watchman never wanted to be whispered about, much less make the official "book".

"It is." He allowed the frown of frustration he hadn't dared allow to be seen during the earlier briefing to show. "Fuercon managed to liberate the Cassius System," He paused and nodded as Baudin started almost imperceptibly in surprise.

"Sir, you have confirmation on that?"

"I just came from a briefing with the Prime Minister and his other advisors on just that." He waited a moment to let that sink in. "Before you ask, I did not have prior warning from our friend on Fuercon."

Baudin nodded once, his expression grim.

"She has been a disappointment for us both," Baudin said.

This time, Watchman nodded. While he had approved Moreau as their operative, Baudin had been the one to recommend her. The fact she continued to fall short in carrying out her orders looked bad, not only for her but for Baudin as well. That was one reason why Watchman would let Baudin redeem himself by dealing with her. If he failed, well, Watchman would deal with him personally. No one disappointed the Intelligence Czar twice.

"Deal with her. Make sure her mission is completed and no loose ends are left." So simple and yet open to interpretation. How Baudin responded would tell him a great deal.

"Do you want me to make a statement with her?"

"No, not this time." Much as he would like doing just that, it presented too much danger.

"Disappearance or accident?"

"Suicide. She's been sloppy and things very well might be traced back to her. Let them end with her as well." He paused, thinking hard. "We can't let her activities lead back to us, Martyn. Suicide would be preferable because it would end all inquiries, especially if she leaves a note. Her reputation for being ruthless when it comes to business is well-known on Fuercon. I have little doubt that most everyone would accept the explanation that she had been profiteering from the war.

"However, if you need to take more *direct* measures to get information from her, I will understand. As I said, I want no loose ends left. How you do that, I'll leave up to you."

"And what of Sorkowski and the others she used and who are now about to stand trial?"

For a moment, Watchman didn't respond. It would be best if the former admiral and those charged with him were removed from the equation. Unfortunately, the fallout from such action would be worse than leaving them alive. One *accident* could be overlooked. But more than one, especially when the targets were in custody, would only bring unwanted attention, attention Watchman and his allies couldn't risk turning in their direction.

"Confirm that they can't lead the Fuerconese back to this office. My gut tells me they can only lead back to Moreau. If that is the case, then they can live. If not, well, we will deal with it when we have to. Moreau, for the moment, is your main concern."

"I understand, sir." Baudin stood. "I will be off-planet by end of day."

"Very good, Martyn. You know what I expect. Let me know when it's done."

4

Ashlyn slid out of bed, not bothering to call for lights. It might be early but she had been unable to fall back to sleep. Who was she kidding? She had been unable to sleep. She might have dozed a little, here and there, but her mind had not rested. Now, with everything playing over and over again in her head, she might as well get up and try to get some work done.

Ten minutes later, she closed the doors to the small room that had become her study since her return from Tarsus. She knew she should find an apartment for her and Jake. She also knew she wasn't ready, not yet. After two years of what could only be considered solitary confinement, of only seeing those in charge of keeping her prisoner, she needed to be around her family. More importantly, at least to her, she wanted Jake to have the stability living with her parents gave them both. Maybe after the war was over, assuming she survived, they would find themselves a nice apartment somewhere. Until then, they would stay where they were.

"I see you got about as much sleep as I did."

Ashlyn looked up and shook her head to see her mother standing in the doorway. Then she smiled slightly. The fact she had not heard her mother open the door proved she was finally starting to relax and trust again, at least where her family was concerned. That had been very difficult when she had first returned from the penal colony. Distrust, even of those she knew had nothing to do with the false charges that had been brought against her, mingled with that sense of waiting for the other shoe to drop. Having been shoved into a fire-fight without warning had done nothing to help either. At least that nightmare was over, her conviction purged and she had been returned to duty.

Only to face another nightmare, one she had suspected but hoped had been nothing more than the product of her own paranoia.

"Kind of hard to relax after looking at all this." Ashlyn waved her hand at the comp display and the notes she had made as she reviewed the data General Okafor had given her.

"Agreed." Brigadier General Elizabeth Shaw, looking nothing like the seasoned Marine she happened to be in her deep blue kimono, closed the door behind her before moving to sit in one of the two chairs situated before the desk. "But it is what you and Richard have been warning us about, even if it comes from a quarter I doubt even you had considered."

"Believe me, I most definitely hadn't suspected it."

"None of us had." Elizabeth paused as a knock sounded at the door. A moment later, the door opened and Marie Leclerc, the family's long-time housekeeper, entered. She carried a tray with coffee, mugs and an assortment of fruit on it. After serving, she left the study, telling them to let her know if they needed anything else.

"How does she do it, Mom?" Ash grinned as she poured coffee for the two of them. "How does she always know the moment one of us is up?"

"I have no idea. I asked your father once. He suggested that she has somehow managed to tag each of us with transmitters that signal her the moment we leave our rooms."

"However she does it, I'm glad for the coffee. I need it this morning." She blew across the top of her mug and took a careful sip before sighing in contentment. Then she turned serious again. "When did you find out?"

"About an hour before you did."

"Ouch." Ashlyn winced as she realized that meant her mother wouldn't have been up for long, if at all, when Okafor contacted her.

Elizabeth nodded, her expression grim. "Speaking of which, we are expected in the Commandant's office in an hour and a half."

Ashlyn nodded. She had been expecting the summons. "Uniform?"

"BDUs."

Another nod. It made sense. If she and her mother showed up in anything else, questions would be asked. "All right. I told Lucinda that I would be late today."

"How did you manage to slip your handlers?" Now Elizabeth smiled and Ash grinned in return.

"She and MJ are accompanying Bravo Company on a training assignment and should be preparing to rendezvous with First Fleet, 103rd BatCruRon. I arranged it with Admiral Collins yesterday after getting Bravo's latest ratings."

"Very good." Elizabeth nodded and then grinned mischievously. "And it keeps you from having to explain what's going on and why you look so tired and worried."

"Only from the two of them. You know Luce. She put Talbot on notice that he is to be my shadow until she gets back."

"She's only doing her job," Elizabeth said.

"I know, but I don't have to like it."

"Then you might as well contact him and tell him to meet us at the Commandant's office."

"Ma'am?"

"Don't look at me. Her aide commed me a few minutes ago. Said I was to make sure you and I, as well as our XOs, were present at the meeting." She held up a hand. "And no, we aren't free to brief them ahead of time."

"Should I call Lucinda back? I can send Talbot in her place. In fact, it might be better if I did."

For a moment, Elizabeth didn't respond. Ashlyn waited, recognizing the expression on her mother's face. Elizabeth was weighing her request, not at her mother but as her commanding officer. "Do it."

Hoping she managed to catch her XO before Ortega left for the 'port, Ashlyn sent the message. Then she turned her attention back to her mother. "Is there anything else you can tell me?"

"No. You know as much as I do about what's going on."

She doubted it, not that she would say so. Instead, she leaned back sipped her coffee. If they had to be in the Commandant's office in less than an hour and a half, they didn't have much time to waste.

"Mom, I think you need to call Kate home. I have a feeling things are going to get very bad before this war is over."

"Your father and I talked about it last night."

Ash nodded. Not once did she think her mother had broken confidence and told her father what was going on. But her father had been a Marine, a Devil Dog, like the two of them. He knew how to read the signs. More importantly, he understood the realities of war. He would want his youngest daughter home, hopefully well away from the fighting, especially with Ashlyn and her brothers, as well as Elizabeth, all on active duty.

"And?"

"He sent word to her before we went to bed."

"Let me guess. He used the same code then that he used when we were growing up and one of you wanted to let us know there was trouble and we were to get home ASAP." Back then, it had usually meant one or the other of their parents had been ordered to ship out. Once her father retired from the Corps, it had been used to warn the children that war was breaking out or heating up and that they were to return to Fuercon as soon as they could.

"Good." She hoped her sister would understand and return to the home system without delay.

"Unless we want to be late, we'd both better get ready." Elizabeth stood and started out the room. Then she stopped and turned to look back at her daughter. "Ash, we will get to the bottom of this."

She nodded, understanding all her mother left unsaid. "I know, Mom."

Even if Intel didn't, she would. She had a feeling in the pit of her stomach that the data they had recovered on Cassius Prime was somehow tied to what happened to her and her people. If that were the case, she planned to find out why. She owed it to those who had died following her as well as to those sent to the penal colony with her.

An hour later Ash stood in the same conference room she had been in just the day before. Unlike then, the room felt crowded. An ensign she didn't recognize moved around the room, offering those gathered coffee or tea. The lieutenant from the day before stood near the head of the table and she guessed he was making sure everything was ready for the briefing. Admiral Collins caught her eye and nodded once, his expression as grim as she felt. Then he turned his attention back to Admiral Miranda Tremayne. Standing nearby were their XOs.

Also present were Elizabeth and Lt. Colonel Rico Santiago. They stood a few feet away, softly talking. Ash had no doubt her mother was grilling the Intelligence officer. Not that she blamed Elizabeth. She would give just about anything for a few minutes alone with her former commanding officer. She had served with Santiago when she was fresh out of the Academy. They had stayed in touch over the years, even after he transferred to Intel. Like so many others, Santiago had worked behind the scenes to clear Ashlyn and her team. She owed him even though she knew he would disagree.

"What's going on, Ash?" Ortega asked softly as she joined Ashlyn. "I was halfway to the port when I got your message."

Ash gave a quick jerk of her head, motioning for her XO to come with her. Not that there was any real privacy for them in the small conference room.

"I can't tell you, Luce." She held up a hand when Ortega opened her mouth to interrupt. "I *can't*." She stared at her XO until Ortega nodded slightly, understanding reflected in her eyes. "You will find out soon enough. Listen closely and be ready to ask any and all questions you have. I promise we will discuss this once we're done here."

Assuming, of course, that they were allowed to discuss it even then.

Before anything else could be said, the door slid open. Almost immediately, Elizabeth called everyone to attention. As she did, Klingsbury, Okafor and President Harper entered the room, followed by their aides and the President's security detail.

"Have a seat, everyone," Harper told them as he took his place at the head of the table. Okafor moved to the chair on his right and Klingsbury the one of his left. "We have a lot to discuss, so let's get down to work."

Ash waited as those senior to her were seated before taking her seat at the table. As those junior to her sat, she waited. What new bombshells were the President and the others about to drop on them?

"Yesterday, Secretary Klingsbury, General Okafor and I met with Admiral Collins and Colonel Shaw. At that time, they were ordered not to discuss the reason for that meeting. You are each going to be read into the situation. Fuercon's war with the Callusians has taken a turn none of us anticipated, as you are about to see."

He nodded to the lieutenant and the lights went down. A moment later, the holo display came to life. Ash wasn't surprised when the vid she and Collins had seen the day before filled the display. Even though she had watched it several times already, she did not look away. Maybe this time, it would give her some of the answers they were all looking for.

———

"Now you see why I said the war has taken an unanticipated turn," President Harper said as the lights came back up.

"This has been verified?" Captain Jareau, Collins' XO, asked. "Sir."

"It has." The President looked to Santiago and nodded. "Colonel?"

"This is one of a number of items retrieved by our forces when we retook the Cassius System," the Intelligence officer began. "From what we have been able to determine, the Anubis, as well as the other ships in the Callusian force, downloaded much of their logs before leaving the system. Under orders from SecDef, I formed a team and we have been going over everything our people found."

"Sir, I'm not questioning you or your people, but is there any way this could have been faked?" Concern filled Ortega's voice. Ash heard it and understood. If what they suspected was correct, they were about to find themselves fighting a war against not only the Callusians but a so-called ally as well.

"It is real, Captain, much as I wish it weren't." Santiago punched a command into his virtual keyboard and the holo display once more came to life. Frozen before them was the image of the Midlothian "advisor". "We have identified him as Commander Bernard Hughes. You will find all the information we have on him in the data that has just been sent to your stations. Unfortunately, it isn't complete because, as Admiral Collins and Colonel Shaw were told yesterday, we haven't wanted to alert our *allies* to the fact we might be onto them."

"Do we know if he is there as a sanctioned agent of the government or if he is acting on his own?" Tremayne asked.

"Ma'am, we don't have a confirmed answer to your question."

And that, Ashlyn knew, was the polite way of saying they had suspicions but no solid proof.

"In the information found on Cassius Prime, did we get any schematics or other similar information about the enemy ships?" Ash asked.

"Would that help?" Harper asked in return.

For a moment, no one answered. Then, a smile playing at the corners of her mouth, Tremayne nodded. "I think I know what the good colonel is getting at. All of us in this room have been part of discussions about the changes in how the enemy has acted since hostilities resumed. She might be a mere Marine." Now she grinned and Ashlyn fought the urge to stick her tongue out at the woman she had known most of her life. While her parents had been proud Ash followed in their steps when she joined the Corps, Tremayne had always made it clear she hoped her godchild would join the Navy. "None of us could put our finger on why, but the enemy has changed tactics, and they have had ships and weapons more advanced than they should have been able to get their hands on, even under the farce of the cease fire."

"So, if we know more specifics about the ships or their weaponry, we might be able to trace them back to the Midlothians," Jareau finished for her.

"Exactly." Ash frowned in thought and then turned in her chair to face Santiago. "Well?"

"Negative, at least so far. We are still deciphering some of the data you and your people managed to secure."

"How do we proceed with this information?" Collins asked. "And can we read our staffs in yet?"

Everyone looked to the President. He, in turn, looked to Okafor, his expression grim. "Admiral Tremayne and Second Fleet will be shipping out by end of week. Once you are out of the system, Admiral, you may brief your senior officers. The rank and file do not need to know. Not yet, at any rate. You may, however, tell your personal staff with the proviso that they understand they are not to discuss this matter with anyone you do not personally approve."

"Understood, sir." The redhead made a quick note on her datapad.

"Admiral Collins, First Fleet is going to resume its position as system defense. That allows your ships to finish making repairs."

"I understand, sir, and had already issued orders along those lines pursuant to our discussion yesterday."

"Excellent." Now the President looked at Ashlyn and she fought the urge to swallow hard. Something about his expression worried her. For a moment, the paranoia flared. She stomped it down, reminding herself that he had fought for her freedom as much as any of the others in the room had.

"Sir, let me," Okafor said almost gently. "It's for me to do."

"Ma'am?" Ash gave a quick, almost imperceptible shake of her head as she felt Ortega stiffen at her side. At least she wasn't the only one worried by the sudden mood change.

"This next bit affects the Marines more than anyone else," Okafor said, her expression grim. "And the Devil Dogs more than most."

Ash looked quickly at her mother. Her worry increased to see Elizabeth's brow furrow in concern.

"Liz, Ash, I received word on my way here that SecDivSecBat Alpha Company was ambushed on what should have been a routine mission. Colonel Pawlak and more than a dozen others were killed before relief arrived."

For a moment, the world stopped. Tears burned Ashlyn's eyes, but she refused to shed them. Paul Pawlak had been her CO when she first joined the Devil Dogs. She had moved up the ranks under his leadership and one of the proudest days of her life had been he handed the battalion over to her. By all rights, he should have been kicked upstairs to Division headquarters. Instead, he had been transferred to SecDivSecBat to bring them up to the same quality as the Devil Dogs.

And now he would not be coming home, one more casualty of a war that should have been ended years ago.

"Has his family been notified?"

"Not yet, Ash. I wanted to wait until you had been told."

Ashlyn nodded. Okafor's response didn't surprise her. The Commandant knew her well enough, and knew her relationship with Pawlak, to understand that she would want to be there when her former CO's family was notified. Then she would have to break the news to her own son, Pawlak's godson.

"Thank you, ma'am. I will see to it as soon as we finish here."

"*We* will see to it," Elizabeth put in firmly.

"The pertinents have been sent to you," Okafor said. "I don't have to tell you that this has hit the Warlords hard. They are basically down a company and have lost their CO. We need to shore them up until a new CO is in place."

Ashlyn nodded, already guessing what Okafor was about to say.

"Colonel, Delta and Gamma Companies are to reinforce the

Warlords. As much as I hate to do it, Captain Ortega, you will accompany them. I need someone out there who can understand what the Warlords are feeling but who will also keep them striving for Devil Dog discipline until a new CO is put in place." Now it was Okafor's turn to hold up a hand to prevent interruption.

"Before you say anything, Captain, I understand that you want to be here for your CO, especially with the courts martial of Sorkowski and the others coming up. However, you are a Marine and you will obey your orders. Besides, you were effectively Hammer's XO after Colonel Shaw and the others were framed. So you know what he would expect of the battalion. *I* expect you to continue doing what he started."

"Yes, ma'am."

"Besides, your colonel is going to be dirtside for the course of the trial and probably for some time after that. By the time the Devil Dogs are ready to ship back out to the front lines, you and the two companies will be back."

Ashlyn wasn't too sure, but she knew better than to say so.

"Now, with the President's pardon, I don't want to delay notifying Hammer's family any longer than we already have."

"Of course, General." Harper stood and waited as the Marine contingent followed suit. "General Shaw, Colonel Shaw, Captain Ortega, you have my sympathies. Colonel Pawlak was a hero and he served Fuercon well. Please extend my condolences to his family."

"I will finish our part of the briefing afterwards," Okafor said and called them to attention.

Ashlyn braced to attention and saluted. Somehow, the day had just gone from bad to nightmare. What else could go wrong and did she really want to know?

5

"What are you going to tell them?"

Ashlyn looked at her XO and gave a half shrug. The last few hours were a blur. She had gone from the briefing to the apartment Pawlak shared with his wife. Fortunately, their son was home from university. The moment Paul, Jr., answered the door, he had known. Ash had seen it on his face. Instead of reacting, the young man had looked from General Okafor to Elizabeth and then to Ash herself. With a nod, he asked them in. Once he had shown them to the den, he had gone to find his mother.

Latrice Pawlak, like her son, knew the moment she saw the three why they were there. A single tear had trickled down her cheek. Then, her hand grasped in both of her son's, she had asked what happened. Okafor told her what she could, including the fact her husband's body had been recovered and would be returned for a burial with full military honors. Then she and Elizabeth had excused themselves, telling Ash they would wait for her outside. She thanked them before turning her attention back to Latrice.

Half an hour later, she rejoined the others. They had ridden in silence back to Okafor's office. Once there, the Commandant sent for lunch and they had gotten down to work. Now it was time to tell the battalion not only about Pawlak but about how the Devil Dogs would respond.

"The truth. Not only about Hammer and the rest of it but also about Bravo Company. Now is the worst time possible for us to be at anything but our best."

Ortega nodded, her expression grim. "What are you going to do about Bravo?"

For a moment, Ash studied her XO, her best friend. She knew there was more to Ortega's question than just wondering if she planned on changing her orders about having Bravo out on training maneuvers now that Delta and Gamma Companies were leaving the home system. If only she had the answers.

"I have to know what's going on with them, Luce. You know that." She waited until Ortega nodded. "But with Delta and Gamma – and you – leaving the system, I have to rethink things." She blew out a breath. God, she wished there was an easy answer but, in war, there rarely was. "Send orders for Anderson Talbot to return here ASAP. Copy their orders to Noffsinger and the CO for the 103rd BatCruRon. I'll prepare a private dispatch for Noffsinger. I want him to understand that this doesn't mean the maneuvers for Bravo Company are cancelled. I'll have to rely upon him to give me feedback."

"Ash."

She shook her head. She knew every objection her XO was about to make and then some. But what choice did she have? "Lucinda, I will keep on top of what's happening. However, I am not sending you, not to mention Delta and Gamma Companies, off without a senior NCO we both trust watching your back. The Warlords are good but they will be shaken right now by the loss of Hammer and the others. They need to know there is a solid command structure to rely upon until the Commandant gets Hammer and the others replaced. So don't argue with me about this."

"All right. I'll admit to being relieved to have one of our own senior non-coms with me."

"Me too." Ash smiled slightly. One hurdle cleared. How many others would spring up before the Callusians were finally defeated?

"So, XO, who would you prefer watching your six? Adamson or Talbot?"

For a moment, Ortega did not reply. "I'd be comfortable with either, ma'am. Under the circumstances, I think Adamson would be best."

"Agreed."

"Besides, Talbot has been with you since your return from Tarsus. I'll feel better with him watching your six while I'm gone."

"In other words, you are going to have a *chat* with him before you ship out about how he is to make sure I don't so much as stub my big toe." Ash smiled to take any sting out of her words.

"I won't have to. He had that chat with me before he and Adamson left with Bravo Company."

Ashlyn grinned, imagining the conversation. Her staff – her friends – had made it their unofficial duty to make sure nothing else happened to her. It didn't matter if she wanted them to or not. As they had told her in not so many words on more than one occasion.

Before anything else could be said, Ortega frowned. Then shook her head. As she did, Ash bit back a smile. She recognized the motion from their years at the Academy. Her XO wanted to say something else but wasn't sure she should. Well, that was easy enough to deal with.

"Spill it, Luce. What else is on your mind?"

"Ash, do you think Midlothians have sold us out?"

And wasn't that the question of the day, the year and even the decade?

"I don't know." She climbed to her feet and moved to stare out the window. Instead of seeing the Academy grounds below with the latest crop of cadets hurrying to class or drilling under the watchful eye of upperclassmen, she saw all the potential problems such a betrayal could hold. "I don't see the advantage for the government to betray us. Still, stranger things have happened."

"That's certainly true." Ortega joined her. "But it does make things more difficult. There may not be any Midlothians in either

First or Second Fleets, or the attached Marine detachments, but there are in other branches of our military."

"I know. All we can do is assume – and hope – the President and the others take that into consideration." She blew out a breath and then glanced at her wrist unit. "The battalion should be gathered. My mother reserved the auditorium for us. Let's get this done."

"And then?"

"I'm giving everyone leave until 0600. Those who knew Hammer will need time to deal with the news. The rest, well, they can use the time to prepare for an increase in our training. I have a feeling the shit is going to hit the fan and much sooner than any of us anticipated."

Ortega nodded. "Be honest with me now. Are you all right?"

"I'm about as all right as you are, Luce." She let her sorrow show for a moment, knowing her friend would understand. "It's not going to be easy to tell the battalion about Hammer. It's going to be harder to tell Jake. You know how much he adored Hammer."

"Hell, Ash, we all did. He taught each of us what it means to be a Devil Dog."

"He did. Now we owe it to him to pass on that knowledge to those who come after us." She closed her eyes and offered up a quick prayer for her mentor's soul. "Now, let's go tell the Devil Dogs what is being asked of them this time."

With that, she turned on her heel and left her office, her XO hurrying after her.

––––––––

THE DOOR SLID shut with a muted swoosh. In the silence the followed, the snick of the locking mechanism engaging seemed almost unnaturally loud. It was followed almost instantly by a soft hum that signaled the activation of the portable privacy shield. From where she stood, hidden in the shadows across the room, Evan Moreau nodded in satisfaction. She had spent a great deal of money on the system. Lives depended on its ability to ensure no prying eyes or ears intercepted their conversation. More importantly, her life depended on it.

Not that Raoul Frietas realized it. Over the course of their *business* relationship, she had come to understand that he rarely gave such security precautions more than a passing thought. He carried his own portable unit that he always made a show out of using. One part of her wondered how he had managed to survive as long as he had without being more careful. But another part was glad he wasn't more suspicious. It made getting information from him so much easier.

A frown touched her lips as Frietas all but sagged against the door. She didn't miss the way he checked to make sure the locks had engaged. Nor did she miss the way his right hand patted a slight bulge in his jacket pocket, as if making sure something was still there. Suspicion mixed with a healthy dose of professional paranoia flared. Had he actually come to their meeting armed?

If so, why?

Moreau took a half step back, moving deeper into the shadows cloaking the far end of the room. As she did, she checked her own weapons. Her movements were slow, calculated to do nothing to draw attention to where she stood. She would not step out until she had a better feel for what was going on.

Frietas turned away from the door. As he did, he blew out a shuddering breath. For a moment, he lowered his head, almost as if in prayer. His chest rose and fell in quick, shallow breaths. Fear rose off of him, so strong Moreau could smell it. Swallowing hard, she waited, wondering what had gone wrong.

Not willing to take any chances, she reached into her jacket pocket and entered a command code by touch into her datapad. If everything went as it should, the room's security had just been increased. No one would be able to enter or leave without her approval. More importantly, she would be notified if anyone or anything entered the floor the room was located on. It wouldn't be much but it should be enough to let her deal with Freitas.

Now all she had to do was find out what had Frietas so spooked.

"All right, Raoul. Why the SOS?" Moreau asked as she stepped into the pool of light illuminating the middle of the room.

He started nervously and spun in her direction. Seeing how his hand moved toward the bulge in his pocket, she acted. Before he could respond, she closed the distance between them. Her hand closed firmly over his wrist, stopping him from reaching for whatever he had hidden. As he looked at her, he blanched. Good. He had seen she would not let him do anything foolish, to either of them.

"Easy," she soothed. "And I'll ask again. Why the SOS?"

"I-I wanted to let you know that everything went as planned." He motioned for her to be seated at the table in the center of the room.

She nodded, noting how his hand trembled. Something had rattled him and that worried her. Perhaps it was time to move up the timetable on dealing with him, especially if he was losing his nerve.

"What is it, Raoul? What is worrying you?" She sat and watched as he joined her.

For a moment, he said nothing. Instead, he poured them each a glass of wine from the bottle she had ordered when she reserved the room. For the first time, he did not immediately drink. Whatever happened had worried him enough that he obviously did not trust her. Well, she could handle that. She gave a slight nod and lifted her glass, taking a sip and relishing the vintage. He might choose not to enjoy it but she had no such compunctions.

"I'm waiting," she prompted as she sipped again.

"I heard about Kannedy."

Surprised, she wondered what he had heard – or what he was implying. Then, seeing how he waited for her response, she nodded once. "A tragic accident."

"Was it?"

She carefully placed her wine glass on the tabletop. When she looked at him, the color drained from his face.

"Are you suggesting it wasn't, Raoul?"

She spoke softly. Her gaze never wavered as she studied him. Sweat pricked out on his forehead. The fear she had sensed in him when he first arrived returned full force. She saw it in his quick intake of breath, in the way his hand fisted on the tabletop before he hid it out of sight under the table. What it meant, she wasn't sure. All she knew for certain was he could no longer be trusted. Fear made him a liability. She would deal with him as she had Kannedy. There wouldn't be a corner dark enough or a hole deep enough for him to hide in, in this system or any other.

"No." He looked like he might be sick at any moment. "The news shook me, that's all."

She could believe that.

"It shook me as well." She leaned back and set her wineglass down. "But accidents happen. You know that."

He nodded and she sensed reluctance in him. "I only wondered if the government had found out what he was up to and took the easy way out."

She frowned. The suggestion was plausible, at least under the previous administration. She had no doubt there were members of the government, not to mention military, who would deal with traitors in the most expedient way possible. What bothered her was that Frietas had thought about it. Could he be worried about meeting such an end himself?

More importantly, if so, why?

"As far as I know, it was just that – an accident."

"Are you sure?"

She fought the urge to frown. Who was he to doubt her?

"I am." She reached across the table and lightly rested her hand on his. As she did, she saw him fight the urge to flinch. Frustration flared as did determination. The last thing she needed was him running to the authorities and telling what he knew. "Raoul, you know my sources would have let me know if we had anything to worry about."

"And his files?"

"Scrubbed."

Just as his would be as soon as she dealt with him. Then she had better figure out why this mission had gone so badly wrong. If she didn't, Kannedy and Frietas wouldn't be the only ones losing their lives. Since she preferred living to the alternative, she had to act fast.

"Now, what else is bothering you, Raoul?" She leaned forward, elbows on the table, chin resting on her fists.

He sipped his wine and she knew he was trying to figure out what to say. "There's been a change in management on the Council."

"Again, not that unexpected. Harper has been cleaning house since he took office."

He nodded. "True but Lydia Matthias is known for not only coming in and shaking things up but for rooting out not only inefficiency but security risks as well."

"Then I suggest you make sure you don't appear to be either."

She didn't care if he heard the threat behind her words or not. It didn't matter. His days – no, his hours – were numbered. He simply didn't know it, yet.

"I assure you, there is nothing that will lead her to me. I was simply warning you in case you had anyone else there who might not be as careful as I am."

"No worries, Raoul. There are no others."

He opened his mouth to say something and then closed it. For a moment, she wondered what he'd been about to say. Then she shrugged it off. It didn't matter. He didn't matter. Not any longer.

"Is there anything else you need to tell me?" she asked.

"Not at the moment."

She checked her wrist unit and stood. Gentleman that he was, Frietas followed suit, just as she had known he would. They stepped around the table until they stood close enough to shake hands. "Keep your head, Raoul. I would hate to hear that something happened to you."

She reached for his hand. Before the import of her words sank in, he reached for her hand. As the fingers of her right hand closed around his, she gave her left arm a slight shake. The hilt of her blade fit perfectly in her hand. She stepped closer, leaning in as if to whisper something to him.

"Sorry, Raoul, but you are a loose end," she said softly as she slid the blade between his ribs, twisting it to do the most damage.

He took a short step back. Shock filled his expression. He opened his mouth to cry out but only a soft gasp escaped his lips. Gently, she lowered him to the floor. As blood flowed from the wound, pooling on the floor at his side, she quickly searched him. Without a word, she pocketed the small stunner he'd brought with him as well as his other electronics. Then she sat back on her heels, watching as the life slowly drained away with each beat of his heart.

"Don't worry, Raoul. You will be reported as the unfortunate victim of a terrorist attack. A bomb will go off, damaging the building but destroying this room and most of the floor in just a few minutes. You will sadly be caught in the explosion."

"H-have in-insurance."

"Which will be gone before your body, what will be left of it, is identified." She stood and carefully wiped her hands on one of the napkins. Then she dropped it and her now empty wine glass into her bag. Even though the explosion would destroy everything in the room, she didn't want to risk any residual DNA being left behind to be found during the investigation.

"I'll be sure to make a generous donation to your favorite charity once your death is announced."

As she left the room, she closed and locked the door behind her. A simple command sequence once she was safely outside would deal with the mess that had been Raoul Frietas. All she had to do was find a way to finish her mission before her handlers decided she, too, had become a loose end.

6

"What now?"

Anton Dorescu glared at his first officer as the hatch slid shut behind the younger man. Only one thing would cause him to risk his commander's wrath. Something else had happened. Such announcements no longer surprised Dorescu. The mission, and the *Anubis*, had been plagued with problems from the beginning. Worse, as long as Command kept his hand tied with their idiotic directives, the problems would only grow worse.

How many times had he been forced to intercede in matters that should never have arisen? How many of his crew had been reprimanded – or worse – by the new constraints put on them? And all because idiot politicians who had never seen battle, much less been on the front line, decided they needed new allies. Allies that would not let them fight the sort of battle they knew how to win.

Worse, to accomplish the new goals, Command had saddled him with four *advisors*. He had no doubt at least some of his superiors fully expected him to deal with the four in such a way they presented no threat to the real mission. So far, he had managed to do just that with three of them. Two had met their ends as a result of injuries suffered "during the course of battle". The fact those injuries had actually been caused by friendly fire didn't matter. None of his people had any use for their Midlothian *brothers*. Scuttlebutt had it the crew was posturing to see who would get the assignment to remove the last advisor from their midst.

Unfortunately for Dorescu's peace of mind, Bernard Hughes was much smarter and had a more finely honed sense of self-preservation than the others had possessed. Worse, he made no attempt to hide his suspicions about what happened to his fellow Midlothians. Dorescu suspected he was somehow managing to report back to his handlers without going through the ship's comm. That meant they would have to be very careful in how they dispatched him. They could not risk the Midlothians complaining to the powers that be. Dorescu might not appreciate having Hughes looking over his shoulder and questioning his every move but he did like the improved weaponry and systems they had received from the Midlothians. Not even he would risk losing the technical support of their new allies, at least not until they had defeated Fuercon. Then he wanted to be leading the attack force sent to show Midlothian where the power really rested.

In the meantime, he had to find a way to deal with Hughes. If he didn't, the crew would. While that might be the easiest way of handling their so-called advisor, the potential for crew unrest to lead to mutiny was too great. If he did not handle Hughes, neither of them would live long.

Damn the man!

Bad enough Hughes told him – Him! – how to conduct a successful mission. Worse, Hughes refused to let his people take their rightful rewards once they completed a mission. He would not let them bring onboard the slaves they wanted, slaves they had earned. Nor would he allow them the ancient right of pillaging. What incentive did his people have to continue the mission if their wallets and entertainment were curtailed?

And why, by all that was holy, did Command go along with such orders?

Worse, at least as far as Dorescu was concerned, was the fact he could not explain the change in orders to his crew. All they knew was their once strong captain was now hamstrung by a foreigner who refused to let them be the warriors and conquerors they were. Dorescu knew he was lucky not to have had a knife slipped between his ribs already.

"For once, nothing is wrong," Pyotyr Kovacz said as he took the seat Dorescu indicated. "At least nothing more than usual." He gave a half-shrug.

"And?"

"We have received new orders."

Dorescu sat up, his interest piqued. Since being ordered to leave the Cassius System, the taskforce had been engaged in hit-and-run missions, harrying the commerce channels and not much else. Hopefully, the new orders would give his people something other than their discontent to focus on.

"We are to translate to the Dathamay System as soon as Commander Rouhipour arrives with the 357th taskforce. Command included an ETA for the 357th of end of the ship's week."

Dorescu nodded, a thoughtful look on his expression. The Dathamay System was unallied in the current war. The last intel he had seen on the system had been sparse but so, according to the data, was system security. That meant it would probably be easy pickings. Better yet, it might be the perfect place to deal with Hughes in a very permanent fashion.

"Our orders once there?"

"We join forces with the 114th Taskforce 22nd BatCruRon under the command of Captain Mahmoud. You will be senior officer, sir." Now Kovacz grinned, an evil gleam lighting his eyes. "Our orders are to take the system and hold it. Use it as an example of what will happen to all systems that refuse to capitulate to our rule."

"Any word about our *guest*?"

"We are to take no overt action against him. Command wants nothing to happen that might strain our relations with our allies. However, accidents do happen, especially on ships in the middle of battle."

"Excellent, my friend. I leave the arrangements to you."

With that, Dorescu swung his chair around so he could stare out the viewport. He could trust Kovacz to make sure the *accident* appeared to be exactly that. Over the years, his first officer had carried out a number of similar missions for him. Now he simply had to make sure no one in the crew did anything foolish before Kovacz was ready to put his plan into action. But for now, he needed some release and knew his friend did as well. Hughes may have tried to deny them all their rewards, but he hadn't been entirely successful.

Thankfully. Otherwise, Dorescu would have been forced to kill him before Command was ready for him to.

Even so, that didn't make their orders any easier to swallow. There were still so many slaves to be had, so much plunder to be found. And it was all denied to him and his crew. They should be rich men by now. That was the natural order of things. The conquerors had the right to anything or anyone within the lands they defeated. Hughes had denied that bounty to them and Dorescu resented it. He had railed against it as well, reminding Hughes of the potential for mutiny if the men were denied all of their bounty. The Midlothian had reluctantly agreed to a little reward. It wasn't much but soon, very soon, much more would join it.

For now, Dorescu planned to enjoy what little he had been allowed.

He activated his comm. "Send my latest toy in and then make sure the First Officer and I aren't disturbed," he ordered.

A few moments later, the hatch slid open. One of Dorescu's personal guards entered, leading a young woman by a chain connected to a heavy metal collar. The collar was the only thing she wore. Her eyes glazed with panic and remembered fear as she saw the men sitting across the room. A moan escaped her lips and she collapsed into a heap on the floor. Ignoring her, Dorescu snapped his fingers and held out one hand. The guard crossed the room, dragging the woman after him. Then he handed the end of the chain to his commanding officer.

"I'll send for you when we are done." Dorescu waited as the guard left. Then he tugged on the chain, forcing the woman to crawl to him. "We shall enjoy this one tonight, Pyotyr. We have earned this." He laughed cruelly as the young woman shuddered in fear.

"This and so much more."

"Soon, Pyotyr, soon."

Kovacz nodded and leaned forward to watch his captain begin his *games*.

Captain Bernard Hughes, Midlothian Space Navy, stepped into his quarters and sighed in relief as the hatch slid shut behind him. Even as he did, he cast a quick look around the outer room to make sure nothing had been disturbed since he had last been there. Then, one hand sliding into his jacket pocket where a mini-pulsar rested, he moved into his bedroom, searched it and the adjoining head. A few months ago, he would have felt the fool for taking such precautions but not now. Not when his life depended on being paranoid.

Damn Watchman for forcing him into the position of having to accept this assignment!

Be honest, Barney, he didn't do anything but be himself. Your fear of him and his position put you here.

Just as it put him one step ahead of the executioner.

Satisfied there were no unexpected *visitors* or surprises waiting for him, Hughes returned to the outer room and dropped onto the sofa. For almost as long as he had been onboard the *Anubis*, he had known Dorescu and the crew wanted him dead. At first, he had tried to convince himself that, no matter how much they resented him and his fellow *advisors*, they would not act. Then, as first one and then another and then yet another died, he knew his days were numbered. What the Callusians did not realize, however, was that he had no intention of making it easy for them to kill him. He hadn't survived as long as he had by being careless.

He had wasted no time in planting listening devices around the ship. Fortunately for his continued survival, Dorescu had not expected him to take such action. He certainly hadn't expected one of the devices to be planted in his own quarters. The information gathered as a result confirmed Hughes' suspicions. The Callusians had no intention of following their orders as laid out by their Midlothian *advisors*. Instead, they planned on using the improved ships and technology provided by the Midlothians to finally defeat Fuercon and its allies. In the course of accomplishing that, Dorescu also planned on making sure his r shipboard advisor perished in the fight.

Unfortunately for them, Hughes did not plan on falling into their trap. But he was no fool. He knew he couldn't be on guard every hour of every day. So, he had put his own failsafe measures in place, designed to activate if anything happened to him. His own superiors would not approve but, after seeing what happened to his fellow advisors, he did not care. Survival became the goal for the mission. Everything else had to come after that. He couldn't accomplish his mission if he wound up dead.

———

"Present arms!"

Master Sergeant M. J. Adamson's voice rang out across the tarmac. It was followed instantly by two companies of Marines, Devil Dogs each and every one, obeying. Hands snapped up in a synchronized salute. Adamson studied the assembly for a moment before executing a perfect about face. She marched with parade ground precision to where Ashlyn stood with Lucinda Ortega.

"Ma'am, First Division Second Battalion Delta and Gamma Companies stand ready for inspection."

"Very well, Master Sergeant." Ashlyn turned her attention to her executive officer. "Captain, these are your companies. The inspection is yours."

Ortega was too good of an officer to break discipline but Ash saw the flash of frustration in her friend's eyes. Too bad. She hadn't wanted to put the companies through an inspection before they shipped out. She remembered how much she had hated such inspections, especially when they were only for show. But Ortega had insisted. Worse, she had brought both Adamson and Talbot to back her up.

At least Ash understood part of their reasoning. Fuercon and its allies had not expected to find themselves at war so soon. Knowing the Devil Dogs were on-planet had some – civilian and politician alike – wondering if the military feared the fight would soon come to the System. Ashlyn understood their concern. After all, it had not been that long ago when an attack was run against the Capital. She still suspected there was more to that brief attack than they knew and that worried her more than she wanted to admit.

"You have done your company commanders proud today, Devil Dogs," Ashlyn said once Ortega finished the inspection and reported the results. "More than that, you have done yourselves proud. In a few minutes, you will board the shuttles at the edge of the tarmac. That will be the first step in your journey to join up with the Warlords. When you do, I know I don't have to ask you to not only remember that you are Devil Dogs, the best in the Corps, but also that Colonel Pawlak was one of us. He might have been transferred to the Warlords but he will forever be a Devil Dog. Honor his memory as well as the memories of those who perished with him."

Her mother had once told her the burden of command wasn't the planning and execution of ops. It was knowing that there would come a time when you had to order someone to take actions that would result in their death. There would inevitably come a time when someone had to make the sacrifice so others could live. As an office, she would have to make that call. The higher the rank, the more often that call would be made. The only way to live with it was to make sure her people did not die in vain and that their deaths were avenged.

Ooh-rah

"Take the fight straight to the enemy and ram it down their throats. We didn't ask for this war. We didn't resume hostilities. They did. Now show them how foolish they were to violate the truce. Show them that Fuercon and its allies will no longer be satisfied with simply holding the line. Show them that we intend to end this war and do so in such a way they will never again be foolish enough to come at us with weapons instead of diplomacy.

"You are Devil Dogs. Go give the enemy hell!"

"Ooh-Rah!"

"Captain Ortega, Master Sergeant Adamson and your Company commanders will lead you wisely. Listen to them and heed their orders. Most of all, never forget that you are Devil Dogs, the best of the Corps."

With that, Ashlyn braced to attention and saluted the two Companies. She held that position until the last rank had marched past on the way to the shuttles. Then she lowered her hand and turned to face Ortega and Adamson.

"I don't know what you're going to find when you get there. My hope is that Hammer managed to bring the Warlords up to something close to our standard. My fear is that you may be walking into a trap. So keep your eyes and ears open and your guard up." She motioned for them to walk with her. "Once you are off-planet, Luce will brief you on some intel we have been given, MJ. It doesn't apply directly to your mission but it very well may impact it. If either of you see or hear anything that concerns you, report back to me immediately."

"Understood," the two said in unison.

"And, before you say anything, I promise to be careful," she continued. "With the courts martial beginning next week, I will be spending most of my time at HQ. Talbot has already received orders, not only from the two of you but from my mother and General Okafor, to be my shadow. So don't let what might be happening here distract you."

"No promises," Adamson said with a cheeky grin.

Ashlyn grinned and shook her head. She had expected them to say something similar but she'd had to try. "Take care and no unnecessary risks." Now she pinned them both with a firm look. "I have a feeling that things are about to heat up and I want you both with me when they do."

"As you told the Companies, Ash, we're Devil Dogs. We will do what's needed," Ortega said. "Now we had best get onboard. It wouldn't do to set a bad example before we are even off-planet."

"And excellent point, XO." Ash reached out to shake first Ortega's hand and then Adamson's. "Dismissed."

The two braced to attention and saluted. As soon as Ash returned their salutes, they nodded once. Then they hurried across the tarmac to the waiting shuttles. Ash watched for a few moments before turning away. Instead of hurrying back to her office, she stood rooted in place, a slight smile on her lips to see what looked to be the rest of the battalion standing to one side of the tarmac. Pride filled her to know they had come to see their fellow Devil Dogs off.

"All right, everyone. Don't you have better things to do than hang around the port?" She grinned to take any sting out of her words.

"You heard the Old Lady. Back to work!" Talbot ordered, his grin matching hers.

"Old Lady, huh?" she teased as he moved to her side. "Let's go, Master Guns. There are some things I need to brief you on now that you are officially my shadow."

"Thank you, ma'am."

She glanced at him, surprised. "For what?"

"For not bitching about it."

"Kevin, even if I wanted to – and I do – I know better. There are too many unknowns right now."

Unknowns he would soon be read into.

7

―――――

"On your feet, Admiral."

Rear Admiral Alec Sorkowski (ret.) no longer winced at the disdain in the guard's voice. He had heard it too many times and from far too many people since he had been forced to retire. That had been bad enough. At least he had thought so. Then the day came when the JAG officer and others arrived to arrest him – Him! – and all because of that bitch Ashlyn Shaw.

"Either get on your feet or I'll tell your attorney you didn't want to see him."

Gritting his teeth, Sorkowski did as ordered. He waited as the security field was lowered and the corporal motioned him out. The moment he stepped into the corridor, a second guard stepped into view. Too familiar with what would happen next, Sorkowski held his hands behind his back and waited for the restraints to be applied.

As if he had anywhere to go should he be lucky enough to escape their custody and find a way out of the security building before someone cut him down.

Without another word, the guards escorted him to the lift. When the doors slid shut, he breathed deeply. It had been days, maybe even more than a week, since he had been out of his cell. Then, like now, it had been to *confer* with his attorney. Confer! What a laugh. There had been no conferring, only orders from the attorney about what he was to do and say, not only when his court martial convened but for the rest of his life. How long that life might be depended on him – and on his keeping his mouth shut.

So what now?

Once inside the conference room where he would meet with his attorney, Sorkowski couldn't even pace, no matter how much he wanted to. For the first time since his arrest, he was being treated like he presented a danger to anyone who might come into his presence. His wrists remained secured behind his back. His ankles had been secured to shackles that were bolted to the floor at the base of his chair. All he could do was wait and wonder what had happened to cause such a change in circumstances?

It wasn't long before the door to the room once again opened. Shock washed over Sorkowski as first Thomas O'Brien and half a dozen others were led inside. Each of them were his co-defendants and it was the first time he had seen any of them since his arrest. He watched in silence as they were forced into chairs around the table and then secured in the same manner he was. Something was about to happen but what?

And did he really want to know.

"There will be no talking without permission," the corporal who had escorted Sorkowski to the room said. "Any violation of this rule will result in immediate removal from the room. You will each note on the record that you understand and only that you understand."

One by one, they answered in the affirmative. Most looked at the tabletop, refusing to make eye contact with the guards. O'Brien, foolish as ever, looked as if he might argue. Then he seemed to deflate before saying he understood.

"Ensign?" Corporal Sikes prompted.

"Yes, but – " Ensign Julia Jicha, Sorkowski's former communications specialist, said.

"Get her out of here!" Sikes ordered.

"No, wait!"

"You knew your orders," Sikes said simply as two of his fellow Marines freed her from the shackles and pulled her to her feet. "Return her to her cell." He waited until the door shut behind them, closing off the woman's protests. "Now, Admiral, your turn."

"Yes."

What else could he say? Much as he wanted to protest their treatment, he knew better. It would only serve to have him removed, just as Jicha had been. He couldn't risk that, not until he found out why they had all been brought together. Something was going on and he had a sick feeling in the pit of his stomach that he wasn't going to like it.

Each of the prisoners had been under Sorkowski's command at the time of that disastrous mission. All had been party to his reports against Shaw and her Marines. Not that they'd had much choice. It had been either support him or face having JAG look too closely at their extracurricular activities in the sector. Some would have lost more than others but he had made sure they each understood the consequences would be much more serious than a simple dishonorable discharge. Their best bet for surviving with their careers, their reputations and their bank accounts intact was to throw Shaw and her people to the wolves. Unfortunately, Shaw had refused to be the sacrificial lamb.

A few minutes later, the door once again slid open. In stepped his attorney, followed closely by Lieutenant Liu. Sorkowski drew a quick breath before hissing it out. Not good. Not good at all. Why in the name of all that was holy was his attorney there with the prosecuting officer? More importantly, where were the attorneys for the others?

It was tempting to beat his head against the tabletop. If he did it long enough and hard enough, he might just beat himself unconscious. At least then he would be free of this nightmare for a little while.

"Ladies and gentlemen, I am here on behalf of each of your attorneys. Lieutenant Liu has something he wants to say to each of you. I recommend you listen closely to what the lieutenant has to say. Once he is done, he will leave the room and we will discuss what he said.

Until then, I suggest you keep any comments or questions to your-selves," Kurt Sorensen said as he took his place at one end of the table.

Sorkowski narrowed his eyes and studied the man. Small, wiry with a shock of white hair, Sorensen looked more like an accountant than a veteran of years in the courtroom. In their previous meetings, Sorensen had been direct, his message clear. Sorkowski was to do as he said. No questions, no deviation. Now, however, there was some-thing about him, a sense of nervousness that only served to increase Sorkowski's worry.

"I will do my best to answer your questions once Lieutenant Liu has left the room. Then we will proceed from there," Sorensen continued.

It all sounded good but Sorkowski knew better. He knew Sorensen wouldn't let him or anyone else talk to the JAG officer. That had already been made very clear, to both himself and to O'Brien, and in the most painful of ways.

"Do you each understand?"

Once they said they did, Lieutenant Liu moved to the other end of the table. For a long moment, he studied each of them. As he did, Sorkowski did his best to show no reaction. He knew Liu's reputation. The lieutenant had no use for anyone he felt had betrayed their oaths to Fuercon and, as far as Sorkowski had learned, he had a perfect conviction record.

"I won't take long. What I have to say is very simple," the JAG officer began. "I have a one-time offer and it is good for only the first person to speak. If you give a full and truthful statement, if you answer each of my questions without hesitation, I will take the death penalty off the board where that person is concerned. I will also recommend on-planet confinement instead of confinement at the Tarsus military prison. It might not sound like much, but I assure you, it is the only way one of you will avoid a date with the executioner."

"Lieutenant, you are asking them to turn on the others. I can't recommend that to any of them." Sorensen looked at the younger man, a hint of regret on his expression. Not that it fooled Sorkowski. He knew the attorney would choose which of them got to make the deal and the rest would be told to keep their mouths shut. Their lives and the lives of those they cared for depended on it.

"That is your prerogative, Mr. Sorensen, just as it is mine to withdraw the offer." He held up a hand before anyone could say anything. "But I won't – yet. You have half an hour to decide who, if anyone, will take the offer." With that, Lieutenant Liu left the room, closing the door behind him.

Almost instantly, everyone started talking at once. Sorkowski let the others ask their questions and demand an explanation. None of that mattered. Even Lieutenant Liu's offer didn't matter. What did was why his attorney was there and why the other attorneys had agreed to let him stand in their places to represent their clients in this matter.

"Quiet!" Sorkowski snapped a few moments later. He waited as the others complied. "Tell me, Sorensen, why?"

"Why what, Admiral?"

"Why are you here and none of the other attorneys? What Liu presented means you cannot represent all of us without a major conflict of interest. So what else has happened that we do not know about?"

A slight smile touched the attorney's lips. Something about it only increased Sorkowski's sense of wrongness about the situation. Damn it, he hated being in the dark.

"Let's simply say that, as Lieutenant Liu has given one of you a lifeline, our respective *friends* have sent a message that you are to remember where your loyalties lie."

With that, he got to his feet. As he moved around the room, he placed small datapads in front of each of them. Even though they sat far enough apart that they could not see what was displayed on their neighbor's units, Sorkowski knew it was the same thing. It was enough to turn his insides to liquid. Their so-called friends were tying up loose ends and making it clear they were just as expendable.

"You will note the authorities are writing off the first death as an accident and the other as murder by an as yet unknown whore. They aren't wasting time or resources in investigating what happened."

The implication was clear. No one would waste time investigating any *accidents* that might happen to them either.

"I will also remind you that while Lieutenant Liu made an offer, you have seen nothing in writing. So my recommendation to each of you is to think long and hard before you even consider making a deal. I promise you it will come back to haunt you, in more ways than one." With that, Sorensen collected the datapads and then signaled he was ready to leave.

"What the hell are we supposed to do?" O'Brien asked softly as the door slid shut behind Sorensen.

"Keep our mouths shut unless you want to end up like the others."

Maybe that would be enough to keep their mouths shut until after he had a chance to get word to Liu that he was ready to talk.

———

A KNOCK SOUNDED at the office door. Sighing heavily, the redhead looked up from the trial brief she had been studying. As she did, she frowned. She had left orders not to disturb her for anything short of an all-out invasion. Despite that, Lieutenant Liu stood in the doorway waiting for her to acknowledge his presence.

Leaning back, Major Alexandra Quintana motioned the young man into the office. He nodded in response and did as she instructed. When he shut the door behind him, she looked at him in surprise. Then, before she could ask for an explanation, he extended a data disk, a slight smile of triumph playing at the corners of his mouth.

"Talk to me, Jianyu," she said as she motioned for him to take one of the two chairs before her desk.

"Major, you really need to have a look at what's on that disk." He grinned like a kid who had just been given the best present ever. "I guarantee you'll find it very interesting."

"Care to tell me what's on it?"

"Just a little case you assigned me and in which you have a passing interest in, ma'am."

"Jianyu," she all but growled. One of the reasons she liked the young man was his somewhat perverted sense of humor, something he didn't let most people see. But it was also one of the reasons he often drove her to distraction when she was in the middle of trial prep. Like now. "You know I'm under the gun here on the Horne case. Just tell me what you've got and why it required interrupting me."

"Major, I had an interesting meeting this morning with Kurt Sorensen."

That was enough to have Quintana sitting up. She reached for her datapad and quickly called up everything she had on Liu's caseload. Not that she needed to. The fact he mentioned Sorensen could mean only one thing. There might finally be some movement on the case against Alec Sorkowski and his co-defendants.

"And?" she prompted.

"Let me backtrack a moment first."

She ground her teeth together, wishing he would get to the point, before nodding.

"I have been working closely with not only Colonel Shaw but with other members of the Devil Dogs, past and present. I've also looked into her counsel for her court martial. I've included that information on the disc. It will make for interesting reading and, in my opinion, it will warrant new charges being filed. This time against the former Lieutenant Benton Cross."

Quintana pursed her lips and nodded. While his news wasn't exactly welcome, neither was it unexpected. But the thought that a member of her beloved JAG could have betrayed a client was something she had never hoped to see. Unfortunately, it made sense, especially when considered with everything else she knew about the case.

"All right." She fingered the disk thoughtfully. As much as she wanted to view its contents right then, she couldn't. She had to finish preparing for the Horne case. "I'll look at this later. In the meantime, tell me what has you so excited. I know it isn't the news about Cross."

"As I said, I had an interesting meeting with Sorensen this morning, a meeting he requested."

Quintana listened closely as Liu described listening in growing disbelief to Sorensen as the attorney said he had been asked by the other defense attorneys in the Shaw case to speak on their clients' behalf. Yes, he had confirmed with each of the attorneys before agreeing to the meet. Yes, he had those confirmations on record.

"Jianyu, everything you've said so far raises red flags. What did Sorensen want?"

"He wanted to know what sort of deal I'd be willing to offer for a guilty plea."

For a moment, she couldn't say anything. After months – no, years – of trying to make sense out of what happened with Ashlyn Shaw and finding those responsible for framing her and the others, could it be that simple?

"I'm sensing there is a *but* in there somewhere."

"There is, ma'am."

She waited, wondering what Sorensen had up his sleeve.

"He told me the attorneys wanted the deal to be for only one of the accused. They would leave it up to the accused themselves to decide which one."

"What. What?" It didn't make sense.

"I know. I felt the same way and told him I would need to consider if we would offer any of them a plea bargain. Then I verified again that he was speaking for each of the other attorneys. It didn't make sense and it still doesn't. But it does get better."

"Do I want to know?"

"You do." Another grin, this one a bit more reassuring. "I met with him and the defendants. The deal was simple. The first one to give a complete and honest statement about what happened, to answer all our questions, etc., would have the death penalty removed from the table and I would recommend confinement on-planet."

"And?"

"I left him to discuss it with the defendants."

She counted to ten, very slowly, before speaking. "Jianyu, please tell me you didn't interrupt me just for this."

"No, ma'am. While we did not listen in on their discussion, we did have the cameras going. Security, you know." He grinned and something close to glee lit his eyes. "Their discussion was short and sweet. He handed out datapads to each of them and then spoke for a few minutes. Then he left. They clearly did not like what he had to say. Some of them were all but pissing themselves. You could read the fear on their expressions. Considering the *accidents* several of them have suffered, I figured he was telling them to keep their mouths shut."

She nodded. Those accidents had caused her to order increased security around each of the defendants, no matter how removed they might have been from the initial charges leveled against Sorkowski and O'Brien.

"The defendants were returned to their cells. By the time I returned to my office, I had a message waiting from Corporal Sikes. It seems the moment they were away from the others, Sorkowski started demanding to speak with me."

"Interesting."

"What is more interesting is the fact he is the only one who has made the request so far. The others, from what their escorts reported were in varying stages of denial and fear."

"Make sure the guards keep a very close watch on them then. No more accidents or anything else."

"Already done."

"And Sorkowski?"

"He is being brought to my office in a few minutes. I wanted to let you know what was going on and see if you had any instructions."

"Exactly what you'd expect. Get it all. I want to know everything about what led up to the charges being filed against Shaw, the reasons behind it all and who that bastard has been working with." She leaned back and thought for a moment. If they played this right, they might be able to avoid airing their dirty laundry in public. It might not be as satisfying for Shaw but it would be best for both the Navy and the Corps, especially now that they were back to war. "I want that bastard to talk about the accidents that have befallen him and the others and who is behind them. Most of all, find out if there is any possibility his compatriots on the outside might make a try for Shaw or anyone else associated with the courts martial."

"Understood." Liu stood and then paused.

"Something else on your mind, LT?"

"If, as I suspect, Sorkowski is about to open up, I recommend we move him into isolation until he can be relocated."

"Agreed. I'll make sure that is in the works. Depending on what he tells us and what we are able to verify, he will be moved to another facility and his new location will not be disclosed until everyone responsible for what happened have been arrested and prosecuted."

"Thank you, ma'am."

"Report back to me as soon as you finish with Sorkowski."

"Yes, ma'am."

Quintana watched as he left her office. Once alone, she shook her head. Lieutenant Liu was one of the best JAG offices she had ever worked with. That was why she had initially put him in charge of looking into the case against Shaw. When it became evident she and her people had been victims of a conspiracy, Liu had continued the investigation. The fact Shaw had been willing to work with him had weighed heavily in the decision to let him continue building the cases against the conspirators. Now it appeared Quintana's faith in the man was about to pay off.

But that was for later. Even as she turned her attention back to the case prep when had been working on when Liu arrived, her right hand reached for the data disk. It was going to be very difficult to ignore it until she finished the task at hand.

―――――

"HAS SOMETHING HAPPENED?" Evan Moreau asked simply, sounding for all the world as if she was merely asking about the weather.

Beneath the surface of calm, however, her emotions stormed. How could things have gone so badly so quickly?

This mission had been a nightmare from the very beginning. She should have known better than to take on something that forced her to stay in place for so long. She worked better when it was an in and out job. Locate the target, learn their habits and then take them out. No muss and no fuss. Not this time. This time she had let greed and the desire for personal vengeance overrule common sense. Because of that, she had been in place for years, not weeks or months. Had she gotten sloppy? Possibly, not that she would admit it. No, the fault lay with those she had been forced to work with. Now, as she had begun to fear, it was all crumbling around her.

"Sit."

Kael Paulus sat – no, sprawled – in the chair opposite the one he indicated she take. He looked relaxed, almost casual. But Moreau wasn't so sure. For one thing, he had taken the position at the table she normally took: back to the wall, chair positioned so he could see all entrances without appearing to be on guard. Then there had been the flash of anger in his eyes and the way his right hand fisted once where it rested on the tabletop before relaxing. Something was wrong. But what?

God, she hated not having all the data. Too much could go wrong.

Tempting as it was to simply get up and walk out, she wouldn't. Not until she knew why he had insisted they meet without delay.

"So?" She leaned forward, forearms resting on the table. Years of working covert operations helped school her features into nothing but mild interest. She had to keep him from realizing how worried she was, at least until she knew what was going on.

"You have a friend arriving soon." Paulus reached for his glass and sipped.

Moreau's mouth went dry. She had no doubt what Paulus meant, but she had to be sure.

"Really?" She forced herself to look interested. Paulus was not one of those she had recruited during the mission. He had been her intermediary with her real employers. The fact he was warning her could mean he understood the handicaps she had been operating under and was giving her the chance to clean up the mess before she was taken out of the picture or it could be a ruse. So she had to go carefully.

"Really." He sat up and leaned in, his expression earnest. "You have been careless lately. There are too many bodies stacking up and people are starting to ask questions. I might have been able to keep the attention off of you but for two things. Those two actions may have signed both our death warrants."

He spoke softly, almost casually and that, she knew, proved just how angry and worried he was. Damn, her worst fears appeared to be coming true. But she wasn't done for yet. Not by a long shot.

"I don't follow." Maybe if she knew exactly what actions he referred to, she would be able to alleviate at least part of the damage.

"Don't play me for the fool, Moreau." He all but hissed out the words. "I told you at the time that our mutual friends would not approve of an attack on the capital just because you needed to clean up the mess with Shaw. Your personal feelings where she is concerned have clouded your judgment from the beginning. You relied on those not loyal to our cause to deal with her and they failed. Instead of making examples out of them, you dug a deeper hole by bringing more people into the conspiracy just so Shaw would not see another day of freedom. Then, when you learned she had been brought back here, you hired mercs – and incompetent ones at that – to attack the security complex. You didn't think how that might impact our friends' plans, did you? All you saw was a chance to clean up a mess you caused because you let your emotions get in the way of the job."

He shook his head, his eyes flashing with anger when she started to interrupt. Instead of saying anything, she inclined her head, signaling him to continue. Even as she did, she seethed. He might think he knew everything about her and why she had acted as she had. Well, she would soon enough disabuse him of that idea. But it could wait until he'd had his say.

"Then there was that so-called terrorist attack on the Rising Star Hotel."

"There is no way our mutual friends could have found out about that and then dispatched someone here who would arrive soon."

If he was trying to scare her, he would soon learn how foolish that could be.

"Think!" he snapped. "Your actions with the mercs focused the idiots here on system security. That does not fit our friends' plans." He ticked the point off on one finger before moving to the next. "Then there is the fact that several of your, shall we say, business partners, have met with untimely accidents. Next is what happened at the hotel. Finally, and much more important, is the very disturbing news I received this morning. It seems that despite your best efforts, Sorkowski has made a deal with the authorities."

"What?"

That broke through her calm. Everything had been in place. The message had been delivered, often painfully, to not only Sorkowski but to the others charged with him as well that they were to keep their mouths shut. Failure to follow that simple order would result in not only their deaths but the deaths of those they cared for. The example her people had made of Thomas O'Brien had almost killed the former Marine officer. But it had done the trick – at least she had thought so.

Damn it, why hadn't Sorensen warned her? If Sorkowski talked, sooner or later the idiots with JAG and Naval Intelligence would put together enough about the conspiracy surrounding what happened to Shaw and her people to start looking closer at what had been happening on Fuercon. Worse, that investigation would eventually lead them to her employers and that, without a doubt, would be the final signature on her death warrant.

Somehow she had to stop that from happening. Not only that, she had to do it before this *friend* Paulus mentioned arrived on-planet. She had no doubt now that whoever it was had been sent to make sure she never had the chance to tell the authorities what she knew.

"How long?"

Would it be enough time for her to either clean up the mess or get away?

"Any day." He lifted his whiskey and sipped again. "The question is, what do you plan to do about it?"

For a moment, she said nothing. Her eyes narrowed and she looked at him closely. Was he asking out of concern or so he could report to whoever was coming from Midlothian?

"The first order of business is to check with Sorensen to confirm what you heard about Sorkowski. If true, I will make sure the Admiral learns just how foolish it is to even think about double-crossing us." She leaned back and considered what to say next. Paulus was no fool. More importantly, he knew how she operated. Unless she missed her guess, he probably knew more about her than she wanted. That meant she had to proceed carefully where he was concerned. He was as much of a killer as was she. "As for the rest of it, I can make all those concerns disappear in short order. Just keep our *friend* off my back for a week. That's all the time I need."

"You will not do anything without first consulting me." He pinned her with a firm look.

"Understood." She didn't like it but what choice did she have?

"Now, I suggest we both get back to work. There is a lot to do and not much time in which to do it." He stood and waited as she did the same.

When he motioned for her to proceed him out of the room, she hesitated. Then she pointedly turned her back on him and walked away. He wouldn't try anything here, in a room off the main dining room of one of the most popular restaurants in the capital. No, it was his none-too-subtle way of telling her to watch her back. Well, he didn't have to remind her twice.

8

"Good afternoon, Mrs. LeClerc." Elizabeth Shaw handed the housekeeper her briefcase. Then she cocked her head to one side, listening. "Is she here?"

"Yes, ma'am. She arrived home half an hour ago." Leclerc looked past her employer to where Lieutenant Liu stood and her eyes narrowed. Seeing it, Elizabeth fought her smile. She recognized the look all too well. Marie Leclerc was ready to morph into protector mode, much as she had with Ashlyn and her siblings had been children. Since Ash's return home, the housekeeper had once again taken up the role.

"Good." She reached out and placed a gentle hand on the woman's arm. "It's all right, Marie. I know why the good lieutenant is here."

"Ma'am." For a moment, Leclerc said nothing. "The Colonel is at the pool taking her afternoon swim."

"Then we will join her there." She glanced to where Liu stood slightly apart from them, as if giving them a moment of privacy. "Lieutenant, you know the way. Go ahead. I'll join you shortly."

He nodded and moved past them. As he did, Elizabeth turned her attention back to the housekeeper. First things first.

"Marie, I promise this is not going to upset Ash," she said as Liu disappeared from sight.

"I hope not, ma'am. She's had a hard time the last few days."

Elizabeth nodded. "A hard time" was putting it mildly. The closer they got to the beginning of the courts martial, the more strain she saw in her daughter's face. She understood why Ash had been working herself into exhaustion. It wasn't simply because Ortega and two Devil Dog companies had left the system. It wasn't even because she still grieved for the loss of Paul Pawlak. Even the so-called terrorist attack the week before did not account for it. Elizabeth understood because she had been there. Ashlyn's nightmares were too close to the surface and they returned every night. The only way to defeat them was to be so exhausted she fell asleep instantly.

But that only delayed the demons. They still came in the dark of night, disturbing her rest. Not that Ash had said anything. She didn't need to when she spent every free moment she could with Jake, as if afraid they would once again be forcibly separated. Not when she was the last to retire for the night and the first up come morning. Marie had reported that Ashlyn had been up before her the last couple of days and no one in the household got up before the woman if they didn't have to.

"Thank you for loving her as much as I do, Marie." She gave the woman's hand a quick squeeze. "I'd appreciate it if you'd pull a tray together for us. We might be a while." And she had missed lunch, something her stomach reminded them both of by rumbling loudly.

With that, she followed Liu through the house. As she did, she reached for her comm. She had a feeling Kevin Talbot would be nearby but she wanted to be sure. The master gunnery sergeant had been left specific orders by Ortega to be Ashlyn's shadow and right hand while she was out of the system with Delta and Gamma Companies. That meant he had taken to bunking in one of the spare rooms at the house most nights. Those nights he wasn't there, he made sure another of the Devil Dogs was. No matter how much Ash protested, he remained firm, backed by Elizabeth's own orders that her daughter was to be constantly guarded until the courts martial had been concluded.

A slight smile touched Elizabeth's lips as she stepped outside. Liu stood to the right of the door, Talbot at his side. Seemingly oblivious to their presence, Ashlyn swam the length of the pool at the far in the deck with strong, smooth strokes. Her skin almost glowed with a healthy tan. Muscles rippled with each stroke. With the exception of the band of white in her dark hair, this was the Ashlyn of old. At least physically. Mentally and emotionally, she would never be the same. No one could be after all she had been through.

But, as Elizabeth was beginning to suspect, Ashlyn would be a stronger, more determined woman and officer as a result. While that boded well for those who served with her, it meant her enemies would find themselves facing a foe who would not give up until one of them was dead.

Elizabeth picked up the towel Ash had tossed over the back of one of the deckchairs and walked to the edge of the pool. "Good swim?" she asked as her daughter levered herself out of the pool.

"Mom!" Surprised, Ash almost slipped back into the water. Then she climbed to her feet and accepted the soft towel her mother extended to her. "I didn't know you were home."

When she stiffened, Elizabeth knew she had seen Liu waiting behind them with Talbot. "Easy, Ash." She spoke softly so no one could overhear. "It's good news. I promise."

Ash lifted the towel to dry her hair, not that it fooled her mother. Elizabeth knew she was giving herself a moment to think.

Ashlyn lowered the towel and studied her mother, her expression serious. Then she motioned for them to have a seat at one of the tables. Almost immediately, Mrs. Leclerc appeared with beer for both of them. Then she disappeared inside the house once more.

"What is it?" Ash asked softly, eyes dark with concern.

Before answering, Elizabeth motioned for the men to join them. "Ash, Lieutenant Liu came to see me this afternoon. He came directly from a meeting with Major Quintana and General Okafor. He had been briefing them on information he just learned about the events leading up to the false charges being filed against you and your people, not to mention the mission that preceded those charges."

They waited as the housekeeper once again appeared. She placed a tray on the table and promised to bring drinks for the men. Then, just before turning to go inside, she rested her hand on Ashlyn's shoulder, a reassuring gesture that had the young woman reaching up and grasping her hand in response.

"I thought that had already been covered." Ashlyn looked at Liu and Elizabeth frowned to see her pale slightly.

"So did we, ma'am." He gave a slight shrug. "But, as your mother alluded to, some new information came into my possession earlier today and it will impact the courts martial of all involved."

———

"And?"

Ashlyn swallowed hard against the gorge rising in her throat. What new information could the JAG officer have that required an unscheduled meeting? The last time something similar happened, she had found herself on the wrong end of a conspiracy. Surely history wasn't about to repeat itself.

No, it wasn't. It couldn't. Her mother would not be a party to it. She had to remember that. Not that it helped – much – when she remembered the past.

She forced herself to breathe deeply and remain calm. She had to let Liu explain. Then she could decide what, if anything, to do.

"Tell her," Elizabeth said firmly as she looked across the table to where the JAG officer sat.

He nodded once. As he did, Ashlyn felt a glimmer of hope. He did not look worried. Instead, there was something close to triumph on his face.

"Yesterday, I received word from Kurt Sorensen asking for a meeting. With Sorkowski's court martial about to begin, I figured it was Sorensen's standard posturing, trying to figure out exactly what evidence we have against his client. What I wasn't prepared for was him asking if I would entertain the possibility of a plea bargain."

Ash felt her eyes widen in surprise. If Liu had been surprised by the question, she was stunned. Never had she expected Sorkowski to admit he had done anything wrong.

Liu sipped his beer before continuing. "It gets better – or stranger. I'm still not sure which."

Ashlyn frowned.

"Sorry." He shook his head and took another sip before continuing. "Ma'am, he wasn't there to ask about a deal for Sorkowski. According to him, he was there representing the attorneys for all the accused. They wanted to know if I would offer and one-time deal for the first of the accused to speak up. He would go with me to meet with the defendants and I would explain what I wanted and what I was willing to give as a plea bargain. Then I would leave him to discuss it with them."

"What? That doesn't make any sense."

"Exactly." Liu went on to explain how he had spoken with the other attorneys and they confirmed what Sorensen said. "I thought maybe they were doing this because they are civilian attorneys and most of them aren't familiar with military proceedings. Still, what they wanted was so far out of the norm for even civilian trials that it didn't feel right."

"And?"

"I met with them. I offered a very short-term deal. The first to agree to tell me everything, and back it up with proof, would have the death penalty taken off the table. That was all. Then I left them to discuss it with Sorensen.

"I didn't expect anything to come of it. Everything about it seemed off. All I knew for sure was Sorensen spoke with them for a few minutes. During that time, he showed each of them something on datapads he had brought with him. Then he left and the guards prepared to take the prisoners back to their cells."

"I take it something happened. You wouldn't be here just to tell me that."

"You're right, Colonel." Now he smiled, a predatory smile she recognized. It was the same one she had seen when he realized the cases against Sorkowski and O'Brien were coming together. "The moment he was away from his fellow defendants, Sorkowski demanded he be allowed to see me. He was the only one to do so and, looking at the vid of all of them as they were returned to their cells, they were all terrified. Whatever Sorensen told them scared the hell out of them."

"Do I want to know?" She looked at her mother.

"You do."

She drew a deep breath, held it, exhaled. "Lieutenant?"

"Colonel, Sorkowski admitted everything. He even told us where we could find more evidence tying him to what happened to you and your people as well as to taking bribes, looking the other way so smuggling operations would continue in the sector, and setting up training exercises and patrols to avoid certain areas of the sector when shall we say less than friendly ships were scheduled to move through.

"The data and his confession make it clear O'Brien was in on it all. The junior officers and non-coms involved mainly took part in the smuggling and bribery operations. Although, a few of them were also involved in what happened to you and yours. He also led us to evidence that directly links some of the former Administration to what happened."

"There's more, isn't there?" Her stomach churned and she pushed her beer away. How deep did the conspiracy against her and her people go?

"There is."

Now Liu looked to Elizabeth. Seeing it, Ashlyn frowned. What could be so bad the JAG officer did not want to be the one to tell her?

More to the point, did she really want to know?

"Ash, you will be getting the full report later, after it is presented to SecDef and the President. From what Sorkowski told Lieutenant Liu and Major Quintana, combined with the data he has led them to, proves what some of us have suspected. What happened to you and your people is tied to the war."

"Callusian or Midlothian?"

"When it happened?" Liu asked and she nodded. "Callusian."

"But?"

"We now believe that the attack on the Capital, as well as the accidents O'Brien, Sorkowski and the others suffered, were arranged by a Midlothian operative here on Fuercon."

For several long moments, Ashlyn sat as silent and unmoving as a statue. She had expected Callusian involvement. It was the only thing that made sense. If Sorkowski and O'Brien had been worried only about hiding their ties with smugglers, they would have found some way to either keep Ash and her people away from any activity that could have revealed what was going on or they would have managed to convince Pawlak to recall them. She and her fellow Devil Dogs had been with the taskforce as a temporary assignment. Hell, the two could have suspended their activities until the Devil Dogs had returned to base.

Even knowing there was a Midlothian hand in the current war had not prepared her for this. It also led to the same questions she had asked when that bit of intelligence had been shared: how long had the Midlothians been working against Fuercon and its other allies and was the Midlothian government involved or was someone else pulling the strings behind the scenes?

"Colonel, we have reason to believe that the Midlothian operative has personally targeted you," Liu continued.

As the news sank in, Ashlyn felt as if she had taken a full stun beam to the body. Her throat closed and she couldn't breathe. Blood pounded almost painfully in her ears, deafening her. What had been a peaceful scene just moments before now swam sickeningly before her as her stomach churned dangerously. She pushed out of her chair and stumbled to the edge of the deck. Once there, she fell to her hands and knees, shoulders heaving and tears streaming down her cheeks as she emptied her stomach onto the grass.

How long she knelt there she didn't know. Stomach still churning, throat raw, she finally climbed to her feet. Absently, she brushed her hands against her thighs before scrubbing away her tears. As if from a distance, she heard her mother softly telling Liu and Talbot to stay where they were.

Why target her? It simply didn't make any sense. She could understand General Okafor or even her mother being targets. You impacted your enemy's fighting force more by taking out senior officers, especially those as well-respected as the Commandant and Elizabeth. But her? She was a Marine, nothing more and nothing less. Kill her and someone else would take her place, just as she had taken Pawlak's place when he had been transferred.

Had she seen or heard something while part of Sorkowski's taskforce that could identify the operative here? That was the only thing she could think of to explain why she had been targeted. If so, it could explain why the former administration had not acted to investigate what happened. That was especially true if a member of the administration was the operative. But it was almost too much to take in, much less believe.

If she was wrong and she didn't possess knowledge of who the operative was, why go to so much trouble just to get her out of the way? What had she done to scare someone that badly? And how deep did the conspiracy run?

And who the hell was behind it all?

"I'm all right, Loco," she said softly as Talbot hurried to help her to her chair. "Really," she confirmed when he continued to watch her in concern.

As she reached once more for her beer, Ashlyn saw how badly her hand trembled. Worse, she knew the others saw it as well. Then her mother was kneeling at her side, gently turning Ash's face so they looked at one another. For a long moment, her mother said nothing. Then she nodded and gave Ash a reassuring smile.

"So what's next?" she asked as she turned her attention back to Liu.

"Sorkowski is being moved. As Major Quintana said, we don't

want to risk him suffering any sort of fatal *accident* between now and morning."

"What happens then?"

"Then, assuming everything goes as planned tonight, there will be a press release from Major Quintana detailing new arrests that have been made as well as detailing the evidence that led to said arrests." He leaned back in his chair and smiled in satisfaction.

"I think you'd better explain," Ashlyn said firmly. "And you had better not be here to say you suspect any of my people."

"No, we don't suspect any of your people." He paused and she waited, her expression grim. "Colonel – Ashlyn, I swear to you. You and your people are not under suspicion. In fact, if everything goes as planned, we may finally understand everything that happened to you and others over the last few years."

"Do you know who the Midlothian operative is?"

"The short answer to your question is not yet. We have the identity of someone, Sorkowski's contact. What we don't know is if she is a deep operative or someone working with them. But we will find out. We're going to move on her tonight."

"Her?" Ashlyn looked from Liu to her mother and back. "Who?"

"The name we have is Evan Moreau."

Moreau. Ashlyn closed her eyes, thinking hard, trying to recall if she had ever come across the name. With a shake of her head, she opened her eyes. If she had crossed paths with this Moreau, she didn't remember. Of course, she knew from her time working with Rico Santiago that operatives never used their own names, not if they planned on living long. That was especially true if they were under deep cover. So her money was on Moreau not being the woman's name, at least not the one she had been born with.

"I take it you don't recognize the name," Elizabeth said softly.

"No." Another shake of her head. "I won't ask to be included in the take-down, Lieutenant, but I want at least one of my people there."

For a moment, the JAG officer said nothing. Then, his expression serious, he nodded. One corner of his mouth quirked up oh-so-slightly and Ashlyn chuckled softly. Liu had finally figured her out. Or maybe he finally realized it was better to keep her in the loop than to risk her, or any of the Devil Dogs, from taking matters into their own hands.

"I was hoping you might loan me the Master Gunnery Sergeant and one or two others, Colonel," Liu said. "Not only will we be moving on this Moreau but also on several others, some who had been under Sorkowski's or O'Brien's command at the time you and your team were sent into the ambush and some who were here, making sure their activities weren't discovered."

"How many do you need?" As she spoke, she saw Talbot produce his comm-unit. No doubt he would send for not only those she gave the assignment to but also someone to stand in for him as her bodyguard until he returned.

"Major Quintana is sending out four teams once I leave here. We wanted to let you know what was happening before we made our move. The two of us spoke and would appreciate it if you sent three of your Devil Dogs with each team."

"Master Guns, send word to the squad that they have special duty tonight. With Captain Ortega away, contact Lieutenant Moran that he has the command."

"Roger that, ma'am." Talbot stood and moved away from the table to make the contacts.

"How does Sorkowski's change of heart impact the upcoming courts martial?" Could luck finally be on her side and she would not have to testify?

"In most cases, I would say the other defendants would have their attorneys begging for plea deals once they learn Sorkowski has broken ranks. But I think we both realize there is more going on here than we know – yet. So, continue to assume we will be going to trial day after tomorrow but don't be surprised if we don't."

She nodded once, her expression grim. The one thing she knew for certain was Liu was right when he said more was going on than they knew. She hoped they found out what before it blew up in their faces again.

"What can my office do to help, Lieutenant Liu?" Elizabeth asked.

"Nothing yet, ma'am. Major Quintana told me to let you know that she will be reporting to both you and the Commandant as the arrests are made and what, if anything, we learn as a result."

"Very well." She looked up as Talbot rejoined them. "Master Guns?"

"General, Colonel, the squad will be ready to move out within the hour. Where do you want us to stage from?"

To anyone who did not know him well, he might have been asking about the weather. But Ashlyn wasn't fooled. Nor did she suspect her mother was. Talbot looked forward to the upcoming op. Not that Ashlyn blamed him. Part of her, a very large part, wished she was going with them. But she understood why she could not. Liu and Quintana wanted to give the defense team no reason to question the arrests or any information gathered as a result. So she had to be satisfied with sending Talbot and the others to make sure nothing went wrong.

"If it is all right with General Shaw, I would like to stage from here," Liu said.

"Of course."

"Thank you, ma'am."

"With your permission, Colonel, I'll inform the squad and make sure Mrs. Leclerc knows they will be arriving shortly."

"Go," Ash said and watched as he made his way inside. "Now, Lieutenant, what else can you tell us? I assume there is more on you mind than what you've said so far."

Even if she wasn't sure she wanted to hear it.

"There is, ma'am." He pushed his beer to one side. "From what Sorkowski has told us, there were some minor and not so minor members of the former Administration who were aware of his activities and turned a blind eye for the right remuneration. That is what the Major is looking into right now and why she did not come with me."

"Did they have anything to do with what happened to my daughter and her command?" Elizabeth's voice turned hard. Ashlyn had a feeling if Liu answered in the affirmative, her mother might decide to go along with Talbot and the others to *help* with the arrests. That, Ash knew, meant busted heads and more if anyone resisted – not that she would blame her mother one bit.

"Ma'am, we are still trying to figure that out but I think it safe to say at least some of them were involved in making sure the Colonel and her people were tried and convicted. Even if they had nothing to do with sending them into the ambush, they helped cover up what happened.

"I have studied the information available to us about the ambush until I can quote it in my sleep. The problem has always been that all the intelligence we had dealt with what happened on your end, Colonel. We never had much more than suspicions about what might have been going on here. Thanks to the information Sorkowski is giving us, and the fact we can confirm most of it through other sources now that we know where to look, we can finally make a move locally.

"What concerns Major Quintana and me the most is how it is starting to look as if what happened to you is somehow tied in with the intelligence your people seized on Cassius Prime. From what we have determined based on Sorkowski's information, there was not only an active movement here to undermine the peace negotiations during the last war in such a way the Callusians could continue acting against us.

"Ma'am – Ashlyn, we don't have concrete proof yet but it is starting to look like Sorkowski's and O'Brien's smuggling and turning of a blind eye was being used by the enemy to give them a route to our allied systems that they knew would not be patrolled. You and your Devil Dogs put that in jeopardy so you had to be taken out of the equation. The only way that could be done without too many questions being asked was to make it look like you had gone rogue and innocents had been killed as a result. It wouldn't be the first time it had happened to a Marine and probably won't be the last.

"Sorkowski admitted the plan had been for you and your people to die in the ambush. They purposely gave you bad intel, knowing you would be walking into a trap. When you survived and they realized you had already been raising questions about how they were acting, they devised the plan to bring you and the other survivors up on charges. Now everyone involved with what happened will face justice. I promise you that."

"And this Moreau?"

"She is the wild card we haven't figured out yet. Hopefully, she will be smart enough to cooperate once we have her in custody. In the meantime, you will find orders from General Okafor that you are to have security with you at all times. She is taking this potential threat as serious as Major Quintana and I are."

"I don't like it but I will do as ordered."

At least as long as she had a say in who her shadow happened to be. She knew her people, her Devil Dogs, would understand the need to find out how deep the conspiracy ran and would help her cut it out, just like you cut out a cancer. More importantly, they would recognize the need to keep her family, especially her son, safe. No matter what happened to Ashlyn herself, little Jake had to be protected.

"Now, General, if there is somewhere I can work until the others get here, I'd appreciate it. I want to make sure all the necessary warrants are in place. Then I need to report back to Major Quintana."

"Of course, Lieutenant." She reached for her comm-unit and a moment later, Mrs. Leclerc appeared. "Marie, please show the lieutenant somewhere he can have a little privacy."

"This way, Lieutenant."

"Ash," Elizabeth began once the two had disappeared inside.

"Don't, Mom." She pushed to her feet and stepped away from the table. "I know, intellectually at least, that what happened wasn't my fault. Hell, I've spent the last three years almost learning to accept that. Now I have to wrap my mind around the fact that not only is one of our supposedly loyal allies trying to help our enemy destroy us but that there is someone working for them with a personal grudge against me. Hell, Mom, life is a whole lot easier in battle."

"I know, love." Elizabeth stood and moved to her side. "But look at what we do know now and realize that at least part of it is about to come to an end. With Sorkowski not only pleading to the charges against him but cooperating with JAG, we are finally getting the information we need to not only bring every one of the bastards responsible for what happened to you and your people to justice but to hopefully ending the war once and for all. I have a feeling it won't be long before you and the rest of the Devil Dogs ship out."

Ashlyn nodded. Part of her hoped her mother was right.

"Now go brief Talbot and tell him I expect a full report when he gets back."

9

"**D**amn it!"

She slammed her palm against the control panel next to the door, locking it. How she had managed to hold her temper in check on the interminable ride home was a miracle. All she had wanted was to kill someone, anyone. She didn't care if it was the cabbie who had brought her from the restaurant – and probably the only thing that saved him was that he wasn't a "him" but an it. The company's use of 'droids to give their passengers the feeling they were being driven was one reason she normally liked using them. Tonight, however, the lack of conversation had kept her from ripping the droid's head from its shoulders. – or anyone else.

No, that wasn't quite true. She had a very definite list of people she wanted to kill, slowly and painfully if possible. It started with Sorkowski and O'Brien. If they had shown an ounce of competence, Shaw and the others would have been killed three years ago. That would have prevented everything that happened since then. Unfortunately, she had learned they were much better at turning their heads away from illegal activities and collecting bribes for doing so than they were with dealing with trouble.

Following close behind those two were Sorensen and Paulus.

Sorensen had failed, something she had not thought possible, to keep his client in line. How could a man so accomplished fail her so completely? It wasn't as if he hadn't been more than handsomely paid for what should have been an easy assignment. Nor was it something he hadn't done before. She had made sure of that before first approaching him. Obviously, she had misjudged him and his devotion to his family. Either that or he didn't believe she would carry through with her threats. Well, she would soon teach him how foolish he had been to let his client go rogue.

A slight smile touched her lips as she opened the safe hidden in her bedroom closet. If she played her cards right – and she would. She always did, no matter what her handlers thought. There were simply times when even the most carefully laid plans became derailed – she would be able to take care of Sorensen and make it look like Paulus had been involved. Let the so-called diplomat explain that away when the Fuerconese started investigating. He might be able to hang onto his diplomatic immunity but, if her guess about the current state of affairs in the Midlothian government were right, they would toss Paulus away like so much trash.

Paulus.

She cursed the day he had inserted himself into the mission. For almost three years she had operated on her own, confident that she would be able to complete the job without problem. After all, this was a long-term assignment, one that required a deft hand and a sharp knife, both figurative and literal. Her Midlothian employers had chosen her because it was exactly the sort of thing she excelled at. Besides, being a Fuerconese citizen, born and raised, her presence on-planet and as part of the business and political sectors would not be questioned.

Then, without warning, Paulus had shown up a year ago. Before she could protest – or even check with those who had initially employed her – he had presented her with proof Watchman not only knew of his presence on Fuercon but approved. Worse, Watchman said she was to take orders from Paulus the same as she would from him. At the time, Moreau had assumed Watchman was simply firming up his control of things on Midlothian, even if it was only behind the scenes, and did not want his attention diverted. That even made sense. But, over the course of the last six months, she had found herself wondering more and more if the Intelligence Czar meant to terminate her at the end of the assignment, no matter how it turned out.

Now it looked like her paranoia had been well-founded.

To hell with both of them.

If Paulus thought she would sit still while he chose the time and place – not to mention manner – of her death, he was sadly mistaken. She would neither wait patiently for the executioner nor would she go about her daily business as if nothing was wrong. She had been in the assassination business long enough to know not only what her handler expected her to do but what this new "talent" would expect as well. After all, she had been the one brought in to deal with *little problems* more times than she could remember. That experience could keep her alive – at least as long as she-did not get careless.

That meant getting away from her apartment without Paulus knowing. No doubt he had someone already in place, watching to see where she went. It didn't matter. She had prepared for such an eventuality long ago. When she walked out the building's front entrance in just a few minutes, anyone watching would see exactly what she wanted them to. They would see a woman on her way to dinner or a night on the town. There would be no heavy bag, stuffed with everything she owned. No, all she would take was the clutch she had carried when she returned home and her briefcase. Of course, inside would be weapons and money, all she needed until she made her way to the first of a series of safe houses. Every move had been carefully planned as soon as she realized Paulus was not going to leave her alone to do the job she had contracted for.

Once safely hidden away, once she was convinced no one had managed to follow her, she could take the time needed to plan her next move.

One thing was certain. If she did not find a way to not only complete her assignment but to prove her value to the Midlothians, she would spend the rest of her life looking over her shoulder. That was not how she planned to live her retirement. But that was for later. One step at a time, starting with getting away from the apartment while she still could.

Then she could figure out the best way to do the job and get a little vengeance along the way.

————

TALBOT casually strode down the street. As he reached the corner, he stepped into the shadows. From there, he took up a position where he could study the entrance to the building across the street without anyone noticing. As he did, he pulled his data unit and called up information on the building. He had already studied all the pertinent information but, as he had learned in the previous war, it never hurt to double check everything before beginning an op.

"Loco?"

Hound and Tank, the squad's heavy weapon specialists, moved silently into the shadows from the opposite end of the street. It wasn't long before the rest of the team was there, including Lieutenant Liu. The JAG officer had remained silent as Talbot went over the op with his people. Until they had Moreau in custody, he was simply along to observe.

"Tank, Boomer, Brigit, you're with me. We're two couples out to meet a friend. The rest of you, take your places. Let's seal the building up and make sure she doesn't give us the slip."

Corporal Annaliese Fekete, the squad's demolitions expert, and Lance Corporal Faith Connery, the comms operator, stepped forward. Talbot looked them, as well as Tank, over and nodded once. Few looking at them would see anything but four people out for a good time. There was no hint they were military, except for their bearing which he knew would change as soon as they stepped out of the shadows. This was not the first time any of them had needed to blend in with civilians and it would not be the last. But, in many ways, it was the most important of those missions to date.

"The rest of you have three minutes to get into place. Signal when you're set."

Talbot watched as the others slipped out of the shadows and moved in different directions. The tactician in him nodded in approval. None of them would take the most direct route to the apartment building. Instead, they would circle around or back, making sure they had not picked up a tail or unwanted attention. In the meantime, all he could do was wait.

Exactly three minutes later, everyone had reported in. They were in place. Time to put the next phase of the op into action.

Talbot nodded and the four stepped out of the shadows. As they did, Talbot reached for Connery's hand and settled it in the crook of his arm. His lips twitched with a smile as Tank slid an arm around Fekete's shoulders. She leaned into him, her arm snaking around his waist. Satisfied, Talbot waited for a break in traffic and led them across the street in the direction of the apartment entrance.

All they had to do was get past the doorman. If they could, and if they could do so without him alerting the target, they might just be able to pull this off.

"May I help you?" the uniformed doorman asked almost as soon as they stepped onto the sidewalk in front of the entrance.

"You sure can," Connery said as she stepped closer to him. Talbot almost choked as she smiled and batted her eyes as the doorman. "It's my cousin's birthday today and she is refusing to let us buy her a drink. Says she has work or something she needs to do. But it's her birthday. We can't let her be alone."

"Ma'am, I'm not sure I can help you." The doorman looked to the others. Before he could say anything, Talbot nodded.

"We know we're asking a lot, but it would mean the world to my partner here if you'd let us in. I promise all we'll do is use the house comm to contact Evan and try to convince her to come out with us. If she doesn't agree, we'll leave."

"Even if I could let you in – and I can't. You should know that. – it wouldn't do you any good. Ms. Moreau left about two hours ago. I guess she had plans after all."

"Brigit, that's good news," Fekete said, as though she were reassuring her friend. "Now can we go get some dinner? I'm starved."

"Did she happen to say where she was going?" Connery asked, still playing the concerned cousin.

"No, ma'am."

Talbot thanked him and the four walked down the street, talking about where they wanted to eat and what they wanted to do afterwards. Once they were out of earshot, Talbot signaled the others.

"The op is a no-go. The target left the building two hours before we arrived." Frustration filled his voice.

"Move to the next target," Lieutenant Liu instructed them. "Moreau may be in the wind now but we will find her."

Damn straight they would.

Half an hour later, Talbot and the others, all except for Connery and Liu, were shown to a table at a sidewalk café across the street from their next target. To anyone looking on, they were nothing more than a group of friends out for the night. No one would guess they were very angry Marines who wanted nothing more than to commit some mayhem. That impression was reinforced when they ordered drinks and decadent desserts.

Over the course of the next two hours, they watched the building, waiting for the target to return home. From time to time, reports would come in from Connery and Liu. They had managed to locate the target as he left his office. Now they were following at a discreet distance, making sure he didn't pull a vanishing act like Moreau had. If they were lucky, this part of the op would soon come to a successful conclusion.

"There."

Talbot nodded to the expensive aircar settling down in one of the parking spaces down the street from the building across from them. Like Moreau's apartment building, the security for this one was tight. But they had already taken care of that, at least Liu assured them he had. If not, things could get very bad very quickly.

Kurt Sorensen appeared from the back of the aircar. As he leaned down, probably paying the driver, Talbot tossed enough money onto the tabletop to cover their bill. As he did, everyone stood. Then, laughing and joking, they started across the street. By the time Sorensen approached the building's main entrance, the group was close enough to stop him. Instead, they watched as he stepped inside, nodding to the doorman without really looking at him. which was all for the good since the regular doorman had been replaced by one of Liu's men.

"Go," Talbot said softly. Instantly, everyone but Tank and Hound peeled off. They would make sure Sorensen went to his apartment did not slip out of the building before Liu could arrest him.

"The lift went straight to his floor. There are two other apartments on the floor. One is empty, undergoing reno for new owners and the owners of the third are enjoying a night at the theater," Liu's man reported. He paused, his head cocked to one side. Then he gave a nod. "The lift has been locked down. He's not leaving the floor unless he tries to take the stairs and alarms will sound if he does."

"Did he seem worried about anything?"

"Negative, Master Guns."

"Good. Make sure no one tries to go up after us."

The man nodded and watched as the small group made its way to the lift. At Talbot's signal, he released the lift. A few moments later, the doors slid open. Talbot motioned everyone inside. As he did, he frowned slightly. This part of the op was going almost too smoothly. Not that he would complain. That had been part of the beauty of the plan. Even if Sorensen thought there might be trouble, they were doing the one thing he most likely would not expect. They were coming to him in the one place he would feel the most secure. Whether he let them in or not didn't matter. Liu had secured a master passcode that would get them inside. Talbot planned to use it and make sure the attorney did not have a chance to get away – or worse.

"We're in position, Loco," Connery reported as the lift came to a halt.

"Hold. I'll leave comms open. Monitor and react accordingly."

As they stepped off the lift, Liu appeared from what Talbot assumed was the vacant apartment. A moment later, the JAG officer handed him the passcode. Together, they walked down the corridor in the direction of Sorensen's apartment. Thick carpet muffled their steps. Soon, very soon, they would have the man in custody and, hopefully, more answers to the questions that had haunted the Devil Dogs for three years.

At least Talbot hoped so.

"Brigit, kill the pickups. Let's not give him any more warning than we have to," he ordered.

"Done. He will be deaf and blind, technologically speaking at least."

"LT." He held the passcode ready and looked at Liu for his cue.

Liu nodded. Talbot used the passcode and dove through the door the moment it slid open far enough. One hand held his weapon and the other his credentials. Behind him, Liu entered the room, followed closely by Tank and Hound. Sorensen stood rooted in place, his expression frozen in shock, as Talbot motioned for Tank and Hound to secure him. Once they had, they began checking the apartment, making sure no one else was present.

"What the hell is this, Liu?" the attorney demanded. "I'll have your commission and your head for this."

"I don't think so," the JAG officer said. "Kurt Sorensen, you are under arrest for conspiracy, interference with an investigation, bribery, accessory to murder, and treason." Liu went on to read Sorensen his rights, ignoring the man's protests.

"You can't do this!"

"I can and I have," Liu countered. "However, if you would prefer I leave you with these gentlemen, I will."

Sorensen looked from Liu to Talbot and then to Tank and Hound as they reappeared from the rear of the apartment. "Who the hell are they? If you think you can coerce me into saying anything, you're sadly mistaken."

Instead of answering, Liu looked at Talbot and nodded once. Talbot stepped forward until Sorensen took a step back and fell onto the chair behind him.

"Master Gunnery Sergeant Kevin Talbot, First Division, Second

Battalion Fuerconese Marine Corps and company. You might know us better as members of the Devil Dogs."

"Ooh-Rah!" Tank and Hound said.

Sorensen paled. His opened his mouth to say something but nothing came out. When he cleared his throat and tried again, Liu stepped forward. At his signal, Tank and Hound lifted Sorensen to his feet.

"Let me put this in terms you can understand. Your former client has told us everything about your so-called representation of him. I have talked with the other defense attorneys and I know how you coerced them into letting you speak for them at our earlier meeting. My office has evidence, and has confirmed it, to prove you have been in a conspiracy with one Evan Moreau to keep all those, and especially Sorkowski and O'Brien, charged in relation to what happened to Colonel Shaw and her people, from telling what they know. We know that you were not representing the best interests of your client but of your real employer, Moreau.

"Now, before you think you can hand her over to us, we have enough evidence already to arrest and convict her. Unlike you, however, she anticipated trouble and has disappeared. I promise it is only a temporary reprieve for her. For you, your only hope to avoid the executioner is to cooperate fully. Or, if you prefer, I will leave now and let these Devil Dogs have a conversation with you. It is your call."

"You can't!" Panic filled Sorensen's eyes.

"I can and will." Liu stepped forward, his expression hard. "You betrayed your oaths as an attorney. Worse, you betrayed your home and government. You sold your soul to the enemy and for what? Money, influence? As far as I'm concerned, you are an enemy combatant. That means and I can and will do as I said."

"Please, give me a chance. I know things, things you can't have discovered without me."

Liu stood there, staring at Sorensen. Talbot had to give it to him. The JAG officer looked as if he were actually considering what the them said. What Sorensen apparently hadn't figured out was that this had all been a carefully planned encounter. Liu would never, no matter how tempting it might be, give the attorney over to the Devil Dogs. But he wasn't above making the threat, not if it led them to more conspirators. As for Talbot, he didn't care if it meant they would finally be able to punish everyone involved in betraying Ashlyn and the others under her command three years earlier.

If they also happened to get a little payback in the process, all the better.

———

CAPTAIN ANDREW HENDRICKS surveyed the room, eyes dark and intense. He missed nothing, not the smallest detail about those nearest his charge. Even so, his expression remained neutral, almost relaxed. Years of experience had taught him the importance of at least appearing unconcerned. His life, not to mention the President's and the lives of the rest of the security detail, depended on what he observed. So, if an enemy happened to underestimate him, all the better. Such underestimation would lead the enemy to make mistakes and those mistakes gave him the edge.

And that edge very often meant the difference between life and death, something he knew all too well.

Not that Hendricks expected any trouble. He simply didn't believe in taking unnecessary risks. That was especially true where the President was concerned.

As his eyes once more swept the room, a soft, almost inaudible beep interrupted his thoughts. He listened closely to the report coming through his earbud. As he did, he reminded himself not to react. It simply wouldn't do to throw his head back and give a battle cry no matter how much he wanted to. Too many people would wonder why the head of the President's security detail suddenly acted as if the battle had been won. While that might not exactly be the case, things were finally falling into place and soon, very soon, some heads would roll figuratively if not literally.

Lifting a hand to cover his mouth, Hendricks quickly acknowledged the report. His eyes danced and his pulse pounded as he glanced in the President's direction. Their eyes met and locked for one brief moment before the President arched one dark brow in question. Speculation filled the man's eyes. Recognizing it and anticipating Harper's unasked question, Hendricks nodded once. Then he stepped away from the door, making his way purposefully across the room in the President's direction.

As he neared the head table, the two Marines stationed behind and to either side of the President almost imperceptibly braced to attention. Hendricks quickly signaled for them to stand easy. Too many eyes had already been drawn to the table by his approach. He almost laughed at how those closest to the President strained to hear what might be said, even as they tried not to look like they were eavesdropping.

"Captain," the President said simply as Hendricks stopped at his side. Nothing about him showed anything but polite interest in what his security head might have to say.

"Mister President," Hendricks acknowledged before bending to whisper in Harper's ear.

"Thank you, Captain," Harper said softly a moment later. He dabbed at his mouth with a linen napkin before continuing. "Please give my regards to the Major and ask her to keep me informed."

"Of course, Mister President. Do you have any other instructions?"

For a moment, Harper remained silent. Hendricks recognized the thoughtful expression that crossed the President's face and understood. Part of the man wanted to leave the dinner and return to his office so he could monitor what was happening. Another part knew he needed to stay. It would not do to start people wondering why he had left a state dinner early. Unfortunately, Hendricks saw no way around that. The information Major Quintana had sent and the implications of what it meant required both she and Colonel Santiago, and who knew how many others, brief the President before news leaked about what had been happening that evening.

"Have the 'car brought around, Captain," the President said softly, hiding his mouth behind his napkin. "Then send word to the appropriate parties, asking them to join me at the Residence. Full media blackout until we know what we are dealing with."

"At once, Mr. President."

"Andrew, don't worry. This is good news, or it will be in the long run," Harper said softly. "You know that."

"I do, sir." Hendricks turned to the Marine guard and, using the hand signals that were as much a part of their communication protocols as the spoken word, instructed them to send for the President's car. As they carried out his orders, he turned back to the dining hall, his eyes alert for anything out of the ordinary. Now was not the time to get careless.

"I apologize for the interruption, Ladies and Gentlemen, but the duties of my office rarely allow me an evening off." Harper spoke easily, almost casually.

As the President spoke, Hendricks let his eyes rest briefly on each of the man's tablemates. Of the seven, only Admiral Collins failed to smile and laugh lightly in response. Instead, First Fleet's commanding officer sat back, for all appearances relaxed and almost a little bored. But Hendricks knew better. He recognized the tautness in the man's posture. Collins might be Navy but he was a warrior and he recognized on some instinctual level that trouble was afoot.

"Is everything all right, Mister President?" the small, too thin woman sporting the garish makeup and unnaturally yellow hair currently favored by the younger members of Fuerconese society asked from down the table.

"It is." Harper smiled, that easy smile he used in public to assure everyone there was nothing to worry about. "Captain Hendricks was simply letting me know that a diplomatic pouch I've been expecting has arrived." Now he turned his attention to Collins and smiled a little regretfully.

"Admiral, as much as I hate to say it, I'm afraid we must cut the evening short and get back to work."

"Of course, Mister President."

"Ambassador Zakarian, please accept my most profound apologies. Unfortunately, duty calls."

"Of course, Mister President," the olive-skinned man seated opposite her replied easily, understanding reflected in his hazel eyes.

"The rest of my party shall remain to represent the Admiral and myself," Harper continued as he stood. "Thank you for a wonderful evening and I look forward to the opportunity to repay your hospitality."

With that, the President stepped away from the table, his Marine escort immediately assuming their places around him. As Collins joined them, the escort spread out, ready to protect both men. At the same time, a quick thrill of excitement ran through the Hendricks. Like a prize racehorse sensing the finish line ahead, he knew they were finally nearing the end of their search for the truth about what happened to Shaw and her people. Soon they would learn exactly who was at the heart of the conspiracy. When they did, they might also learn just how deep the betrayal by the Midlothians ran.

Then and only then would they be able to effectively fight back.

10

Ashlyn sighed heavily and leaned back, stretching her arms high above her head. Beyond the large window behind her, the night sky was broken by occasional flashes of lightning that danced across the horizon. The violence of the approaching storm resonated with the pounding deep inside her skull, a pounding caused not by the weather or even by the number of reports she had reviewed over the course of the evening.

No, it was caused by something much more primal than that.

Turning her chair away from the desk, Ashlyn stared outside. A bright flash of lightning, followed almost instantly by a deep roll of thunder, filled the air. Rain beat against the windows. Below, security 'droids patrolled the grounds, undisturbed by the rain or wind.

She had put Jake to bed several hours earlier. Not long after that, her parents had retired to their suite on the other side of the house. Since then, Ash had done her best to focus on the reports she would be expected to present at the meeting of FirstDiv's battalion COs the next morning. Try as she might, her attention wandered. So much rested on what Talbot and the others discovered that evening. She might finally have the answer to why she and the others had been betrayed. As important as that was, it paled in contrast to the realization that they might finally learn how deep the betrayal by Midlothian ran.

The potential harm of such a betrayal was more than she cared to think about just then. Midlothian had been one of Fuercon's most trusted allies for more than a century. It had been privy to much of the Administration's – current and past – plans to defeat the Callusians. If it had truly turned against Fuercon, things were going to get much worse before they got better. The possibility of having to go to war with Midlothian turned Ash's stomach. The casualties would be so much greater because they would have to make an example of their former ally. Not only would the military lose more good men and women but the civilian loss would be high.

That was war, but she never liked the idea of non-combatants being killed simply because they had the misfortune of being used as shields by their government.

But that was a worry for the future. Now her concern was for her people, for Talbot and those he had tapped to go along with him as he helped Lieutenant Liu execute the warrants he had secured based on the information from Sorkowski. Even though she knew Talbot would take care, she could not help wondering if the former admiral, one of those she held most responsible for what happened to her and her squad, might not be leading them into a trap. It would be just like the man, especially if he thought it might save him. Still, Liu had been convinced his information was good. She had to trust the JAG officer.

Not that putting her worry aside was easy. It was far from it, in fact.

Talbot's continued absence and the lack of an update were the real reasons Ashlyn's head felt as if it might explode at any moment. It was also the reason she had thrown herself into the stack of reports. She had hoped concentrating on them would not only prepare her for the morning meeting but would keep her distracted until Talbot returned. Unfortunately, it had not.

Damn it, why hadn't she heard anything? Had something gone wrong?

If it had, she would be as much to blame for it as she had been for what happened on the mission that led to her and the others being court martialed. She had known something was wrong, not only with her orders but with how Sorkowski and O'Brien were operating. She had even sent her concerns up the chain of command. But she hadn't pressed the issue. She had not been able to imagine the two men actually turning a blind eye to the smugglers operating in the sector, much less think they might be betraying Fuercon and its allies. That failure to recognize what was happening had led to the loss of some of those under her command as well as the courts martial of the surviving members of the team and herself. She would not be able to live with herself if something happened to Talbot or any of the others this time.

Damn it, why hadn't she told Liu to use his own people?

Stop it! You know Loco won't do anything to put himself or the others in danger.

But did she really? She had seen the almost pathological need to avenge what had happened to her and the others reflected in his eyes. She had seen it and recognized it. So, against her better judgment, she had all but given him her blessings before he left the house with Liu.

Now, as her doubts and fears rushed over her, she gritted her teeth in frustration. Would she never be allowed to return to a life where she didn't have to worry about those she cared for falling on their swords for her? More important in a way, would those very same friend and family members ever get past the need to avenge what had been done to her and the others? Didn't they realize what it would do to her if anyone else suffered because of her?

Turning away from the window, Ashlyn glanced at the clock. A frown tugged at the corners of her mouth to see it was almost midnight. Too much time had passed. Something must have gone wrong. Otherwise Talbot would be back.

Before Ashlyn could convince herself she needed to go in search for Talbot and the others, she heard the sounds of a vehicle approaching the house. A few moments later, the soft chirrup from the security panel downstairs broke the silence enveloping the house. Ashlyn turned away from the window. As she left the study, anticipation and something else – fear or worry, she wasn't sure which – filled her. If they had managed to accomplish what they set out to do . . ..

Moving quickly, forcing herself not to break into a run, Ashlyn made her way to the second-floor landing. Her heart skipped a beat in expectation and relief to see Talbot, his back to her, standing before the security panel. She watched closely, holding her impatience at bay, as he activated the house's security system. Then he turned and started for the stairs. When he looked up and saw her, he nodded slightly. For a moment, her heart seemed to stop. Had they failed? Then she saw the satisfaction reflected in his eyes. Hope flared once again.

"Master Guns, please join me in the library."

With that, Ashlyn turned and disappeared down the hall. As she did, she frowned thoughtfully. Talbot looked much as he did at the end of most missions. But then, little ever really ruffled him. That was one of the many reasons he was such a good Marine. It was also why she trusted him not only with her life but with her son's. Still, there had been something about his expression that worried her and she wondered yet again if something had gone wrong.

As she entered the study, Ashlyn grinned to herself. Talbot had made it clear from that first day when the Capital had been attacked that he was there to help her however he could. There had been times when, over her objections, he had made sure she ate or slept. He had kept her, on more than one occasion, from doing something that could have sent her straight back to the Tarsus penal colony. Now she would do whatever she could to make sure he was all right, whether he liked it or not.

A smile tugged at the corner of her mouth as she realized just how much she needed this opportunity. Talbot would never fully understand how great a help he had been those first few weeks after her return to Fuercon. After so long at the penal colony, after being betrayed by the Corps and the government, Ashlyn knew she had been little more than an animal. Oh, she had put up a good front in an attempt to hide her anger and fear from the others but Talbot had seen through it. He never said a word, but he had been there whenever she needed him, no matter what or when. He had kept her focused on duty when the thirst for vengeance would have had her risking everything just to get a little of her own back. More than anyone except her parents and son, Talbot had been her anchor as she found her way back to humanity.

"Have a seat, Kevin," she said gently as he entered the study.

Without waiting to see if he obeyed, Ashlyn turned to the antique butler's table and poured two glasses of whiskey. As she turned, she shook her head to find Talbot still standing just inside the doorway. She handed him one of the glasses and settled on one end of the sofa resting against western wall. Then she cocked an eyebrow at him in question. Talbot hesitated another moment. Then Ash shook her head, giving him her best "I'm your CO and this isn't a request," look. Smiling slightly, almost apologetically, he inclined his head and moved to the chair nearest her.

The silence stretched between them for several minutes. Recognizing her companion's need to collect his thoughts, possibly even come to terms with whatever he had seen or done that evening, Ashlyn leaned back and sipped her whiskey. As she did, she watched the master gunnery sergeant through lowered lashes. She had no doubt he understood what she was doing and why. Now she wanted him to see how much the decision to let him go with Liu had worried her as well as seeing how relieved she was he was home safely.

"Are you all right?" she asked simply as she placed her glass on the table at her elbow.

"I am, ma'am," he assured her, a satisfied smile lighting his features. "My apologies if I worried you but things took a bit of a left turn on us."

"Oh?" She cocked her head to one side and looked at him in questions. That things had not gone exactly as planned didn't surprise her. She had learned long ago few plans went off without a hitch of some sort. For a moment, she said nothing else, waiting for him to explain. When he didn't, she frowned slightly, concern once again flaring. "Master Guns, explain." She was too tired and too aware of everything that could have gone wrong to be patient.

"Sorry, ma'am, it's been a long evening."

He had no idea.

"You will get a full brief tomorrow from Lieutenant Liu and Major Quintana. The LT said to ask you if it would be convenient to meet with them at 0700."

She nodded. It would mean letting her mother know she might be a bit late to weekly briefing of battalion COs, but she was not going to miss hearing what the JAG officers had to say. She hoped her mother would understand.

"But the short version is we missed Moreau. From what the doorman at her building said, she left a couple of hours before we got there. My take is she is on the run, not necessarily from us. It could be her handlers decided she was a loose end they can't afford any longer."

Another nod. If Moreau was on the run, they still had a chance of catching her. Not that Ash would hold her breath. She knew how easy it was for someone with the right skills and enough cash in their pocket to find ways in and out of the capital and, from there, off-planet. But at least they knew who they were looking for and, if she knew Liu and Quintana, the alerts had already been sent out.

"We did manage to take Kurt Sorensen into custody. Let's say the good councilor was not pleased to be treated like one of his clients."

"Did you get anything out of him?"

"No, but I have no doubt that will change. He struck me as the type who has to bluster and posture but he will ultimately try to cut a deal to save his own skin. Liu left his own investigators combing through Sorensen's apartment and office. If there is a data trail to find, they'll find it."

Ashlyn sipped her whiskey. As she did, she wondered what the arrest of Sorensen would mean to the courts martial. She feared it would postpone them, even for those the man had not represented. If so, it meant she would be stuck on Fuercon even longer. That did not sit well. She was a Marine, a Devil Dog. She should be on the front lines, commanding her battalion in the fight against the enemy. Instead, it looked like they might remain in-system for the unforeseeable future.

Damn it!

"Anything else?"

"No, ma'am."

"Were any of our people injured?"

"That's a negative, Colonel." He finished his whiskey and set the glass on the table at his elbow. As he did, he grinned and the coils of concern nesting in Ashlyn's stomach eased. "Angel, we might have lost our tempers a bit, and I'd be lying if I said we weren't royally pissed not to get our hands on Moreau, but we're Devil Dogs. We took down the targets without any muss or fuss. These bastards weren't any challenge to us."

Targets?

Ashlyn leaned forward, elbows on knees, her expression intent. "Loco, explain. Targets?"

Still grinning, he nodded in confirmation. "Yes, ma'am. Targets."

"Master Guns, I swear if you don't get to the point, you will be walking night watch for the next month."

"You wound me, ma'am." He laughed and then held up a hand to keep her from saying anything else. "Sorry, ma'am, but you know how it's been. The rest of us have wanted to do something, anything to make the bastards responsible for what happened to you and the others pay. Tonight we took the first step in doing so."

She listened closely as he reported on the rest of their evening. After taking Sorensen into custody – and hearing how Liu had offered to leave the attorney in the gentle care of her Devil Dogs instead of arresting him brought a smile of her lips. She would have loved to have been there to see the expression on his face when presented with that possibility. – Liu had remained behind to begin the search of the attorney's apartment. Talbot and the others reported to Quintana. She had been waiting for them near the Midlothian embassy.

For more than an hour, they had waited. Then the JAG officer indicated a man just leaving the embassy. He was tall and thin but moved like a fighter. Instead of taking one of the waiting aircars, he simply walked away from the embassy. Every half block or so, he would pause, as if looking in a shop window or checking his comm-unit. It hadn't fooled any Talbot. The man had been checking for a tail. What he had not anticipated was the fact Talbot had put two of his team on the rooftops and they were relaying the man's position to the rest of the team.

"We tracked him to a bar in a part of town where you wouldn't expect someone like him to be found, at least not willingly," Talbot continued. "Quintana figured it had to be a meet but no one joined him and we did not see any sort of info drop take place. She said she would get with Colonel Santiago in the morning to set up surveillance on him."

"Why him? I assume you found something linking him to either Sorensen or Moreau."

"Sorensen had been in contact with him more often than he should have been, especially since he denied knowing him."

"Interesting." She thought for a moment. The morning briefing with the JAG should prove interesting. "All right, Loco. Go get some rest. If I'm supposed to meet with Liu and Quintana at 0700, we both will need to be out earlier than usual."

"Yes, ma'am."

"And, Kevin, thank you. Make sure the others know how much I appreciate all you did tonight."

"No need, ma'am. They know."

Ashlyn watched as he slowly left the study. He had given her a lot to think about and even more questions to ask when she met with Liu and Quintana. But all that had to wait for morning. In the meantime, she needed to leave her mother a message explaining why she might be late for the battalion COs briefing. Then she'd better get some rest. Morning would come all too early.

11

"**B**egging the Colonel's pardon, ma'am, but are you supposed to be meeting with JAG first?"

Ashlyn couldn't blame Talbot for sounding confused. She had reread the message from her mother three times that morning before deciding she hadn't read it wrong. Instead of giving her permission to meet with the JAG officers, Elizabeth had left instructions to be in her office at 0700. Apparently, according to the message, they had something they needed to discuss. That did not bode well, at least not based on her experience as a daughter. Whenever Elizabeth wanted to "discuss" something, it usually meant Ash had broken one of her parents' rules. What it meant with Brigadier General Shaw, she wasn't sure – and wasn't sure she wanted to know.

"There's been a change of plans, Master Guns." She handed over her comm-unit so he could read her mother's message. "Any thoughts?"

"No, ma'am." He pressed the control on the door next to him that raised the privacy screen in the aircar. Ash frowned, wondering what he did not want their driver to overhear. "Honestly, ma'am, too many and it is all speculation. The first thing that came to mind is that last night's activities are coming back to bite us."

Damn it. That worried her as well. At least she had a record of what Liu told them the day before – not to mention the fact her mother had been present. But that didn't mean her people, men and women who acted out of loyalty to her, might not be in trouble for their actions. If anyone tried coming for them, they would find a fight on her hands. She had learned a lot since her own court martial. She'd played by the rules then. That was a mistake she would not repeat of last night's efforts were backfiring on Talbot and the others.

"Did you keep a record of your activities?"

"Aye, ma'am, and I ordered the others to as well." His expression spoke volumes. Unless she missed her guess, he had also made sure they each had made copies and secured them just in case they would be needed later.

"Good." She frowned as the aircar slowed. Soon they would have to get out and any chance of speaking privately would be over, at least until they could get to her office. "You will let me do the talking, Kevin." She held up her hand when he started to protest. "We don't know what is going on and, let's be honest, we are anticipating the worst based on what happened to me. Hopefully, we are wrong. If not, well, let's just say I know how to fight this battle now."

He nodded, but she knew he would do whatever he could to protect her. Of course, that was only if she let him.

Ten minutes later, they waited to be shown into Elizabeth's office. As they did, Ashlyn stared out the window. She wanted to pace, to burn off some of the nerves knotting her stomach but she wouldn't. If anyone happened to be watching, she would not let them know how this unexpected summons worried her. She would not give them anything they might use against her or Talbot.

"You may go in now, Colonel," the lieutenant manning the desk next to the door to Elizabeth's private office said.

Ashlyn squared her shoulders and turned away from the window. As she did, she felt Talbot's eyes on her. When he reached over to carefully adjust one shoulder seam, she smiled slightly. Leave it to the Master Guns to make sure she did not appear before their division CO with so much as a seam out of place. With a nod of appreciation, she crossed the anteroom. Like it or not, it was time to find out what was going on.

The moment she stepped inside, Ash came up short and braced to attention. She had expected her mother. What she hadn't expected was to find not only Quintana and Liu there but General Okafor as well. Surprise had her swallowing hard even as she sensed Talbot bracing to attention one step back and to her right.

"Lt. Colonel Shaw reporting as ordered, ma'am!"

"Stand easy, both of you," Elizabeth said. "Have a seat." She waited as the lieutenant appeared in the doorway to see if they needed anything. Elizabeth instructed him they would have coffee and then she waited as he left, closing the door behind him.

A moment later, a knock sounded at the door. When Elizabeth called out for the newcomer to enter, the door slid open and Colonel Rico Santiago, head of Intel, entered. Before he could brace to attention, Okafor told him to relax. He nodded his appreciation and then took the chair next to Ashlyn's.

"I really hope someone is going to tell me what's going on and soon," Ash said. "Right now, I don't know whether to relax and listen to what you have to say or make a break for it."

For a moment, her mother and Okafor looked at her with almost matching puzzled expressions. Then her mother cursed softly before moving around the desk. For a moment, it looked like she might go to Ashlyn. Instead, she leaned against the desk, her expression contrite.

"I – we – didn't think. I'm sorry." She frowned and shook her head when Ashlyn started to say something. "I promise, you want to stay and listen. You are in no trouble, nor is the good Master Gunnery Sergeant."

"Thank you."

So why had they sent for her?

"If I may?" Quintana waited until Okafor nodded. "Colonel, I'm sure Talbot briefed you on what happened last night."

"He did."

"Lieutenant Liu will be sending you a complete report once it has been finalized. However, suffice it to say that enough evidence was found last night to confirm our suspicions about not only those already charged with regard to the conspiracy against you and your team. Sorensen started singing like a bird once he figured out we weren't bluffing about the evidence we already had against him.

"The good news is that it appears there are only a few more suspects we need to take into custody. While I know it may seem like the conspiracy against you and your people was widespread, it really wasn't. I'm not making light of what happened to you, but you were simply collateral damage for most of them. They had been involved with the cover-up of Sorkowski's and O'Brien's smuggling operations and were doing whatever it took to hide their illegal activities."

For a moment, Ash didn't say anything. Part of her wanted to snap with anger at Quintana for the almost casual way she called them collateral damage. Whether the conspiracy had been actively aimed against them or not, good people had died and others had lost two years of their lives because of it. They were definitely more than mere collateral damage.

Then Quintana's words sank in. She had said "most" of those involved had been trying to hide their illegal activities and Ash and her team had simply been collateral damage as a result. That implied at least one of those they had evidence against had other motives. What and could it be something personal?

"Ash, I've reviewed all the information Captain Quintana and Lieutenant Liu have complied," Rico Santiago said. "I even agree with their take on it. For whatever reason, Moreau has targeted you. My people are digging into her history, trying to find out what connection you might have with her. There had to be a motive and I promise we will find it."

"There's more. Just tell me."

"There is more," he said and then paused as the lieutenant returned with coffee for everyone. "The short version is, Sorkowski's information led us to a former Academy instructor who is now in Logistics. This former instructor has benefitted greatly from Sorkowski's illegal activities. In fact, he had been the station commander before Sorkowski took over for him. He is also the one who, when Sorkowski said you and your team had been assigned to the sector, said he had better take you out of the picture if he wanted to keep his activities secret."

"Who?"

"More importantly," Talbot broke in. "Has he been arrested?"

"And who is it?"

"He is being picked up as we speak," Quintana said. "JAG is taking care of it because we don't know – yet – how deep his involvement goes. My gut says it goes no further than his own activities and Sorkowski's with regard to the smuggling and taking bribes to look the other way. But if he is involved with the Midlothians, we don't want to tip our hands. So far, they aren't aware that we are on to them."

"And that is how we need to keep it," Okafor said. "And that comes directly from the President. He wants us to keep digging, to find out exactly who is involved in the conspiracy against Fuercon. He will not let anyone, not even Midlothian, get away with selling us out to the Callusians. That said, he knows the danger of having to go to war with someone we thought an ally. So he has tasked us, especially Colonel Santiago and Captain Quintana, with determining if those working against us represent the Midlothian government or a faction of it or something else. In the meantime, we will continue to keep out eyes and ears open and he is taking steps to make sure they do not have any further access to operational data that can be used against our forces."

"That still didn't answer Talbot's question," Ashlyn said.

For a moment, no one spoke. The looks that passed between Santiago and Elizabeth worried her. Obviously, they were worried about how she would take what they had to say. That was bad, very bad.

"Rear Admiral Jonathan Lawrence," Quintana said.

Ash hissed out a breath and bared her teeth. Lawrence! She still had nightmares about him. He had made no attempt to hide his opinion of Marines, including the fact he did not feel the hallowed halls of the Academy should not be sullied with their presence. For one full year, she had been forced to endure his insults and open attempts to flunk her out. The fact he had failed, first in an astrogation class and later in naval tactics, only seemed to spur him on. She received more write-ups and demerits from him than she had from her other instructors combined.

Now, years later, he was back, doing his best to ruin her career and, in the process, causing the deaths of some of those under her command. She had no doubt about that. Nor did she have any doubt he would pay, one way or another, for what he had done. She would see to it, even if it was the last thing she did.

Damn him!

"You're sure?"

"We are. We now have the transmissions between him and Sorkowski. Those led us to other records, enough to convict him on many of the same charges that Sorkowski and O'Brien face."

There was so much she wanted to say but this was neither the time nor the place. Later, when she and Talbot were alone, she could ask him what he knew. Until then, she had to trust the JAG officers and the others to make sure Lawrence paid for what he had done. Still, there was one question she could ask, one she wanted them to make the man answer before he would be allowed to plead out.

"Why? I want to know why he targeted me and my people. There is more to it than simply trying to cover his ass." She probably shouldn't curse but she didn't care. Her words were mild compared to what she was thinking. "He targeted me in the Academy. Back then, I figured it was just because he hated Marines."

"I've already told them to find out," Elizabeth said. "Lawrence always had a hard-on for Marines. I had the misfortune of being stationed on one of his ships. It was sheer hell, probably the worst assignment I've ever had. If we had actually seen battle and not just a few pirates, I have no doubt more than a few Marines – not to mention his own people – would have considered resorting to friendly fire to deal with him."

"I assure both of you that we will find out what his motivations were and act accordingly," Quintana said.

Ashlyn nodded. She had to trust the JAG. She did trust it, at least these two members of it. Both of them, and especially Liu, had worked hard to not only prove the charges against her and her people had been false but to also bring to justice those behind them. Because of that, she would give them time to find the answers she needed.

Besides, much as she would like to deal with Sorkowski and O'Brien – and now Lawrence – on her own, she would not risk being brought up on charges again. She wouldn't do that to her family, especially her son, and she wouldn't let Fuercon down at a time when it faced a war unlike any it had known before.

"There is one more thing before we take our leave, Colonel Shaw."

Quintana reached for something resting on Elizabeth's desk. Seeing the official looking folder, Ashlyn waited, barely daring to breathe. What now?

"Colonel, I have been in contact with the judge as well as the defense attorneys for the upcoming courts martial. The arrest of Sorensen, as well as Sorkowski's agreement to plead guilty to all charges against him, have changed the tenor of the upcoming trials. The presiding judge has agreed that you may leave a recorded statement about what happened leading up to you and your people being court martialed as well as detailing your time at the penal colony. The defense attorneys have until tomorrow morning to present any questions they wish you to answer. You will not be required to remain on-planet for the trials."

Ashlyn leaned back, not sure what she felt. News that she was no longer grounded was as welcome as it was unexpected. She stammered out her appreciation before the JAG officers requested permission to be dismissed. Ash was still trying to take in what Quintana said when the woman stopped next to her chair and rested a hand on her shoulder.

"Colonel, Lieutenant Liu will forward everything we have learned. Until then, know you have my thanks for all you and your Devil Dogs have done to assist us. I wouldn't have blamed you if you had turned your back on us. My office failed you once. I plan to make sure those responsible pay and, hopefully, your faith in JAG will be restored."

Ashlyn climbed to her feet and extended her hand. "Captain, you and Lieutenant Liu have more than done that. You have my thanks and the thanks of the Devil Dogs for helping avenge our fallen brothers and sisters." After shaking Quintana's hand, she did the same with Liu. "Thank you."

"My turn now," Santiago said as the door closed behind the JAG officers. "My team is taking over the investigation into the Midlothian tie to what's been going on. We have eyes on Paulus. An informant in the embassy says there is a new assistant counsel – spy or assassin in other words – expected. They haven't been able to find out who or exactly when. So we are keeping an eye on all incoming personnel. The President is very determined to find out how deep the Midlothian connection to the Callusians run. Once we have enough proof to act on, we will."

Ash nodded. She did not want to think about going to war with the Midlothians but knew they would have little choice if the proof showed the government had authorized the betrayal. Because of that, she hoped Santiago's investigation showed the enemy to be nothing more than a faction working against both the best interests of Fuercon and Midlothian. If that were the case, they could bring the Midlothian government in to deal with it.

"I understand, Rico. I also promise not to do anything that might compromise your investigation."

"Then on that happy note, I will be on my way. I want to brief my team. One of them will observe the interrogation of Sorensen and Lawrence. I'll keep each of you posted." He stood, braced briefly to attention and then left the office.

Ash sat back, wondering what else they were going to spring on her that morning. She had a feeling the surprises weren't yet over.

"Master Guns, you're dismissed," Okafor said as she moved to sit behind Elizabeth's desk. "I promise we aren't going to eat your Colonel," she added with a grin when Tolbert hesitated.

"Colonel?"

"Go on. I'll touch base when I'm done here. In the meantime, why don't you lead morning PT?"

He nodded, braced to attention and left the office. Once alone with her mother and Okafor, Ashlyn waited. She had a feeling they were about to discuss new orders for the Devil Dogs. Still, after everything that had happened, she wouldn't take book on it.

"Ashlyn, since you have been released from the need to testify at the upcoming courts martial, you and your battalion will be joining the fighting. We all understand why the President has wanted to keep the Devil Dogs here but you are our elite SpecOps battalion. It is time we put you to work," Okafor began. "You will receive your official orders later today but the gist of it is you and the Devil Dogs will be shipping out sooner, rather than later."

"Thank you, ma'am. As you said, we belong in the fight, not dirtside in the home system." News that they were shipping out would help morale. "When do we ship out?"

"Before I answer, let me explain what I have in mind for you and your people." She waited until Ash nodded. "You will not be shipping out to the front, at least not immediately. Our latest intelligence indicates that the Callusians will soon be moving against the Drakkana System. The system has become increasingly important not only because of its location on the shipping route to Ramadian but also for its agriculture production. That is something the Callusians lack, as you know. If they can take control of the system, they not only interrupt the supply chain to several of our allied systems but they gain resources necessary to keep their war effort going."

"General, I'm not questioning your reasoning or the need to protect the system, but is that the best use of the Devil Dogs?"

"Ashlyn, intel leads us to believe the Callusian taskforce heading that way is the same one that attacked Cassius Prime."

She exhaled and leaned back. One corner of her mouth lifted in a slight smile. If Okafor was correct and if the Devil Dogs managed to help hold the system and if they also managed to capture intact at least one of the enemy ships, they might actually get the confirmation they needed to prove Midlothian involvement with the enemy. It was a lot of *ifs* and she knew it. But the potential payoff would be worth it.

Assuming, of course, that the intel was accurate and the ships her Devil Dogs were assigned to were up to the task.

"Very much worth it, ma'am. Any objections I might have had are withdrawn."

"I thought you might feel that way." Now Okafor grinned. "I have one question for you. Your battalion is currently under-strength. I will be issuing orders for Delta and Gamma Companies to return to the fold. But you know as well as I do that it will take time. Are you comfortable shipping out with your current companies and having Delta and Gamma catch up with you as soon as possible?"

"I am, ma'am. I would rather be in place, even under-strength, before the enemy arrives in-system."

"Excellent." Okafor looked at her in approval. Then she glanced at Elizabeth and Ashlyn's stomach did a slow roll. There was something they had yet to tell her and she had a feeling she knew what it was.

Damn it.

"I'm going to be losing Captain Ortega, aren't I?"

"You are," Okafor confirmed. "I'm tapping her to replace Pawlak as CO of the Warlords."

"As much as I hate losing her, she deserves the command, ma'am. My only recommendation is that she have a strong senior non-com, one who will work well with her and who will accept no nonsense from either the enlisted or the junior officers."

"I agree with you, Ashlyn, but I'm worried you might come across the desk and throttle me."

She tried not to groan. "You want Anderson."

"Yes."

"You are stripping me of two of my best people, but I won't object – too loudly, at least. It happens I agree with you. I would recommend you bring the Warlords back in-system." She thought hard for a moment, trying to remember where the different SpecOp forces were deployed. "The Red Dragons can take their place until the Warlords are ready to return to the front."

"Why the Dragons instead of the Fighting Devils?" Elizabeth asked.

"The Devils are more a ground pounding battalion. That is their forte. Give them a target to secure dirtside, and they will get it done. They do some of the best pinpoint strikes, minimizing collateral damage of any of the SpecOp forces except the Devil Dogs. The Dragons have proven themselves more adept at space battles and I would kill to get some of their pilots assigned to the Devil Dogs. They are experts at boarding as well as at taking over orbital platforms."

"I told you." Okafor grinned up at Elizabeth. "I bet your mother dinner at Falzo's that would be your recommendation and why."

Grinning, Ashlyn shook her head. "You two are incorrigible – ma'am."

"Now, you will receive a full briefing packet later this morning. Can you be ready to ship out by the end of the week?"

It wasn't much time but they were Devil Dogs. They would be ready. The hardest part would be saying goodbye to their families. But, as she learned during the last war, it was better to get it over quickly. Drawing it out only made the eventual departure all the harder for everyone involved.

"Excellent." Okafor nodded once. "Admiral Tremayne will be in contact. You will be shipping out with Second Fleet. First Fleet will remain in-system as originally planned."

"Yes, ma'am."

"You will be Marine CO, not only for the Devil Dogs but for those already stationed with the fleet, Ash. Tremayne will inform the current Marine CO."

"Ma'am?"

"Ash, the current CO is young and inexperienced, at least for the sort of mission you are looking at. Tremayne has assured me he will not have any problems stepping aside. My recommendation is that you take him under your wing. Let him learn from you and your people."

"Yes, ma'am."

"Very well, Colonel. You have a great deal to accomplish before you ship out."

"Ma'am, you are a master of the understatement." Ashlyn stood, her thoughts already going to what needed to be done before the Devil Dogs shipped out.

"Get with me this afternoon, Ash. We'll go over what you'll need for the mission. Be prepared to discuss personnel needs at that time," Elizabeth told her.

"Understood, ma'am." She prepared to leave but stopped and turned back. "With your permission, I am not going to tell my people our destination. It's not that I distrust any of them but you know what it's like. Someone will slip up and say something, whether it is to a spouse or parent or friend and then that someone will slip and tell someone else. I'm assuming you would prefer word of our mission not get out."

"Agreed, Colonel. Good call," Okafor said.

"Ma'am, one more thing. I know this isn't my call and I know I probably shouldn't say anything, but I recommend Captain Ortega be promoted upon her return here. The Warlords deserve it and she most certainly does."

"It is already in the works."

"Thank you." Ashlyn would make sure to leave a set of her own rank insignia with her mother along with instructions to offer them to Ortega when she was promoted. "With her permission then, I'll take my leave."

"Dismissed, Colonel."

Ashlyn braced to attention and turned to leave the office. As she thought about all she had to do to get the Devil Dogs ready to ship out, she wondered if it might not have been easier to have stayed on-planet to testify against Sorkowski and the others.

On the March

12

"Ten-hut!"

Talbot's order rang out as Ashlyn stepped off the lift. She paused, not only to give those gathered time to brace to attention but to take stock of her surroundings. Less than a day ago, the Devil Dogs had marched aboard shuttles that would take them to where Second Fleet waited on the outer edges of the system. There had been no fanfare and no public send-off. Anyone curious enough about the sudden departure had been told FirstDivSecBat was about to take part in an extended training mission. As far as the public knew, the Devil Dogs were still in-system and would stay there.

It was also what the battalion believed. Only Ashlyn and Talbot knew the truth. Now it was time to let the other Devil Dogs in on the mission brief. In less than an hour, Second Fleet would leave Fuerconese space. Admiral Tremayne had notified Ashlyn of their departure less than half an hour ago. After a brief consultation, they agreed it was time to let everyone know what they had been tasked to do.

Even then, it would not be a full brief. That would wait until they were closer to their target. In the meantime, however, there were sims to run, duty stations to become familiar with and physical training to complete. Then there was equipment to check and maintain. Such was the life of a Marine.

Ooh-Rah!

"Master Guns, is the Company ready for inspection?" She fought to keep from smiling at the groans that greeted her question. No Marine enjoyed inspections, at least no sane Marine, and that was especially true immediately after shipping out. She knew they were still checking their equipment to make sure nothing had been damaged.

"No one gave you permission to talk!" Talbot snapped. "If the Colonel wants to conduct an inspection, she will conduct and inspection and you will, by God, do me proud or I will make sure each and every one of you spends the next week scrubbing decks with nothing but soap, water and your toothbrush. Am I making myself clear?"

"Yes, Master Gunnery Sergeant!"

"Don't worry." Ash did smile now. "No inspection – today. I would rather you finish making sure all our equipment and gear made it onboard without damage. But that doesn't mean there won't be one in the near future."

"Ma'am, yes, ma'am!"

"Admiral Tremayne has given us permission to continue using this bay as we finish checking our equipment. Master Guns, I expect all personal weapons and gear to be properly stowed by chow time. You have until morning to secure everything else. Let me know what, if anything, was damaged during transport and repair status."

"Understood, Colonel."

"Very well." She held the Company at attention. She had no doubt that on other ships in the fleet, her other Companies stood just as straight and still, held there by their company commanders. "At ease!"

The sounds of boots sliding across the decksole reminded her so many earlier missions. Pride filled her as the members of Alpha Company moved in almost perfect unison in response to her order. She could let them get back to what they had been doing – she knew from experience they would hear everything she said even as they checked their weapons – but she wanted their undivided attention.

"Companies, sound off!" she ordered. As she did, she nodded slightly as the voice of Tremayne's comms officer came over her earbud, letting her know 'links with the other companies had been established. She listened as each one reported in. The absence of Delta and Gamma Companies was obvious. With luck, they would rendezvous with the battalion before Second Fleet reached its destination.

"I'll be brief, Marines. Second Fleet will soon depart Fuerconese space. We have received orders from FleetCom and from President Harper himself to take the fight straight to the enemy. Delta and Gamma Companies have been recalled and should join us before we reach our destination. However, this is war and you should each understand that we may run into trouble before they do. That means, we have to be prepared at all times for anything that might happen. Our ability to adapt is only one of the things that makes us Devil Dogs."

"Ooh-Rah!" Alpha Company shouted.

She smiled slightly, giving them a nod of approval.

"The transit to our target will not be spent getting fat and lazy. We are Devil Dogs after all. You will receive your duty assignments in the morning. When you are not on duty, you will be checking your equipment or working out. There will be training missions and sims that will be run. You will also be shadowing the Navy personnel you have been assigned to back up if we find ourselves in a ship-to-ship battle. By the time we reach our target, we will be back in battle trim. Understood?"

"Ma'am, yes, ma'am!"

"For security reasons, and they will be explained to you later, I am not at liberty to discuss where we are headed. It's not the first time the Devil Dogs have been sent on a mission and we didn't know our destination until we were almost there and it won't be the last. Ours is not to question why -- "

"Ours is to do or die!"

"Ooh-Rah!"

"Company commanders, we will have a briefing at 0630 tomorrow. Your ships' commanders have been instructed to have shuttles made available to transport you to the flagship. Be here." She waited as they acknowledged, one by one, their understanding of her order. "There is one last item you need to be made aware of. Captain Ortega and Master Sergeant Adamson have been transferred to the Warlords. Captain Ortega is being breveted to the rank of Lt. Colonel and will assume command. I know she will do Colonel Pawlak proud. Master Sergeant Adamson becomes the battalion's senior non-com. Now, before you start thinking that means you won't have to face any of the good Master Sergeant's very inventive training exercises, think again. Master Gunnery Sergeant Talbot has spent more than enough time with the Master Sergeant to know how her mind works. More importantly, he and I happen to enjoy the sort of training exercises she put together. I have a feeling that between the two of us, we can make the Master Sergeant proud."

She didn't laugh – quite – as more than a few of her Marines groaned.

"Any questions?"

"Ma'am, why all the secrecy?" Hound asked.

For a moment, she didn't respond. Under most circumstances, she wouldn't. But this wasn't most circumstances. Not by a long shot.

"I can't get into specifics, not yet. However, there has been a security breach dirtside. FleetCom suspected there might be one before our last mission and some of the intel we seized on our last mission confirmed it. Unfortunately, the source of the breach has yet to be identified and confirmed. That means the leak has not yet been plugged. So, until we are well away from the home system, my orders – as well as Admiral Tremayne's – are to keep the details of our mission secret."

"Understood, ma'am."

"Anything else?" When no one said anything, she nodded to Talbot and he called Alpha Company to attention. One by one, she listened as the other companies followed suit. "Marines, I know I don't have to tell you how important it is that we do nothing to tip our hand to the enemy. However, let's be sure we all understand. If I get wind of anyone, and I do mean anyone, breaking security, you will find yourselves before me for discipline before you know what happened. If I do determine you violated orders, you can bet your asses I will kick you out of the Devil Dogs without a backward glance. Then you will be brought up on charges.

"Marines, we are at war, a war unlike any we have faced before – as you will understand once you are fully read into the mission. Until then, think on this. President Harper has made it clear to General Okafor who made it clear to General Shaw who, in turn, has made it abundantly clear to me that we are not only taking the war to the enemy but we will, by God, win the war this time. No more hoping the Callusians start playing by our rules. No more thinking diplomacy will win this fight for us. Our beloved Corps, along with Fleet, has been tasked with finishing what we started in the last war. I told General Okafor she could count of us. What say you, Devil Dogs?"

"Devil Dogs, ooh-rah!"

Ashlyn turned and left the bay, a slight smile on her lips. She had no doubt the cry had sounded from each of her companies. Her only regret was that she had not been able to tell them about their mission and she hoped that didn't come back to bite them. Not that it could be helped. Like it or not, Okafor had been right. Until they knew all the major players in the conspiracy Fuercon, they did not dare do anything that might tip their hand to the enemy.

Now, as much as she would prefer to stay with the Company, she knew she couldn't. They needed time to ask their questions of Talbot and the junior officers who, if they knew what was best for all concerned, would refer the questioners back to the Master Gunnery Sergeant. Besides, she had a briefing with Tremayne shortly and, unless she missed her guess, the admiral would want a status report on how the Devil Dogs were settling in and when they would assume their duties, not only on the flagship but on the other ships as well.

Besides, she had a training exercise or two to design and she wanted to make sure the battalion realized M. J. Adamson wasn't the only one who knew how to put them through their paces.

————

THE LINE of workers moved ever forward. Each step took her one step closer to the security gate. As it did, she glanced around, doing her best not to draw attention to herself. For the last week, security at the spaceport had seemed higher than normal. At first, she had explained it away as a reasonable step, even if one taken too late, to the resumption of hostilities. Non-essential travel had not yet been curtailed but everyone, travelers and those working at the various ports that dotted Fuercon, were having to go through tighter and tighter security checks. So far, it had not impacted her, nor did she expect it to. Even so, the closer she came to the guards, the greater her nerves. So much rested on her simply getting through the gates unmolested.

"ID?"

She handed over her ID and waited. The guard, one she had not seen before, glanced at it and then her. Without a word, he motioned her forward and waited as she pressed her palm against the 'reader. A soft beep a moment later signaled she could remove her hand. On the inside, she sagged in relief to see the green light confirming the ID she had presented. On the outside, she gave her best impression of a harried worker worried about being late.

"You've got a new assignment today, Ms. Vincent. You're to report to the maintenance chief at Hangar 113B. Know the way?" The guard handed her back her ID.

"Yeah, I know the way," she grumbled. "Damned bosses could have told me when I went off-shift. At least then I'd have known to go to the other gate."

He nodded and motioned her to move on. She slid her ID back into her pocket and shifted the strap of her toolbox on her left shoulder. Another line, this one to pass through the security scanners. In some ways, this was more nerve-wracking than the ID check. She trusted her ID. It had been made for her by the best counterfeiter on Fuercon. At least he had been before he finished the work she needed. Then he had simply disappeared. For once, she had not had to take matters into her own hands. Instead, knowing the authorities would soon start cracking down on *businesses* like his, even more so than they had during the previous war, he had packed up and left the planet. She had no doubts that, by now, he was well away from the System. It wouldn't surprise her at all to find him on one of the newer settlements well away from the fighting. The frontier planets always had those looking for new IDs, whether to hide their past or to cover their current activities. Part of her even wished him luck. He had done well by her and there might come a time when she would need his services again.

"You Vincent?" a heavy-set man asked as she entered the hangar.

"Yeah." She handed him her ID and waited for him to scan it. Instead, he shoved it back at her.

"You're late."

"Sorry. Didn't get the new assignment until I got here. You can check with the front gate."

"I don't give a damn about excuses, Vincent. You do the work, we'll forget about today."

"I'm good with that."

"Name's Rounsaville. You can call me Boss, Chief or Mr. Rounsaville. Understood?"

"Sure – Boss." For his sake, she hoped he was simply posturing with a new team member. Otherwise, she might be hard pressed not to make sure he had an on-the-job accident. It would be very easy to do. Almost too easy, in fact. "Where do you want me?"

"We've got a diplomatic shuttle coming in later this morning. Word's come down that they don't want to be held up any longer than necessary clearing the regular security checks. Problem is the main scanner's been acting buggy. You get on the board and figure out what's wrong. If the dignitaries are held up, it will be your ass on the line, not mine."

"Point me at it, Boss."

Without a word, he turned and walked off. She assumed he meant for her to follow. Mid-way across the hangar was the control platform. From there, they could take control of shuttles coming into the hangar, guiding them to the appropriate area within the hangar. Once a shuttle was stationary, security protocols could be then initiated with a simple command.

"You've got two hours."

Before she could respond, he was gone. Not that she minded. The last thing she wanted was someone looking over her shoulder. All she needed was enough time to fix the problem and put her own special bit of code into the system. Then she would know exactly when the Midlothian agent Watchman had dispatched to Fuercon arrived. More importantly, she would know who it was. That information would be enough, she hoped, to let her track the agent and deal with him before he could do the same to her.

They always underestimate you, Evan. That is their fatal flaw – as they will all too soon learn.

———

"TELL ME, Alexander, what is the situation on Fuercon?"

For a moment, the Intelligence Czar said nothing. For all outward appearances he looked like a man simply trying to form his answer in the most concise way. That was just about the farthest from the truth. In actuality, Alexander Watchman was doing his best not to let the fear bubbling inside him show. He might have the reputation for dealing quickly and effectively with those who crossed him, but the man sitting before him was much, much worse. He was, in short, the only person Watchman feared.

And with good reason. They managed to coexist only because they had found one another to be useful allies. But there was no trust between them and certainly no liking. Watchman knew there were those, both on the Council and who operated behind the scenes, who were doing their best to convince Douglas Honesdale to do away with him in a very permanent fashion.

Just as there were those who kept telling Watchman he should do that exact same thing to Honesdale. How many of them were playing both sides? That was a question he would soon be forced to answer, especially if he hoped to see his plans through to fruition.

"The political situation is unchanged. Harper has proven to be much more effective in carrying out his campaign promises than we expected. He also has shown an ability to get his policies through their Congress despite opposition from the other parties." There was no sense in denying something Honesdale already knew. "He has managed to clean house on most of the standing committees, as well as in major governmental departments, and has put in place those who are not only loyal to him but how have, at least so far, shown no weaknesses we can exploit.

"However," he continued Honesdale or either of the others also present could interrupt. "My sources that are still in place have confirmed that Fuercon is continuing do as we anticipated regarding the Callusians. They do not suspect that anyone might be helping the enemy. Because they have not realized there is more to the change in the Callusian tactics, they are continuing to fight the Callusians as they did in the previous war. That leaves them open to the next phase of our plan."

"Good," Honesdale commented in apparent satisfaction. "My only concern is whether they managed to secure any intelligence when they retook the Cassius System. Also, do we know who they took prisoner in the operation?"

"There should have been nothing in the data they seized when they retook the system that could lead them to us. Commander Hughes is too good of an officer to have downloaded anything into the system servers and we all know the Callusians will not admit they are getting help from anyone. It would be a loss of face in their warped way of looking at things to admit they couldn't get the job done on their own." At least he hoped his operative and the Callusians felt that way. His life and the entire plan depended on it.

"As for your question about prisoners, the Fuerconese have yet to release a list of those taken into custody. Part of that is because they have always played such things close to the vest. For another, they are leaving a lot of that sort of thing to the interim government." He shook his head when one of the others started to say something. "However, it is my understanding that the Callusians had pulled most of their forces out of the system before the Fuerconese arrived. Anyone left behind would not be in a position to know of our involvement."

"How confident of this are you?" Honesdale asked.

"I admit I would feel better if our Callusian allies had made sure no one from the *Tarrant* had survived. The possibility is slight they would have garnered any information during the short time they observed the invasion of the system before the ship was fired upon. However, survivors are a loose end and I have never liked loose ends."

"What does your operative on Fuercon have to say?"

Watchman looked at Honesdale, wondering how much the man actually knew. "As I said, I dislike loose ends and she has become one."

"You assured us she was the best for the job." Honesdale spoke softly, almost casually. Not that it fooled Watchman. He knew the man believed it was almost time to make his move.

The fool!

"She was, or so I thought. Up until this mission, she has been the most reliable and most successful of my operatives. For whatever reason, she let this mission become personal. Her focus on Shaw distracted her from the big picture and she got careless. Just as she has been dealing with her own loose ends, I have taken steps to do so where she is concerned. Martyn Baudin has been dispatched to Fuercon with orders to make sure she does not become a problem for us."

"Good," Honesdale commented and others nodded in agreement. "Let's move on to Commander Hughes' latest report. If I remember correctly, he voiced some concerns over the situation onboard *Anubis*."

"He does and I'm afraid his concerns are being repeated almost across the board by our other advisors on Callusian ships,"

Watchman confirmed. "Callusian commanders have never been known for their military discipline. They are used to being able to do what they want, when they want as long as it doesn't go against the general battle plan drawn up by their superiors. Hughes has hinted that Dorescu, the commander of the *Anubis*, has killed the other advisors. If so, then we have to face the very real possibility that Hughes' life is in danger and his mission is in jeopardy.

"The only real concern I have is that the Callusian commanders will revert to the tactics they employed in the last war. If they do, the Fuerconese and their allies will, sooner or later, capture a ship and figure out what we have been up to."

"What steps are you taking to make sure that doesn't happen?" Salina Hatcher, the Assistant Secretary of War, asked.

For a moment, Watchman said nothing. If there was one person more of a danger to him than Honesdale it was Hatcher. The woman's ambition was well known. She was not afraid to do whatever was necessary in her quest for power. Watchman knew she did not trust him. From the first time they met, she made it clear she would like nothing more than for him to disappear, along with his files. Not that it surprised Watchman, considering he had done just that to her father.

"I have sent orders to Hughes and the other advisors to make sure their ships do not fall into Fuerconese hands. Each of them were given – and should have installed – a failsafe code. If they have followed orders, they downloaded the code. Unless the Callusians know what to look for, they will never know it is there. The code is tied to that ship's advisor. As long as the advisor lives, the code remains dormant. However, if the advisor dies, or if the advisor initiates the command sequence, the code will activate and the ship will self-destruct."

"You are positive this is the best way to deal with the situation?" Honesdale asked.

"I am. We cannot run the risk that a few Callusian commanders might put our mission in jeopardy simply because they aren't allowed to rape and pillage the way they want."

"Very well." Honesdale paused and pinned Watchman with a firm, penetrating look. "See to it that the advisors understand what they're to do. I know I speak for the others when I say I want to know the moment Baudin arrives on Fuercon and then again when he completes his mission. When we next meet, we need to be prepared to discuss what their chances would be should we decide to go forward with Operation Kill Zone."

"Agreed." Watchman stood. "I would remind each of you that we had best be prepared to follow through with what we discuss here. We have committed treason by taking the steps we have so far. Any betrayal, any sign of weakness, will be met with swift – and fatal – consequences."

With that, he left the room. As the door slid shut behind him, he swallowed hard. Once again, he had managed to keep Honesdale on his side. All he had to do was maintain the status quo until time to institute Operation Kill Zone. Then Honesdale and the others would learn why he had been so successful in a role that usually meant an early grave.

13

"All right, I think that about covers it," Admiral Miranda Tremayne said. "How are your people settling in, Ash?"

Second Fleet's commanding officer leaned back and studied the two officers sitting before her desk. Captain Justin Montgomery, her XO, looked tired and she understood. He had just come off-duty, standing bridge watch in her stead while she shuttled back to the surface for a briefing with President Harper and several others. Hopefully, she could let Montgomery find his bed before long.

Ashlyn sat next to Montgomery looking even more exhausted. Not that it surprised Tremayne. In the four days since the Devil Dogs moved onboard the various ships with Second Fleet designated to transport them to their target, Ash had worked almost non-stop to make sure her Marines were settling into their new routine. FlightOps had reported the shuttle assigned to the fleet's new Marine CO was getting a workout. Each day she had visited different ships in the fleet. Tremayne knew without asking that Ash was checking on not only her Devil Dogs but the other Marines she now found herself in temporary command of.

"Everything is falling into place, ma'am," Ashlyn said. "Your Marine CO has kept his people in top form."

Tremayne waited for her to continue. From the look on Ashlyn's face, she knew the Marine CO was bothered by something and she had a pretty good idea what.

"Admiral, I have already sent a report back to General Okafor. You should be aware of what it contains."

A frown creased Tremayne's brow. That most definitely was not what she expected the younger woman to say. From the way Montgomery sat a bit straighter and looked at Ashlyn in concern, she knew Ashlyn's words had surprised him as well. Could she have found something that might delay their mission? Worse, had she found a security problem that could scrub the mission altogether?

"I think you'd best explain, Colonel."

"Ma'am, meaning no disrespect to you or to General Okafor – or to my good mother for that matter – but you are each doing a disservice to Major Laboe. He has done a remarkable job with the Marines assigned to the fleet. They are well-disciplined and extremely well-integrated into the crews of the ships they are assigned to. It is my professional opinion that it will not only disrupt the smooth working of your Marines to put them under my command, especially since I am not nearly as familiar with the workings of the Fleet as they are, but that it also undermines the Major's authority and position with them. To them, especially since they do not know what our mission is, it looks like you and General Okafor lack confidence in Laboe."

"I see."

She did and she cursed herself for not thinking of it. When Okafor had discussed the situation with her, she had been the one to suggest putting Ashlyn in command of all the Marines, those originally assigned to the fleet as well as the Devil Dogs. Her reasoning had been sound, if incomplete – as she now realized. She should have thought about how the Marines under Laboe's command would feel. More than that, she should have thought about how it might look to Laboe himself. That was an oversight she would correct just as soon as possible. The last thing she wanted was for one of the best Marine COs she had worked with to think she did not have faith in his ability to command.

"And you are right. However, it isn't my call. Brigadier General Shaw has issued the order and it has been signed off on by General Shaw."

"True, ma'am, but if I may be so bold, your recommendation to rescind that order would go a long way to making it happen."

"Colonel Shaw." She shook her head, one corner of her mouth quirking up as she remembered Ashlyn using that exact same tone of voice and earnest expression back when she had been Lieutenant Shaw and fresh out of the Academy. Now, as then, Ashlyn had a point.

"Before I do that, I think it prudent that we discuss the matter with Major Laboe." Before Ashlyn could object, she sent for him. "Anything else to report?"

"Yes, ma'am." Ashlyn glanced at her datapad and then looked up. "The Devil Dogs have settled in and what repairs needed to be made after the transfer of our equipment have been completed." She went on to detail how her company commanders were beginning sims and other training exercises. Beginning the next ship's day, the Devil Dogs would start working with their Navy counterparts in accordance with their specialties. That way, hopefully, they would be ready to step in and assist should the fleet come under fire on the way to their destination.

"Excellent, Colonel." She held up a finger as her comm beeped softly, signaling an incoming message. "Major Laboe is off-ship at the moment. We will meet with him when he returns at 1800 hours."

"Yes, ma'am."

"Then, unless there is anything else we need to discuss right now, you're dismissed Colonel, with the order to find your rack and get at least four hours shut eye."

"Ma'am." Ashlyn stood, braced momentarily to attention and then left Tremayne's ready room.

"Now, Justin, you are to do the same. I'll brief you at 1700 about my meeting dirtside. You are off-duty until then."

"Aye, Admiral."

Once alone, Tremayne sighed and called up her e-mail. Near the top of the list of messages waiting for her attention was the report Ashlyn mentioned. Even though it wasn't an issue yet, she sent a quick note to Okafor and copied it to Elizabeth Shaw, letting them know Ashlyn had spoken with her and they would be meeting with Laboe later. When they had, she would report back to them what her recommendation happened to be.

Once the message was away, she stood and crossed to the view port on the far bulkhead. The vastness of space greeted her. As she adjusted the image, she smiled proudly as the ships under her command came into focus. Second Fleet boasted some of the newer ships in the Fleet, a necessity after the last war and the way the previous Administration had tried to downsize Fleet to a size where it would have been hard pressed to maintain anything more than System security.

The pride of Second Fleet was its flagship, *her* flagship. *Phoenix Rising* and its sister ships had been on the drawing board for years. The only reason it had not been scrapped, as plans for the others had been, was because construction had already started at the end of the last war and Congress could not justify throwing the money already spent on it down the proverbial drain. So construction continued, slowed to a crawl, but it continued. Shortly after President Harper took office, he ordered construction to ramp up and the result was she now commanded the first ship to launch under the new Administration.

Not that it was really her ship, Tremayne reminded herself a little regretfully. That pleasure actually fell to her flag captain. But she still took pride in the ship and knew just what it represented. The *Phoenix* was, in her opinion at least, the best ship in space to date. She looked forward to seeing the ship in action against the enemy. As long as she and her officers didn't get careless or make too many mistakes, there would be little the Callusians could do to defeat them.

But that didn't mean they were invincible and Tremayne knew it. The ship was new, barely of the Yard. The one advantage Tremayne had was that the crew from her previous flagship had transferred to the *Phoenix* from the *William Donovan*. That meant they not only knew how to work together but the naturalness a good crew had was already present. Tremayne's only concerns centered on the ship. New as it was, especially with all the new tech, problems were sure to arise. She hoped it happened during the last of their shakedown exercises and not in the middle of battle.

To make sure the latter did not happen, she had better get with her flag captain and make sure he understood what she expected, both long and short term.

———

"You wanted to see me, ma'am?"

Talbot stood in the hatch to her small office, a slight frown touching his lips as he looked around. Looking up, she waved him inside. As she did, she recognized his look and gave a quick shake of her head. They would not have *that* discussion yet again. Yes, there were other offices in Marine country she could have taken. Yes, she could have ordered Major Laboe to change offices with her so she had the largest office. But that wasn't her style. Besides, this office was located the closest to the part of Marine country the Devil Dogs had settled. That was important.

"Shut the hatch, Master Guns." Once he had, she motioned for him to have a seat. "Before you give me your report, let me brief you on my meeting with the Admiral."

"Ma'am, is there some other reason than deciding to wait for Delta and Gamma Companies to rejoin us to hold up our departure?" he asked when she finished almost ten minutes later.

"Not that I know of, Loco, and I asked Admiral Tremayne just that. However, I have a feeling there might be something, a suspicion if nothing else. I do know she was called back to the Capital for a briefing and that she is keeping what was said close to her chest. My gut tells me there is more going on than we've been told, possibly more than she's been told yet."

"Agreed." He looked as though he liked the situation about as much as she did and that wasn't much.

"We also discussed the message I sent back to HQ about Major Laboe. While the Admiral isn't ready to recommend the order be rescinded, she has said she will consider it after we meet with the major."

"And that will be when, ma'am?"

"1800 hours." Before he could protest, she cut him off. "Loco, I know what you are going to say and you don't have to. The Admiral has already ordered me to take a solid four down. I have enough time to do that and still get some work done before meeting with her and Laboe."

For a moment, he didn't say anything. Then he nodded once. "I'll make sure you aren't disturbed, after I make sure you do as the Admiral orders."

She didn't know whether to laugh or not. Just then he looked and sounded a great deal like her mother when Elizabeth was making a point. In this case, Talbot was letting her know that he would not allow her to nap at her desk or on the decksole. He intended to make sure she not only made it to her quarters but to her bed and she had a feeling he would not hesitate to contact the Admiral if she balked.

"No need. I know I need rest. We all need some. Send word to all Company COs that I'm ordering a halt to all training and sims until 0800. Regular duty shifts are to continue but no extra duty."

"Understood, ma'am." He quickly relayed her orders, adding that any questions were to come to him as the Colonel would be unavailable until after 1900 hours. "Now, ma'am, I know you have said you haven't had time to consider replacing either Captain Ortega or Master Sergeant Adamson. However, you are not going to have any better time to do so than now, while we are still in-system. More than that, you can't keep pushing yourself the way you have been. We need you at your best when we hit the target, not so exhausted you make mistakes."

She wanted to argue with him but she couldn't. He was right. The problem was, she wasn't ready to replace Ortega. As for Adamson, there could be no replacing her. No one was as warped and inventive when it came to training exercises. But she and Talbot came close.

Besides, the Company did not need a Master Sergeant as well as a Master Gunnery Sergeant. Not yet, at any rate. She knew she had been lucky to hang onto both of them as long as she had.

She did need an XO, however, like it or not.

"You're right, Kevin. I'll even admit I've been dragging my feet on it." A quick laugh escaped her lips at the look of surprise on his face. Clearly, he had not expected her to agree so easily. "Don't look so hopeful. I'm not going to request a replacement for MJ. I think we can handle her duties between the two of us – three, when I get a new XO – and the other senior non-coms."

He nodded, not looking quite as pleased.

"So, Master Guns, do you have any recommendations for my XO?"

If he had looked surprised before, he looked stunned now. She smiled slightly. It was a rare occasion when she managed to get something over on the man. His ability to anticipate her orders – and her needs as battalion commander – were two of the things that made him so valuable. It also meant those time she did surprise him were to be savored.

He leaned back and his expression turned thoughtful. A moment later he opened his mouth and then snapped it shut. Instead of saying whatever had been on his mind, he consulted his datapad. Ashlyn waited, wondering who or what he was investigating. She had a feeling it was a who and she would wager her next month's pay that he was attempting to check on someone's current assignment and how long it would take for them to join up with the battalion.

"Ma'am, in the hope that you might ask for my input, I took the liberty of preparing a list of three recommendations."

Of course, he had. She might have surprised him by asking for those recommendations when she did but he had known she would give in sooner or later.

"Let me guess. You also pulled their records and current assignments."

"Yes, ma'am."

"Then send them on. I will review them after I follow the Admiral's orders and get some sleep." By then she would have her own list as well. It might prove interesting to see how closely his recommendations followed her own.

"It will be waiting for you when you get up," he assured her and she shook her head. He really did know her too well. If he sent the list now, she would review it instead of getting rest.

"Then let's finish up here so I can follow orders."

For the next hour they discussed what sort of training she and Tremayne had planned for not only the Devil Dogs but the entire fleet. Most of it was pretty standard. She planned to put their own spin on it but every exercise was aimed at trying to anticipate possible scenarios they might encounter during the transit to their target. Once they were on their way, she would start running sims for what they might find once they hit the target. In the meantime, she planned on making sure her Marines could fill almost any role needed to keep the fleet from falling in battle.

"Ma'am, you do realize that these last several exercises could end up with you assuming command of at least the ship, if not the fleet?"

If Talbot sounded uncertain, it was nothing compared to what Ashlyn felt. The thought of having to take command of anything larger than a shuttle turned her stomach. She had argued with Tremayne that the most junior Naval officer would still be better suited to command in that situation than she. She was a Marine. She wasn't trained for space command. Just because she had specialized in Tactics, it didn't mean she was competent to step in for a seasoned – or unseasoned – ship's commander.

Dear God, please don't let this be a portent of what's to come.

"I know but I also understand the Admiral's reasoning." Understanding and liking being two very different matters. Of course, she wouldn't say so, not even to Talbot. "Word of those sims is not to leave this office. The Admiral wants them to be a surprise. So if you will let the Company commanders know we will run the planned sims tomorrow at 0900, I'd appreciate it. You have the schedule. The only change on it I have is I want all Companies involved in the first sim. Let them know they are competing against one another."

"Understood, ma'am."

"Then I will leave the battalion in your hands, Master Guns, and find my bed. Once my meeting with the Admiral and Laboe is concluded, you are off-duty until morning."

"Thank you, ma'am. Rest well."

She nodded and stood. It didn't surprise her when Talbot fell in behind her as she left the office. She knew from experience, he would escort her to her quarters and then make sure a guard was set. It wasn't necessary but the regs required it. Only then would he leave. He had done so at the end of each workday since their arrival onboard the *Phoenix Rising* and she knew he would continue doing so until they were groundside once more.

————

"ALL RIGHT, Justin, I think that about covers everything. Send word to the fleet that we have a scheduled sim tomorrow at 1030 hours. We'll split them into the same divisions we'll use as we near the Drakkana System." Admiral Tremayne lifted her arms over her head and stretched until her back popped.

"I'll let them know, ma'am."

"What they won't know, nor are we going to tell Colonel Shaw and her Marines, is that we're going to throw them a little surprise. The sim will actually begin at 0600. Let's see how they react to the change."

"You're an evil woman, ma'am," her chief of staff said with an appreciative chuckle.

"I most certainly am," Tremayne agreed with a grin. "And to prove it, I'm going to change the parameters of the sim as well, something else we aren't going to tell the rest of the fleet until we spring it on them. Our division will be the attackers. I'll lay out our strategy after dinner tonight. I want Baker and Charlie Divisions to be the main defensive force. Let's see how they can work together. They've done a good job trying to batter each other's brains out in the other sims, so now it's time to make them work in cooperation. The other divisions will be either support or with us. Give it some thought and we'll hammer out the final tonight."

"I think we can come up with something appropriate to wake everyone up, ma'am," Montgomery said as the comm beeped softly.

"Colonel Shaw is here. Give us a few minutes. Let me know when Major Laboe arrives," Tremayne said as she stood.

He nodded and left the office. Tremayne watched closely, gauging the interaction of her chief of staff with Ashlyn as they greeted one another. It relieved her to see no tension in their greetings or in the way they shook hands. Good. Not that she had expected anything else.

"Have a seat, Ash," she said as she returned to her desk. "You're looking better."

The dark smudges she had noticed under the younger woman's eyes earlier no longer looked like bruises. That meant she had slept some. Obviously, it hadn't been enough but it was a start. All she could hope was there would be time between now and their arrival at the Drakkana System for all of them to get as much rest as possible. Once in-system, she had a feeling rest would be a commodity they would have to little of. That was the way of war, something she had learned long ago.

"I understand the good Master Gunnery Sergeant finally spoke with you about naming an XO," she began and grinned when Ashlyn shot a look over her shoulder in the direction of the hatch. It wouldn't surprise her at all if Ash had a *little discussion* with Talbot when they were done there.

"That's correct, ma'am. I won't ask how you know. I have a feeling a certain member of my command informed you."

"Only under duress, I assure you. I asked and did not leave him an opportunity to refuse to answer."

For a moment, Ashlyn stared at her, eyes narrowed. Then she nodded once. Tremayne knew it wouldn't get Talbot off the hook, not completely but it had to be enough. Ashlyn wouldn't hold it against the man for answering honestly when a superior officer asked a direct question.

"Have you made any decisions?"

"Actually, I'd like your opinion on one possible candidate, ma'am."

Now it was Tremayne's turn to be surprised. That had been the last thing she had expected. Instead of saying so, she nodded, signaling for Ash to continue.

"I would actually like to discuss the position with Major Laboe. He's a former Devil Dog. Although I've never served with him before, I've reviewed his record and his evals from not only his time in the DDs but also his other commanding officers. I've also talked with those who have served with him in Second Fleet. I think he would be a good fit with not only me but the rest of the battalion as well."

Tremayne leaned forward, elbows on the desktop, her fingers steepled. Of everyone she had considered Ashlyn wanting to discuss with her, her own Marine CO never even made the list. Part of her wanted to deny permission. She not only respected Laboe but she liked him as well. He had been one of the best Marine commanders she had served with. Not only did he understand his duties as the Marine CO, he respected his Naval counterparts and demanded his Marines do the same. He also had the Devil Dog mentality still, years after being transferred to other duty stations. That meant he made sure the Marines with Second Fleet were prepared for almost anything that might happen.

Much as she would hate to lose him as her Marine CO, she also knew she could not stand in his way if he wanted the transfer. Professionally, it would be a step up for him. She had known very few Marines during the course of her career who did not want to be Devil Dogs. Those who had served with FirstDivSecBat and then been transferred to other assignments would do everything they could to get back to the Devil Dogs. The Corps, with very few exceptions, had gotten its best officers from the ranks of the Devil Dogs. To be asked to return to the battalion, especially in the position of XO to the battalion commander, was a career move few would turn down.

"Ash, I had expected any number of names but that one," she said. She waved off any comment Ashlyn might have and continued.

"And I will be honest, I wish I could tell you no. Laboe is an asset to Second Fleet that I don't want to lose. However, I will not stand in his way and I will be the first to congratulate him should he decide to accept your offer. My only qualification for you asking him is that, if he accepts, you assume command of the Marines assigned to Second for the duration of the mission. He can help transition to his second-in-command but I want them under your leadership and his until we conclude the mission."

"I understand your concerns, ma'am, and agree." Now Ashlyn grinned. "I figured you'd say that."

Tremayne shook her head and smiled. She had no doubt Ashlyn had anticipated her response. She was too good of an officer not to have. But that didn't mean Tremayne would let her think she figured everything out.

Even if she had.

"There is another qualification I have to insist on."

"And that is?" Suspicion colored Ashlyn's voice.

"Let me ask you this in return, Ash." Now she leaned back, relaxed and enjoying what she was about to do.

"Ma'am – Miranda, I know that look on your face."

Tremayne's grin widened. This was going to be fun.

"We have both been in situations where a battle has resulted in CIC or the bridge or both being taken off-line. We have also seen that it takes time to transfer command to the next senior Naval officer in the chain of command."

"And?" Ashlyn narrowed her eyes before glancing over her shoulder, as if trying to determine if she could escape the office before Tremayne sprang her trap, whatever it might be.

"Let's just say that some of the upcoming sims might include you having to step in, at least for a short while, until command can be transferred."

"Miranda."

"No, Ash. I'm not kidding. In fact, I am very serious." Once again, she lifted a hand to keep Ashlyn from speaking. "I am not proposing you take over command of the ship, much less the Fleet, for any length of time. For one thing, I don't plan to let us get in the situation where it would be necessary. However, I also believe in planning for the unexpected. If something happens and the normal command of the *Phoenix* is taken out of commission, I want you prepared to step in until the next senior CO can assume command of the Fleet. The chances of it actually happening are very slim because it means that not only have I been taken out of action, but so has Captain Montgomery as well as Captain Vilhjalmsson."

Ashlyn frowned. Tremayne waited, giving her time to consider what had been said. Tremayne knew what she proposed did not align with how many in the Navy thought. To them, the Marines were onboard merely as passengers and, in the case of emergency, Damage Control extra hands. Those who thought that way did not want to admit to themselves or anyone else that the Marines went through much the same training as their Navy counterparts, especially the officers. While Marines would never command most ship classes in the Navy, they already commanded some of the smaller vessels and light attack craft. All Tremayne was asking was that Ashlyn do what she would not hesitate to do if they were talking about a smaller craft.

"I have only one question," the young woman finally said. "Have you cleared this with my superiors?"

Well, at least she hadn't said "no" outright.

"I have. Both your mother and General Okafor agree that it is a good idea and General Okafor is going to talk with FleetCom about making this sort of training standard."

Ashlyn drew a deep breath and let it out. "I guess I don't have a choice."

"No, you don't." The grin was gone. "Now, I haven't pushed before now but I've known you too long not to realize something's bothering you, Ash. What is it?"

Ashlyn blew out a breath and got to her feet. Tremayne watched as she walked to the viewscreen. For several long moments, the younger woman stared at it, much as she would stare out a window. When she turned, there could be no mistaking the fact she had something on her mind. "You know me too well, Miranda."

"And I know you're worried about something more than the little bombshell I just dropped on you. What is it?"

"You mean other than the fact I still wake up in the middle of the night, wondering if JAG telling me they no longer needed my testimony was only a ploy to get me off-planet long enough for them to release Sorkowski and the others? Or how about the nightmares of being back at the penal colony on Tarsus? Then there's that damned sim that keeps replaying in my head with Jake being a potential casualty of war?" she asked with a humorless laugh.

"What sim?" She got to her feet and moved to stand next to Ashlyn. Worried, she reached out and touched Ash's arm, waiting until the young woman looked at her. "Ash?"

"Before the Devil Dogs' last mission, we were running some pretty standard sims – at least they were supposed to be. I had set up the sims, with input from Talbot and Adamson, and they had been approved by not only my mother but General Okafor as well. At first, there were no problems. The last sim we ran was not one I devised or authorized. Neither had anyone further up the chain of command. Long story short, someone changed the sim to recreate that last mission before my court martial and did so without notifying me. If that wasn't bad enough, the sim ended with that bastard adding Jake in."

Dear God, no wonder Ashlyn still had nightmares about it. Anyone would. That last mission had been bad enough. Ashlyn had lost members of her team. Civilians had been killed but not because of anything the Marines had done. Ash had not known then that they had been set up. Nor had any of them expected the courts martial that would follow and the two years in the Tarsus penal colony. The fact Ash hadn't killed whoever was responsible spoke volumes for her self-control Tremayne wasn't sure she'd have been able to stop herself.

"Ash, we've talked about this before." Well, they had discussed everything but the sim. Now she understood Ashlyn's attitude when it came to unscheduled sims she had not set up personally. "You should also know that the JAG will not betray you. Those who did are no longer wearing a uniform. They no longer have the right to practice law and, at least one of them, will soon be sitting in a cell just as you and the others did.

"As for the rest of it, I understand your doubts. You'd not be human if you didn't have them. But they are unfounded. The fact you are here, back in uniform and with the promotion you deserved long ago – not to mention the fact you are now in command of the Devil Dogs – ought to tell you that."

"I know, Miranda, just as I know you think I'm being unreasonable for blaming myself for what happened to my people. You're probably right. But that doesn't change any of it. However, I promise it won't interfere with me doing my duty. The nightmares aren't as frequent and knowing we are finally taking the battle to the enemy helps."

"It does." For a moment, Tremayne stared out the viewport. As she turned back to her desk, Captain Montgomery commed to let her know Major Laboe had arrived. "Laboe's here. Let's see what he has to say. I'll let you start off and we will play it by ear from there."

"Sounds good," Ashlyn said and then grinned. "Want to place a bet on what he says?"

Before Tremayne could reply, the air was split with the shrieking of red alert. As Tremayne activated her comm, demanding a report, Ashlyn sprinted out of the office. Trusting her to coordinate with Laboe, Tremayne listened as reports began pouring in. As she did, she ordered Montgomery to send someone for her 'suit. Better to be prepared than regret it later.

14

———————

"Status?" Anton Dorescu demanded as he strode into the ready room.

The moment he entered, the six men seated around the table quickly climbed to their feet and braced to attention. He held them there, his gaze going from one to another. As he did, he made no attempt to hide his displeasure. If that weren't enough to warn them he was out for blood, his scowl and brusque demand for a report should have – as he'd intended. They were about to enter a critical point in their mission and he would not let anything distract him from their goal. If that meant culling a few officers – and *advisors* – he would do so without hesitation.

"We are at the launch coordinates, sir," the slender, dark skinned man sitting just to the right of the head of the table said when Dorescu's gaze settled on him. When Dorescu continued to look at him, he swallowed hard before continuing. "CIC reports that our preliminary probes confirm the information provided by our *advisor*. Location of all enemy assets appear unchanged."

Hearing the disapproval in the tactical officer's voice at the mention of the Midlothian officer, Dorescu bit back his own growl of disgust. He had quickly tired of the man and all the demands he placed on the crew. They were Callusian, the best warriors in any of the nearby sectors. Who was this Midlothian to tell them what they could and could not do? His people were not warriors. They were, at best, merchants who flipped sides the moment the tide of battle turned. Worse, they were not men enough to do so openly. They liked hiding in the shadows, thinking they were so much smarter than everyone else. Well, he would soon prove to at least Hughes how wrong they were.

The thought of what he wanted to do to the Midlothian brought a slight smile to Dorescu's lips. When the time came, he would not have to get his own hands dirty, unless he wanted to, of course. He had informed his senior officers about the true nature of Hughes' presence onboard *Anubis*. Their attitudes mirrored his. They would use the man as long as necessary and then they would do away with him. If a few of them wanted to have some fun with the man, all the better. It would teach him how foolish he had been to accept this mission. His eventual death would serve notice on his superiors that the Callusians were not to be underestimated. They would take what they wanted from the Midlothians and then deal with them as there would soon deal with Fuercon and its allies. The thought of enslaving the pampered Midlothians made putting up with their agent almost palatable.

"Good." He waved for the others to take their seats. "And what of our reinforcements? Have we any contact from them yet?"

"No, sir," a small, compact man answered from down the table. Dorescu watched as he hunched his shoulders. Coward. Lukovic's ability to tap into almost any comms system without being detected was the only reason Dorescu put up with him. "They may be running dark in order to prevent the enemy from intercepting any comms traffic from them."

"True." Not that it helped him just then. He needed to know where they were before he instituted the next phase of their mission. Of course, he wouldn't put it past that bastard Zhukov to hold his ships back until Dorescu's taskforce engaged the enemy. It would be just like Volkov to swoop in at the end of the battle and then demand a share of not only the glory of defeating the Fuerconese but an equal share of any plunder Dorescu's people secured.

"Whether Captain Zhukov and his ships are here or not, we will proceed as ordered." He rested his forearms on the tabletop and studied the holo display of the target system. "I want a running record from now until the end of the mission. Make sure it covers not only our attack and the enemy's response but anything Zhukov and his people do when and if they arrive in time to take part in the mission."

"Understood, Captain," Lukovic replied.

"Make sure each of your departments know their assignments and are ready to proceed. Current time to commencement of attack is twenty hours. May the gods grant us a victory and all the rewards of true warriors," Dorescu said and watched as all but his executive officer left the ready room.

"Captain, the crew is growing restless with the restrictions that have been placed on them. They do not understand that it is not by your order but by that of our *advisor*. When they learn we aren't here to actually take the planet but simply to show them that we can, they will want more. You know that and you know what that means," Kovacz said seriously once they were alone.

"I know. But no worries, the problem will be dealt with." For a moment, Dorescu said nothing more. Then, he nodded and looked at his executive officer, the closest thing he had to a friend onboard. "We may not actually take the planet, but there are still bounties for us to grab while here."

"Sir?"

"Think, Pyotyr, think." Now he did smile, a predatory, evil smile. "We will be going against their ships, ships we will damage and destroy because they will not be expecting an attack here, in what is essentially their home space. They have not faced our taskforce and the improved weaponry our *friends* have supplied us. That means there will be survivors we can pick up and use as we see fit. I promise you we will get the rewards we deserve, especially since we were denied so much our last mission."

"And Hughes?"

"Pyotyr, in battle, no one is safe," Dorescu said simply as he leaned back, a satisfied look on his face.

Kovacz mirrored his smile. Dorescu motioned for him to leave. He had preparations to make, preparations he did not care to share with anyone, even his executive officer.

Especially not his executive officer, one how reached that position when his predecessor met with an unfortunate *accident* during a training exercise. Since Dorescu assumed the captaincy in much the same way, he had no intention of making it easy for Kovacz to follow in his footsteps. He planned to live long enough to see the war successfully ended. With his accounts filled, he would gladly turn the *Anubis* over to his first officer. Until then, he would not turn his back on anyone.

EVAN MOREAU STOOD in the shadows, watching as last stragglers of the day left the pub. A slight smile touched her lips as the door opened once again and two men stepped outside. Kael Paulus staggered a little, batting at his companion's hand as the second man reached out to steady him. Not surprising. Paulus had a love for good wine and young men, something she shared with him. Unlike her, he overindulged and now that tendency benefitted her instead of him.

But he was secondary to the man with him. Moreau recognized him. She had first seen him a week earlier when he disembarked from the Midlothian diplomatic shuttle. Any question she might have had that he might be Watchman's "cleaner" had been put to rest when Paulus arrived. His fear had radiated from him until the newcomer said something. Then Paulus bobbed his head up and down before leading him to a waiting air car. A moment later, they sped away and Moreau emerged from the area where she had been working, committing everything she had witnessed to memory.

That had been the easy part. Harder had been discovering who the man was. She could not use any of her usual contacts at the embassy for fear they might say something to Paulus. She needed him to believe she had left the planet. The newcomer would not believe it, at least not at first. But she doubted he would look as hard for her if he had no reason to think Paulus knew where she might be.

Luck had been with her the day before when the same aircar she had seen at the 'port pulled up outside the café where she had stopped for dinner. For a moment, panic filled her. Despite all her precautions, had the Midlothian found her and come to kill her? Her hand under her jacket and moved to the small of her back and the pistol secured there. Part of her wanted to get up and make her escape but she remained at her table. She kept her head down, canting her eyes to the side to watch as the man was shown to a table across the room.

Somehow, she managed to finish her dinner. After paying her bill, she left the café. Tempting as it had been to look back to see if he watched her departure, she had not. Instead, she walked through the café and out the door. There she paused and looked around, hoping she presented the image of a woman deciding between going home or going out on the town. A few moments later, she climbed into a cab and hoped anyone watching would think her gone for the evening.

Instead, she had gotten out of the cab a few blocks from the café and walked back, keeping to the shadows. Then, as now, she waited, looking for an opportunity to strike. It had not come, but it had given her a waiter to question once the man left and the driver of the aircar that had taken him away from the diner later. Neither would be missed until it was too late – for Martyn Baudin and Kael Paulus.

She stepped out of the shadows, watching as the men walked down the opposite side of the street. Late as it was, pedestrians filled the area as last call sounded in local bars and restaurants. To anyone glancing in her direction, she was merely another one of many who enjoyed one last drink before calling it a day. Even if Paulus looked directly at her, he would not recognize her. She had taken great care to alter her appearance. Gone was the businesswoman he knew.

Gone was the tech from the spaceport. Tonight, she was an off-worlder looking for a good time.

If everything went as planned, that was exactly what she would have.

Three blocks later, she crossed the street, keeping her eye on her prey and a group of people she guessed were university students between them. Laughing as one of the students told an off-colored joke, she moved closer to them, joining them. None of them seemed to notice the addition to their group. Instead, one of them passed her a flask and told her to help herself. As he did, Baudin glanced back. Whether he sensed something or simply wanted to check out the commotion, Moreau did not know. To keep from drawing attention to herself, she raised the flask to her lips, as if drinking. Then, she handed it back to the young man who had offered it and smiled provocatively at him.

"Let's get away from here, baby." He slid his arm around her shoulders and tried to pull her close.

"Sounds lovely but I have other plans." She glanced at him, letting him see she meant it, and then she stepped away. When she looked back up the street, she bit back a curse. In just a few short moments, both Paulus and Baudin had disappeared.

Damn it!

She had to stay calm. There weren't many places they could have gone, not at this hour of the night. Trying not to let her worry show, she stepped away from the students as they drifted across the street in the direction of an after-hours club. That left her exposed, but she didn't care. Nothing mattered beyond once again locating her targets. If she failed, she might as well sign her own death warrant.

"Sloppy, Ms. Moreau, very sloppy," a voice said from behind her a few minutes later. "I expected better from you."

For a moment, she considered denying her identity. Just as quickly she knew how foolish that would be. What little she knew of Martyn Baudin, he was just as thorough and just as merciless as was she. If she tried denying who she was, he might kill her out of hand.

If she could keep him talking, she might have a chance, small though it might be, of surviving the night.

The fact he had not killed her already meant he wanted something from her. But what?

More importantly, could she turn that to her advantage?

Still behind her, he nudged her toward the alley to her right. Her heart beat a little faster as she complied with the silent order. The alley presented a much better venue to kill her and escape undetected than the street did. Could that be why he had not struck right away?

"I guess I have you to thank for this little set-up, Paulus." Somehow, none of her nerves or anger showed in her voice as she greeted the man. "Did he tell you he warned me of your arrival?" He would pay for setting her up.

"No, but it doesn't surprise me. We've known for a very long time that he was one of the weak links in the chain here," the man said. He moved to the side, letting her see him and the gun he had aimed at her mid-section. "This won't take long and I promise to make it painless if you answer my questions."

"And if you believe me." She concluded for him.

"True." He tilted his head slightly in acknowledgement. "Consider it professional courtesy."

Professional courtesy!

"What do you want?"

"We'll start with something I'm sure you won't mind telling me. Other than Paulus breaking protocol and telling you of my imminent arrival, has he jeopardized our interests here before?"

Moreau smiled, satisfaction filling her even as Paulus looked from Baudin to her and back again in growing concern. The fool! Had he really believed when Watchman decided it was time to clean house that he would not be included? Baudin was right about one thing. She had absolutely no problem answering his question.

"He has." She wanted to laugh to see fear suffuse Paulus' face. It wouldn't surprise her if he pissed his pants before long. "As you have seen for yourself, he has a weakness for wine and, just in case he was on good behavior tonight, his tongue gets loose when he talks. Add in his weakness for young men and pillow talk and, well, I think you see the potential problem."

"I see. Not unexpected." Baudin seemed to think for a moment before continuing. "If you want a chance to survive this encounter, Moreau, you will do as I say without hesitation and without question."

She nodded. She knew he was toying with her, much as she would if their positions were reversed. Still, if there was a chance . . ..

"While your disguise is quite effective, you need to rid yourself of it – now."

Without a word, she reached up and removed her wig. A moment later, she ran her fingers through her hair. Then she took the cloth Baudin tossed to her. Using it, she wiped away the makeup that had darkened her skin. With that done, she removed the prosthetics that had altered the shape of her jaw and nose. In less than five minutes, she looked much as she did when in the privacy of her own home.

"Very good, but that's not all." He motioned at her hands.

Her mouth hardened into a line. When he continued to wait, she sighed and scrubbed her hands together. It did not take long to remove the micro-thin prosthetics that had given her new finger-prints. Once done, she waited, wondering what else he had in mind.

"Watchman told me you were smart."

He shifted the gun to his left hand. He reached inside his jacket with his right hand and pulled a knife. With a deft flick of the wrist, he gently tossed the knife in her direction. She reached and caught the knife by the hilt, her eyes never leaving his.

"Good. You aren't foolish enough to think you could get to me with that blade before I cut you down."

"So why give it to me?"

"You are going to deal with a mutual problem for me, Ms. Moreau. Kill him." He nodded to Paulus.

"No!"

His eyes wide, sweat beading on his upper lip, he stepped toward Baudin. One hand reached out, as if he was about to plead his case.

Before he could, Moreau acted. She closed the distance between them and drove the blade deep into his chest. The blade slid between his ribs, into his heart. She twisted her wrist, doing her best to ensure the kill. As she stepped back, the knife still in Paulus' chest, the man fell to the ground. A detached part of her mind approved of the kill. She had struck true and he would bleed out in seconds.

"Remove the knife," Baudin ordered.

For a moment, she stared at him in disbelief. Then, seeing how his grip tightened on his gun, she bent and reached for the hilt. Paulus gave a soft sigh, his last breath leaving his body, as she pulled the blade free. Blood dripped from it as she turned to face Baudin.

"Now, Ms. Moreau, you need to cut yourself and make sure plenty of your blood gets on our poor friend there."

She bared her teeth and hissed out a breath. Damn him! Even if he let her live, he had signed her death warrant. He was making her do the one thing no professional assassin ever wanted to do: leave DNA at the scene. Worse, it would be on the victim's body. Once the authorities discovered Paulus, it would not take long for them to identify her.

But what choice did she have? Baudin stood too far away for her to make a try for him with the knife. His gun would cut her down before she could close the distance between them. At least if she did as he said, she had a chance of living out the day, even if it was a very small chance.

She winced slightly as she dragged the edge of the knife across her palm. Blood welled up along the cut, a steady flow she knew would bleed freely until she applied pressure. Knowing he watched her, she stood over the body. Then she knelt and let her blood mix with Paulus'. At Baudin's order, she made sure some of her blood dripped to the ground nearby. Then she stood and turned, wondering what came next and knowing what she would do in Baudin's place.

"Kick the blade over here," he said. When she did as instructed, he bent to retrieve the knife. "It really is too bad you let her personal feelings get in way of doing the job, Ms. Moreau. Mr. Watchman was very disappointed to realize you had let him down." The gun once more rested in his right hand.

"You are both wrong, not that I expect you to believe me."

"No, and I respect the fact you aren't trying to lie your way out of it." He once again inclined his head slightly. "I will give you the choice of how you die. Knife or gun?"

She drew a deep breath. The moment she answered, she would be dead. She knew it just as she knew he would shoot her without a second thought if she tried to flee. The best she could do was try to lure him in close enough to strike out. If she was lucky and if she managed to land at least a stunning blow, she might get away. For how long didn't matter. If she managed to give him the slip, she had a chance of living long enough to get off-planet. Then she could worry about what her next move should be.

That meant she had to choose the knife. She opened her mouth to tell him only to have her words drowned out as sirens suddenly filled the air. Startled, Baudin glanced over his shoulder in the direction of the street. Without hesitating, Moreau acted. She launched herself at him. Her right forearm connected with his jaw, driving his head back. She followed up with two quick punches to the solar plexus. As he staggered back, stunned and winded, she ran. She ran as fast as she could, sliding around the corner of the alley. A shot sounded and she staggered, pain radiating from her side as a dart tore through it. She took the next corner and, seeing a waiting taxi, offered up a prayer of thanks. Then she dove inside, ordering the driver to get her away from there.

She might even let him live. After all, he had helped her get away from Baudin.

15

"Talk to me, people," Miranda Tremayne said as she strode onto the flag bridge, Captain Monroe on her heels. As she did, she quickly motioned for the crew to remain where they were. This was no time for protocol.

"Ma'am, we were running a test of the long-range scanners when we picked up a signal from the new recon platforms," her flag captain, Lars Vilhjalmsson, replied. She looked at his image on the holo screen and nodded. With the fleet at alert status, Vilhjalmsson was on the main bridge. He had command of the ship while the welfare of the Fleet fell to her.

"Do we have an analysis of the signal yet, Lars?" She took her place in her command chair and made an automatic check of her those manning the flag bridge. Like their counterparts on the main bridge, they were busy checking all their readings and planning for possible contingencies.

"Yes, ma'am. I'm feeding it to your terminal now."

Tremayne closely watched as the data rolled across her screen. She sensed more than saw Montgomery doing the same. Without a word, she input the command to bring the latest images from the recon platforms onto the holo screen. She looked from them to the data analysis and back.

"Has CIC run this against the data we have on the invasion of the Cassius System?"

"They are running it now, Admiral," Vilhjalmsson said. He turned away from the pick-up for a moment and spoke to someone off-screen. "Preliminary guess is this is the same element that attacked the system."

"Now ID squawks. Right?"

"That is correct, Admiral."

"All right. My guess is they don't want us to know they are there. That tells me two things. The most important, at least right now, is that they don't know about the new platforms. If they did, they wouldn't have crossed the system boundary. The second is more problematic. If the prelim analysis is correct, this is the same force that attacked Cassius Prime. We know they went in under the guise of a merchant fleet. Based on what we know so far, we have to assume that's not their plan this time. So, are they here to invade or are they here to probe our defenses or are they doing their own recon of the system before the real attack?"

"All good questions, ma'am, ones I wish we had the answer to."

"I know, Lars." She thought for a moment, weighing the options. "Lieutenant Avery, tight beam message back to back to FleetCom. Relay all the data retrieved so far along with my recommendation that they dispatch First Fleet immediately. We'll hold position until we receive further orders, unless the current status changes," she ordered, her eyes never leaving the display. "Then set up a conference with all ship's commanders and their executive officers via link. I want it done within the next ten minutes. In the meantime, take the fleet to battle stations. This is not a drill.

"Captain Monroe, Captain Vilhjalmsson, until we confirm the identity of those ships, we are operating under the assumption they are what they appear to be – the Callusian taskforce that attacked the Cassius System. Captain Monroe, I want you in CIC," she continued, thinking hard. "Captain Vilhjalmsson, get the backup command staff to the auxiliary bridge. We are going to do this by the book until we stand relieved or receive other orders."

"Aye, ma'am," they answered in unison.

"Comms, send for Colonel Shaw and Major Laboe. I want them in the ready room before the briefing."

"Aye, Admiral."

"Lieutenant Gideon, the flag bridge is yours. I'll be in the ready room."

"Aye, Admiral. I have the flag bridge," the man said and moved to take her place.

"Admiral, I am sending orders to Major Laboe to send a detail to both the flag bridge as well as the ship's bridge," Montgomery said softly.

"Agreed." Tremayne knew better than to argue. Montgomery's duty just then was to make sure security for her admiral was in place. "Link into the conference as soon as you're set up in CIC, Justin."

Monroe braced quickly to attention and then left the flag bridge. As he did, Tremayne paused and once again studied the tactical display. At least the ships did not appear to be in any hurry coming further in-system. She would take that as good news and hope it meant they had no intention of coming any closer. The cynic in her said she was being overly optimistic. It was more likely the ships were waiting for someone or something. Tremayne hoped she heard from FleetCom before that happened.

———

"LOCO, REPORT!" Ash said as she stepped into the staging area reserved for the Devil Dogs. Then, seeing the Marines of FirstDiv-SecBat Alpha Company dropping what they were doing to brace to attention, she waved them off.

"The alert has gone fleet-wide. Company commanders have reported in and are awaiting orders," Talbot replied as he pushed through a group of Marines.

Aren't we all?

"All I can tell you is this is not a drill or sim. So we are going to play it safe until the Admiral tells us differently. Finish gearing up and get to your stations. I want the LACs ready to launch soonest. Check and double check comms and weapons."

"You heard Angel!" Talbot lifted his voice to be heard throughout the staging area. "Gets your asses in gear, Devil Dogs."

"Speaking of gear?" she prompted.

"Over here, Angel," Tank said and motioned to the battered foot-locker at his side.

She nodded and crossed to the footlocker. It had been with her during the last war. She would never forget the emotions that had washed over her when the Devil Dogs presented it back to her when she rejoined them after her conviction had been vacated. That, more than almost anything else, had reassured her she would not have to go back to the penal colony. Now it was a reminder to be sure she never considered, not for a moment, turning into the sort of officer Sorkowski and O'Brien had been.

The moment she had the footlocker open, Talbot was at her side. Already in the light armor most of the Devil Dogs wore for space battles, he helped lay out her gear, checking it as he did. Without a second thought, she kicked out of her boots and stripped down to tank and underwear. Modesty might dictate finding somewhere private to take care of getting ready to pull on the armor but that had been drummed out of all of them long ago. Battle conditions didn't care if you were male or female.

She quickly pulled on the bodysuit with its built-in monitors and *plumbing*. As she did, she shook her head. Modesty might not have a place on the battlefield – or in battle prep – but Talbot and several others had formed a human wall around her, giving her privacy to take care of the more intimate parts of gearing up.

"Colonel, the Admiral requests your presence in her ready room ASAP," Connery reported as Ash secured the last seal of her armor.

"Confirm receipt of the message and respond that I will be there in five." She accepted the first of her weapons, a pulser, from Talbot and slid it into the holster at her right thigh. Then she slid matching knives into sheaths at her calves. Two more went into her boots. She slung her battle rifle across her back and nodded as Talbot took possession of her sniper rifle, the newest model available and a present from the company to her at her last birthday.

"Loco, if Major Laboe hasn't sent a detail to the flag bridge, do so. I want a Devil Dog with the Admiral at all times until this – whatever this is – is over."

"Yes, ma'am." He touched her arm and led her several steps away from the others. "Did you have a chance?"

Even though he didn't finish his question, she knew what he meant. "No. We went to alert status before I could."

He nodded and then turned, signaling to Connery. "You're with Angel, Brigit. Don't let her try to shake you."

"Understood, Loco." She looked at Ash and shrugged, a slight smile touching her lips. "Sorry, Angel. You might be our CO and all but the Master Guns scares me more."

"I guess I'll have to work on that then." She grinned slightly and took one last look around the staging area. "All right, Loco. The company is yours. I'll update you as soon as I know something."

With that, she turned and made her way toward the lift, Connery on her heels.

"Ladies and gentlemen," Tremayne began less than ten minutes later. As she spoke, she made eye contact with the four in the Ready Room with her and then with the ship's commanders taking part in the brief via comm. "We have received preliminary instructions from FleetCom. Their analysis of the data confirms our own. Specifically, there is an as yet unidentified force on the edges of the system. They feel the force is closer to taskforce size than fleet size, which works in our favor. They also agree, initially at least, with our analysis that at least some of the ship signatures match those from the invasion of the Cassius System."

She reached out and tapped in a command using her virtual keyboard and the holo display came to life over the table. From where she sat at the middle of the table, Ashlyn studied the holo. The home system was displayed. Different colored lights indicated various ships, merchant and military. Blue flashing lights marked the defense platforms. At the northern apex of the system, green lights indicated Second Fleet's position. Beyond it, mere inches on the display but hundreds of kilometers – or more – red lights indicated the unknown taskforce.

"As you can see, First Fleet is slowly moving into a close defensive position around the home system's center, especially Fuercon." Tremayne highlighted the change in positions. Someone, possibly Captain Montgomery, murmured approval. "They are being careful with it so they don't let the intruders know their intent."

"Reinforcements?"

Ash glanced at the screen inset into the table in front of her. A slight smile touched her lips as she recognized the speaker. Captain Rafe Thrasher. He had been first officer on the *Atlantia*, an aging battle cruiser, during the last war. Two years before the mission that had ended to badly, she and her platoon had been assigned to the *Atlantia*. In that time, she had found Thrasher to be more than capable. Better yet, he had a respect for the Marines lacking in some Navy officers.

"We are on our own, at least for the moment," Tremayne answered. "FleetCom remembers the attack on the Capital not that long ago. We know now that attack had been nothing more than a feint. This may be much the same or it could be a distraction, designed to pull our defenses out of position." She shipped from a white mug and grimaced slightly. "Frankly, ladies and gentlemen, we don't know what this is. These ships may be no threat at all or they may be surveilling the system. That, as I am sure you realize, is the problem."

"Our orders, ma'am?" Captain Vilhjalmsson asked.

"Most of Second will hold position here. The *Birkenhead, Challenger* and *Nagato* are to proceed toward the ships and challenge them. Captain Thrasher, you are in command of this makeshift strike group."

"Ma'am, if I may." Ash waited until Tremayne looked at her and nodded. "Instead of *Challenger*, I recommend sending the *Scimitar*.

That will give Captain Thrasher LAC support and might make whoever is in command of those ships think twice before doing something foolish."

"Captain Thrasher?"

"I admit that the presence of LACs would be helpful, Admiral."

"Agreed." She turned her attention back to Ash. "Colonel Shaw, how do you see using the Devil Dogs?"

Instead of answering immediately, Ashlyn quickly input a series of commands and watched as the latest reports from her company commanders came up on her datapad. A second set of commands followed the first and she looked at the Marine complements assigned to the three ships. A slight frown tugged at the corners of her mouth as she considered her options.

"The Scimitar's Marine contingent is solid, especially with the addition of the LACs and their support teams from the Devil Dogs. Major Laboe has done a standout job with his Marines but Second Fleet's Marine contingent is light, too light for my liking – meaning no disrespect to either the Major or to you, Admiral. I know both of you would have liked more of us jarheads onboard to do the heavy lifting." She grinned as the others laughed softly. Good. She had hoped to take some of the edge off.

"My recommendation is to shift Alpha Company's Second Platoon to the *Nagato*. Lieutenant Lashay is the CO. I'll send Master Gunnery Sergeant Talbot along as well. As for the *Birkenhead*, Third Platoon, Delta Company should be a good fit."

"Agreed, but with modification," Tremayne said after a moment's though. "Major Laboe, you become interim Marine CO for the *Phoenix*. Master Guns Talbot will remain onboard to assist you and to ask as liaison with the Devil Dogs. Colonel Shaw, you will accompany Second Platoon to the *Nagato*. Captain Thrasher, is that acceptable?"

"Aye, ma'am, quite acceptable." The man's blue eyes sparkled and Ashlyn shook her head. Once again, Tremayne had outflanked her.

"Ash." Tremayne waited until Ashlyn looked up from her data-pad. "I want your eyes and ears out there as well as your experience. I can't help feeling this is more than a simply surveillance mission."

For a moment, the Admiral looked at some point beyond the table. Ash waited, recognizing Tremayne's expression and guessing its cause. Unless she missed her guess, the Admiral was about to read in the others on their mission and the suspicions behind it.

"Ladies and gentlemen, what I am about to tell you is not to be discussed with anyone except your XOs until you are told differently."

Tremayne waited, giving those attending via comm to make sure no one could overhear. Once they had signaled they were ready, she continued, explaining the mission to the Drakkana System and why FleetCom had decided to hold Second Fleet back until the remainder of the Devil Dogs could rendezvous with them. Now, looking at the icons for the unidentified ships resting at the System boundary, Ashlyn thanked whatever officer or deity or whatever had made the decision.

"There is a need to maintain secrecy about our mission, ladies and gentlemen," Tremayne continued. "And if it weren't for the Devil Dogs and First Fleet, we might not know – or we might not know until it was too late – that one of our allies has turned against us."

"What?" Captain Montgomery leaned forward, his expression a mixture of anger and surprise. A quick glance around the table, and then at the comm screen, showed the others felt the same. "Who?"

"Each of you know how FleetCom has been troubled by the change in tactics we've seen from the enemy since President Harper declared the truce null and void." Heads nodded. "And then there has been the question of how they managed to upgrade their weapons and, in some instances, managed to get new ships." More nods.

"Colonel Shaw?" Tremayne looked to Ash and she nodded in return.

"When we managed to retake the Cassius System, we discovered something that surprised not only Admiral Collins but Fleet Intel and FleetCom as well. The Callusians had withdrawn the bulk of their ships before we arrived in-system. Instead of finding the task-force that had invaded, we found defense platforms and only a few ships. Dirtside, there were some troops but the Devil Dogs made fairly quick work of the main resistance. Our AARs should be available for your review as soon as the briefing is concluded.

"What we found once we recaptured the capital was that the Callusian ships had downloaded their data, including video records of the invasion, to dirtside servers. We seized all the data and it was brought back to FleetCom. Colonel Santiago and his team have been working on decoding it all."

She glanced at Tremayne who, as if reading her mind, nodded once. Taking that as all the permission she needed, Ash called up the image of the Midlothian officer on the Callusian bridge.

"This image was taken from that record." She gave everyone time to study the image she had sent to their screens. "It has been analyzed and there is nothing to indicate it has, in any way, been doctored. As you can see, it shows an officer in the Midlothian Space Navy. There is no evidence he is there by anything but choice. Our preliminary ID on him is that of Captain Barnard Hughes."

Silence filled the Ready Room. It wouldn't last. As soon as those studying the image overcame their initial shock, the questions and demands for answers would come. All she could do was wait.

And wish she had the answers.

"Do we know if he is still on active duty?" Montgomery asked.

"No." Ashlyn held up a hand to prevent anyone from interrupting. "And that is what makes this problematic and interesting. Colonel Santiago has had to move very carefully in the research into Hughes. Because of the possibility the Midlothian government not only knows about his actions but approves, FleetCom can't just send a request for information about the man. What little they have found speaks volumes, at least to me."

She typed in another command sequence and the information Santiago had sent her about Hughes flashed onto the holo screen. As it did, the tactical display shrank and moved to the lower right corner. That let them keep an eye on it in case there was a change in status but they could concentrate on the data as she discussed it.

"Bernard Hughes was a decorated officer in the last war. Unlike many – most – of the Midlothian officers we dealt with, he had no qualms about being in the midst of the fighting when necessary. His official battle history is appended to the report. I won't take time to go over it right now as it isn't really pertinent to the current situation.

"After the war, there are a few mentions of him in the Midlothian media and one or two entries in his official record. However, a little over a year ago, he seemed to simply disappear. No more mention of him in the media and no official entries into his record. Colonel Santiago and his people are still trying to find confirmation but their read on it is he was pulled into an assignment that had to be off-the-books, at least for a while."

"Our assignment, once we reach the Drakkana System is to prevent the Callusians from moving in. More importantly, if we do encounter the enemy, we are to do everything possible to confirm the presence – or absence – of any Midlothian equipment or personnel. We have the added imperative of capturing at least one ship intact. That is part of why the Devil Dogs are with us," Tremayne said. "As with the information about our target system, you are not to discuss this with anyone except your XOs until further notice. Questions?"

When there were none, she nodded. "Captain Thrasher, get with the others in your strike group and formulate your approach vector and course of action. I expect your report in half an hour. Colonel Shaw, how long do you need to transfer your people to the *Nagato*?"

"Half an hour, ma'am. I need time to brief Major Laboe and my staff."

"Then I'll let you and the good Major get to work. Report when you are ready to depart."

"Aye, ma'am." She pushed back her chair and stood, bracing quickly to attention before leaving the Ready Room, Laboe and Connery on her heels.

16

"Status?" Dorescu asked as he entered the bridge.

Kovacz turned from where he stood studying the tactical holo. Dorescu studied his first officer, noting his puzzled expression. Then he turned his attention to the holo. Kovacz might be puzzled about something but he did not feel it serious. Otherwise, he would have sent for Dorescu. At least he would have if he wanted to continue living. Even so, Dorescu knew better than to make assumptions, especially considering where they happened to be.

As he moved to Kovacz's side, he looked at the holo. Nothing much had changed since he'd last checked it half an hour before. Ships they assumed to be part of First Fleet still sat between them and Fuercon. The defense platforms located closer to the planet still appeared to be in passive mode.

The fools. They should have learned from the last war that they needed to have defense platforms closer to the system's edge. Not that he was complaining. Their current location suited him just fine.

"The ships are still unaware of our presence, sir," Kovacz said. "There has been some shuttle activity between several of them but nothing else."

"Comms chatter?"

"Nothing we have been able to pick up using passive scans."

Dorescu frowned at the holo. Everything was as he'd expected. So why did he feel he was missing something?

He turned and made his way to the command chair. As he did, he pushed down his concerns. The Fuerconese had no idea the ships sitting so patiently, so peacefully on the edge of their system were anything but peaceful. They had to believe it. Why else had they yet to challenge him?

Calm, Anton, calm. He breathed deeply, his expression still. He would not let his concern show.

There was nothing to worry about. He knew it. Just as he knew the source of his doubts – Hughes.

The Midlothian had confronted him – oh-so-respectfully, of course – in his quarters not an hour ago. Dorescu had almost laughed at the *advisor's* outrage. They had their orders and those orders in no way included being anywhere close to Fuerconese space. So why, in the name of all that was holy, was the *Anubis* and the rest of the task-force not only close to Fuercon but actually in-system?

Dorescu had let him have his say. The only reason Hughes still lived was the fact he had shown enough restraint to being his "concerns" to Dorescu privately. One thing he could say for the man, Hughes had learned very quickly how to survive on the *Anubis*. Not that it would do him any good for long. He had outlived his usefulness and soon Dorescu would deal with him just as he had the other so-called advisors.

The look on Hughes' face when he saw the orders instructing them to head to Fuerconese space had been priceless. For a moment, the man went still. Dorescu wasn't sure he even breathed. Then all color drained from his face. He swallowed hard. His hands fisted at his sides. It had not been difficult to guess what was running through his mind. Hughes's first comment when he finally regained the ability to speak confirmed it. He thought Dorescu and his Callusian superiors had lost their minds. The danger of this mission could not be justified, especially considering the possibility of the Fuerconese learning of the Midlothian involvement.

That break in discipline pleased Dorescu. It gave him the justification he needed to drive home a lesson too long denied. Without warning, he'd struck. His fist caught the Midlothian squarely across the jaw. Hughes stumbled back, blood pouring from his mouth. Before he could recover, Dorescu struck again and again. Soon Hughes lay on the decksole, curled into the fetal position in a futile attempt to protect his ribs.

"This is your only warning, *Advisor*," he'd snarled. "Question me or my superiors again and it will be your last act of insubordination." He'd followed the threat with a savage kick to the man's ribs. Then he'd ordered his security team to take Hughes back to his cabin. If they happened to *remind* the man who commanded the *Anubis*, all the better.

"Sir, three ships are breaking away from the main body," the scanners tech reported.

"Course?"

"CIC says they are on a direct approach vector," Kovacz answered a few moments later.

"It seems their commander has gotten curious." He closed his eyes and considered his options. As tempting as it was to open fire on the three ships, he would rather not give the other ships a chance to either counter his attack or send word back to Fuercon for reinforcements.

"Signal all ships to hold position. Prepare for battle but weapons are not to power up until I give the order. Let's not give them reason to suspect we present any danger." He turned in his chair to face the communications officer. "Prepare to squawk the merchant ship ID if they hail us. Let's see what they want."

"Our LACs?"

"Have the crews ready to launch." He turned his attention back to the tactical display. "Designate the oncoming ships as Target Alpha. Rear guard is Target Beta."

"Designations made," Tactical replied.

"Now let's see if they will fall for the bait."

———

"COLONEL, there's a message coming in for you from Admiral Tremayne," the shuttle pilot reported.

Less than ten minutes earlier, the shuttle had left the *Phoenix Rising*. A quick check showed they were less than fifteen minutes away from the *Nagato*. In the time since leaving Tremayne's ready room, she had been busy. She'd briefed Talbot on their current situation and even managed a minute alone with Laboe to ask if he wanted to transfer to the Devil Dogs. His reaction had brought a smile to her lips. After a moment's surprise, he had braced to attention and formally accepted her offer. Even though she had not had time to issue her request for his transfer to her command, she had informed the Devil Dogs. That would, she hoped, keep any problems from arising should he find himself in the position of issuing orders in her stead.

At least Miranda will make sure the transfer goes through if anything happens to me.

"Put it on my screen, Petty Officer," she said, turning her attention to the small communications screen embedded in the bulkhead before her.

She sat back and waited. As she did, she smiled slightly to hear Connery telling the others onboard to hold it down. The lance corporal was there under orders from Talbot to make sure nothing happened to her. So far, Connery was taking the assignment very seriously.

"Colonel Shaw," Admiral Tremayne began as her image appeared in the top right corner of her screen. Ash felt her eyes go wide in surprise to see not only Tremayne's image but those of her mother, General Okafor and the President as well.

"Aye, ma'am." She sat a little straighter in her flight couch. As she did, she hand-signaled Connery to keep everyone away until she finished the comm.

"Colonel, Admiral Tremayne informed me of your request for permission to ask Major Laboe to join the Devil Dogs as your XO. I have approved your request, with her blessing. Consider him a member of your battalion."

"Thank you, ma'am."

"Colonel, I will leave the briefing to the others but know this. You have one priority if this encounter goes the way we anticipate. Protect the system. Everything else is secondary. However, if you and Admiral Tremayne can manage to get us confirmation about the extent of the Midlothians' involvement in what is going on, you would have my administration's undying gratitude."

"Understood, Mr. President."

"Then good hunting, Colonel." With that, his image disappeared from the screen.

"Ash, I've issued orders for Master Gunnery Sergeant Talbot to bring the rest of Alpha Company forward," Elizabeth took up. "Further analysis of the readings from Second Fleet confirm this is the same taskforce that attacked the Cassius System. Once you are onboard the *Nagato*, bring your LACs to launch readiness. I want them clearing their bays as soon as contact with the enemy is made. Do not wait until their weapons go hot."

"Yes, ma'am. Launch readiness confirmed."

"One last thing before I turn this over to General Okafor and Admiral Tremayne. You are not to take unnecessary risks, Ash. You are battalion CO, not a fire team commander any longer."

"I will do what needs to be done, ma'am. I'm a Devil Dog."

"And a stubborn one at that. Shaw out."

Ashlyn watched as her mother's image disappeared from the screen. She knew that was the closest Elizabeth would come to letting her mother's instincts show on an official comm. Hopefully, they were anticipating the worst and would find all their preparations unnecessary.

"Ash, I have issued orders for the other battalions of FirstDiv to be prepared to reinforce your Devil Dogs. They are shuttling to various ships with First Fleet as we speak. Unless and until they arrive, you are now officially in command of not only your battalion but of all

Marines assigned to Second Fleet. Rely on Major Laboe in deciding how best to use them."

"Understood, General. If necessary, they will back us up on boarding parties. I would prefer to leave them onboard their current ships if at all possible to assist the Navy crews and to repel any potential boarders."

"Agreed." Okafor looked off-screen for a moment before turning her attention back. "Ash, Miranda, move quickly. The sirens just went off groundside. Someone screwed up and I assure you I plan to find out who. But that means the enemy will know we're onto them sooner, rather than later. Okafor out."

"Ash, I've issued orders for Captain Thrasher to move in on the enemy location as soon as your people are on board. Once you move, I will bring the rest of the Fleet to full battle readiness and we will begin moving in your direction. I'll leave screening elements behind in case they try to flank us. Until we get reinforcements from further in-system, we are on our own."

"Admiral, you can rely on the Devil Dogs." She motioned for Connery to step in. "With your permission, Admiral, I will go ahead and order the LAC crews to go to launch readiness. I want them in the air before the ships being closing with the enemy."

"Agreed. See to it. Tremayne out."

As the screen went blank, Ashlyn turned to Connery. "All right, Lance Corporal, we have a lot to do in the next few minutes. Transmit my order to the LAC crews. Inform their CO that I want a full update on their status upon arrival. Then contact the comms officer onboard the *Nagato*. I want the platoon tied into the battle net before we dock."

"Aye, Colonel."

"Petty Officer, how long until we dock?"

"Two minutes."

"Make it one." She stood and turned to face the platoon members on the shuttle. As she did, she frowned, wishing yet again they had taken a battle shuttle capable of carrying the entire platoon. Instead, another shuttle followed with the rest of her people.

"Listen up!" She waited until the Marines had focused on her. "Our orders have changed. FleetCom has confirmed that the readings the defense platforms pulled from the ships match those that invaded the Cassius System. Captain Thrasher has been ordered to close in as soon as we are onboard. So hit the decks running. As soon as I have reported in to Captain Thrasher, I'll have a better idea of what our first target will be. Secure for docking."

"Ma'am, yes, ma'am!"

———

Captain Bernard Hughes, Midlothian Space Navy, slowly, painfully crossed to the hatch leading out of his quarters. He almost sobbed in relief as he programmed the locks. It wouldn't keep anyone out for long, especially if they were determined to get in. But it would give him enough time to prepare. He might not live long if they rushed the room but he would, by God, take as many of them with him as he could.

Damn Dorescu and damn Alexander Watchman for putting him at that madman's mercy. How had they not realized the Callusians would do as they wanted at the first opportunity? God, he had been such a fool to agree to this assignment. A damned fool who would pay with his life and there was little he could do about it.

He carefully sat at the small desk across from the hatch. His breath hissed out as his ribs screamed in pain. Dorescu's beating had been bad enough. By the time the Callusian security team finished with him, he knew several ribs had been broken. He was lucky not to be more badly injured. That was little consolation when he knew the pain would slow him, making it even less likely he could survive the next encounter with the Callusian commander or one of his crew.

Yet they had underestimated him, just as Watchman had. At least he hoped they had. He cast a look around his quarters. Nothing appeared to have been disturbed during his absence. Thankfully, his *hosts* appeared to have decided several weeks ago that he no longer represented a threat. It had been that long since they had searched his rooms. That might just work in his favor now.

Relaxing slightly, he slid one hand into his pocket where a mini-pulsar rested. Using his other hand, he levered back to his feet. First things first. He needed to do something about the pain. If this change in missions went as badly as he anticipated, he could not be slowed by his injuries. His life and the honor of his homeworld depended on it.

Ten minutes later, freshly showered and dressed in a clean uniform, Hughes returned to the outer room. Pain no longer threatened to force him into unconsciousness. Now it was a dull throb, something to be endured. Not only did that let him move easier but the pain no longer clouded his mind. He could think and plan and he did not intend to waste a moment.

For more than two months he'd known Dorescu planned to kill him before they returned to the Cassius System. He had suspected it for much longer but he had gotten his confirmation then. Professional paranoia once again served its purpose. He had planted listening devices in the briefing rooms and ready room, on the bridge and even in Dorescu's quarters. Much to his surprise, the Callusians had never found any of his bugs. As far as he knew, they had never so much as done a security sweep for them. That careless, so indicative of the Callusian attitude that no one could best them, would be their undoing. If he was lucky, he would have a hand in it.

His plans were simple. He would make sure Watchman knew what was happening. The Callusians had yet to realize he had been in contact with the Intelligence Czar without going through their communications officer. Nor had they realized he had tapped into their databanks and had been systematically downloading everything he could, not only about their activities but future plans, communications with other ships and Callusian command officers. If those messages reached Watchman, he would know the Callusians had not only murdered the other Midlothian advisors but that they also planned on turning against Midlothian as soon as they defeated Fuercon and its other allies.

But they had underestimated their intended victim. Hughes knew when he accepted the mission that his life very well could be forfeit. He just hadn't expected it to be in this fashion. So, he had his own failsafe measures in place. It wouldn't take much to activate them. A simple command code – or his death – would make sure no one ever learned the role his own people were playing in the new war wasn't discovered by the enemy.

Resting his head against the back of the sofa, Hughes closed his eyes and let his mind go back over the latest meeting with Dorescu. The Callusian had made it abundantly clear he had no use for his Midlothian advisor. Nor did he have any intention of returning to the battle plan drawn up by the Midlothians. His goal was to probe Fuerconese space, testing their defenses and dealing as much damage as he could before withdrawing. This might not be the inevitable invasion of Fuercon but it was the first volley.

It didn't matter that such action would put the Fuerconese on guard, all but ensuring another invasion would not succeed, at least not without high casualties on both sides. In some warped way, it was a matter of honor with Dorescu. But that honor would probably get them all killed.

Damn them all!

17

"Status?" Captain Rafe Thrasher said as he strode onto the bridge.

A tall, almost painfully thin man with graying hair and eyes to match stood next to the command chair. At the sound of the Captain's voice, he braced to attention and his Adam's apple bobbed nervously. From where she stood just behind Thrasher, Ash fought the urge to smile. On their way to the bridge from the staging area, Thrasher had given her a quick rundown on his senior officers. Like her, just before they shipped out, he had found himself without an XO. Lt. Commander Sarah Washington had been transferred to Third Fleet where she would take command of a frigate. Because Second Fleet had shipped out so quickly, that left Thrasher to promote from within. Lt. Commander Aaron Styles had proven to be more than competent as *Nagato's* weapons officer, Thrasher had concerns about him as XO. From what she had seen so far, Ashlyn felt those concerns valid.

"No change in target's position. CIC reports no change in weapons status."

"Very good." Thrasher took a moment to study the tactical display. "Colonel Shaw, may I present my first officer, Lieutenant

Commander Aaron Styles. Lieutenant Commander, Colonel Ashlyn Shaw of the Devil Dogs."

"Lieutenant Commander." Ashlyn shook his hand and glanced around the bridge. each station was manned and most had a second in place to take over if necessary. She nodded in approval before turning her attention back to Thrasher and Styles. "If I may, Captain, how long until we are within weapon range of the target?"

And how long did she have to get her people – and the Marines on the three ships comprising the attack group – ready?

"Six hours at present speed, Colonel," Styles replied.

"Half that, Colonel," Thrasher corrected. "Now that you and your people are onboard, we are going to increase speed. Will that give you enough time to get your Marines ready?"

"It will." Another glance at the tactical display. "Captain, the Devil Dogs are at your service."

"I know better than to try to tell a Marine what to do, ma'am." He grinned and she smiled back at him. from the soft chuckles from several the bridge crew, she guessed they were well used to their captain's sense of humor.

"Then, with your permission, I'll return to the staging area."

"Or course, Colonel. If you or your platoon need anything, let Lieutenant Commander Styles know."

"I will." She stopped at the lift and turned back to the bridge. "Pre-op brief?"

"Assuming no change in status, two hours," Thrasher said.

Ashlyn nodded and, with Connery on her heels, entered the lift.

"One moment, Colonel. What sort of quartering will you require?" Thrasher asked before the lift doors could shut.

"I'll bunk with my Marines, Captain. Some of us will be bunking hot on the attack shuttles. Other will bunk in the staging area, ready to move into any area of the ship where we might be needed."

"I thought you might say that." He grinned again and she saw something in his expression that had her wondering what he had up his sleeve. "I've arranged an office for you off the staging area. There's a head with a shower as well as a cot. Admiral Tremayne instructed me to make sure you get at least an hour's downtime before we go to red alert."

"I would argue, but we both know the Admiral would have our heads if we disobeyed." Not that she appreciated Tremayne's heavy-handed – or maybe it was more underhanded – approach. "You can assure the Admiral I will do as she ordered."

"Thank you." When he looked at her this time, she knew he meant it. She also understood. Tremayne had put him between a rock and a hard place with that order. As fleet commander, Tremayne outranked them both. "If you change your mind about quarters, let me know. I'll have something prepared."

"Thank you, Captain."

With that, she programed the lift for the staging area. She had two hours, one really, to prepare for whatever they might find when they finally reached the other ships. Her money was on battle. If their data was correct, this was more than likely the first real salvo in the new war.

"Tenn-Shun!"

Ashlyn's boot heel had not hit the decksole as she stepped off the lift when the order rang out. Instantly, the members of Second Platoon stopped what they were doing and braced to attention. So, too, did every other Marine in the staging area – and there were more Marines there than should have been. Not that it surprised her. Whenever Devil Dogs arrived at a new posting, other Marines came to check them out. Some wanted to see for themselves if the Devil Dogs were as big and bad as their reputation. Others were recon-necting with former squadmates. Then there were those who came to check out the Devil Dogs' equipment, always the best in the Corps.

"Lieutenant Lashay, report," she said as she crossed to where the young man stood, the platoon sergeant at his side.

"No problems so far, Colonel. We need another few minutes to finish unpacking the gear. Lieutenant Fielder just reported in to confirm that LAC crews are standing by."

"Any problems?"

"Negative, ma'am."

She nodded. She hadn't expected any. The transit, while made without much forewarning, had been an easy one. Much of their equipment had been left on the *Phoenix* because they were looking at only potential boarding and defense action. That meant they did not need the same sort of armament and weaponry they would for a ground assault.

"Very good, LT." And exactly what she expected. "Sergeant, get them back to work. Walk with me, Lieutenant."

She strolled across the landing bay they were using as the staging area, Lashay at her side and Connery one step behind. As they walked, she took in everything going on. The Devil Dogs had immediately gone back to work, checking their weapons and battle armor. Good-natured banter filled the air as they worked. The occasional question from some of the newer members of the platoon was quickly answered by the veterans. Non-coms moved among the enlisted, making sure everything was up to the standard Ashlyn had set.

Good.

What wasn't so good was the number of Marines not assigned to the platoon who seemed to be milling about the area. Under other circumstances, she would not give them a second thought. This was different. The *Nagato* and its sister ships were heading toward ships she knew were hostile. Those Marines should be either on duty or making sure their own gear was ready for what might happen when they made contact with the unidentified ships.

"LT, our orders are simple. We'll be putting the LACs in the air before contact Captain Thrasher contacts the targets. I want your people split into two groups. One will assist with damage control and repel any boarders. The *Nagato* has a full Marine complement, so we will let them handle backing up Naval personnel."

"Yes, ma'am."

"The other group of Devil Dogs are to hot bunk on the attack shuttles. Full battle rattle for everyone in the platoon. That includes you, LT." She made a point of looking him up and down, raising an eyebrow at his lack of secondary weaponry.

"Yes, ma'am." He colored slightly.

Taking pity on him, but not too much, she reached out and gripped his arm. "Lashay, you're a good officer but you need to set the example for your platoon. That means you need to gear up and then make sure each of your people have done the same thing."

He nodded and she didn't miss the way he looked at the way she had geared up. "If I may, Colonel, how many weapons are you carrying?"

"More than I hope I ever need," she said and went on to list everything she had on her, both officially sanctioned and not. When she added the weapons included with the rest of her gear, he shook her head. "Ma'am, I will never again accuse Sergeant McQueen of exaggerating."

Ashlyn grinned. McQueen and Talbot played poker together and she had no doubt the Master Gunnery Sergeant had regaled McQueen with tales of his CO. Some of those tales might even be true.

"Lashay, I learned long ago things happen we can't foresee. That's especially true in battle. So having too many weapons, as long as they don't interfere with the completion of your mission, is never a bad thing."

"Point taken."

"Good. I'll leave you to get your people ready. Once they are in place, tell them to grab some chow and rest. If we are lucky, we've got a little less than three hours before we make contact. Alternate watches between now and then."

"Aye, ma'am."

"Captain Thrasher said he'd made an office available for me down here."

"Yes, ma'am. Far corner, starboard."

She glanced in the direction he indicated and nodded. "Very well. You know what to do, LT. I'll be in the office if you need me."

Lashay briefly braced to attention and then hurried across the staging area to where the platoon worked. Ashlyn watched, Connery now at her side, as her signaled Sergeant McQueen. The platoon sergeant nodded once and made his way to the center of the area. Once there, he glanced to where Lashay stood. When he caught his lieutenant's eye, he nodded once. Seeing it, Ashlyn smiled slightly. The *Nagato's* Marines were about to learn a lesson.

"Sergeant McQueen!" Lashay's voice rose above the sounds of everything else.

"Sir!"

"When does it look like my platoon has grown in size?"

"Because we have a lot of looky-loos, LT."

"Then get them out of my staging area." With that, Lashay turned and moved to what Ashlyn assumed was his footlocker. When he began pulling additional weapons from it, she nodded in approval.

"Now I know all you looky-loos posing as Marines can't be in my beloved Corps. A *real* Marine wouldn't be down here, gawking at other Marines, not even the Devil Dogs, the pride of the Corps. A *real* Marine would be reporting to his duty station or making sure his own gear was ready for anything that might happen. A *real* Marine would not put himself or any of his shipmates, even those poor souls foolish enough to join the Navy instead of our glorious Corps, in danger by not being prepared for battle. So I guess none of you standing around, looking like you want to hide behind your mama's skirts because the mean old platoon sergeant is dressing you down, are *real* Marines."

"He is almost as good as Master Gunnery Sergeant Talbot, ma'am," Connery whispered.

"That he is," Ashlyn agreed as the ship's Marines found the nearest exits from the staging area. "Let's leave them to it."

One hour later, Ashlyn stepped out of the small head in the office Thrasher had assigned her. As she did, she sniffed the air appreciatively. Then she grinned. Lance Corporal Connery stood near the hatch to the staging area. Her expression gave nothing away. It didn't need to. Not when a mug of coffee so hot Ashlyn could see the steam coming off of it sat on the desk. Certainly not when the mug was accompanied by a carafe she guessed contained more of that same lifesaving brew. Most definitely not when a sandwich and a selection of cheeses waited for her as well.

"You may not be trying to join my personal staff, Lance Corporal, but if you keep this up, that's exactly what's going to happen." Ash moved to the desk and reached for the mug. One sip of the coffee told her all she needed to know. This had not come from the Mess. Connery, or someone who loved coffee as much as she did, had brewed it.

"I'm a Marine, ma'am. More importantly, I'm a Devil Dog. That means I know the first rule of war. Keep your CO happy. The fact we both happen to appreciate a properly brewed cup of coffee makes that a bit easier."

"Point to you, Lance Corporal." She lifted her mug in salute. "Have you eaten?"

"Yes, ma'am, and I managed 30 down," Connery answered, anticipating Ashlyn's next question.

"Status?"

"The platoon is in place. Sergeant McQueen is hot bunking with the squads onboard the attack shuttles while the LT is staying onboard to oversee our Marines here."

Ash nodded in approval. Lashay's decision to send McQueen on the shuttles meant he understood the Devil Dogs would listen to the veteran non-com and do as he ordered without hesitation. Unfortunately, that wasn't always the case with junior officers who were not the battle-hardened veterans of the rest of the platoon. The fact Lashay recognized it spoke well of him and of his future with the Devil Dogs.

"Anything else I need to know?"

"Captain Thrasher asked that you join him on the bridge at your convenience, ma'am." Before Ash could ask why she had let her sleep instead of passing on the message, Connery continued. "He said not to wake you, Colonel. Said he would like your insight as we near the targets."

"Very well." She didn't like it but Connery had acted properly by not waking her immediately. Even so, she would have a talk with

Talbot when they returned to the *Phoenix Rising* about what she expected from her escorts, even if a senior officer said not to disturb her. She finished her sandwich and drained her mug of coffee. "Let's go see what the good captain can tell us."

"Aye, ma'am." Connery pressed the control next to the hatch and a soft snick sounded as the locks were disengaged. "Whenever you're ready, ma'am."

————

"Sir, CIC reports the three ships that broke off from the main Fuerconese force have increased speed. At their current speed and trajectory, they will be inside our weapons envelop in two hours," the helmsman reported.

Anton Dorescu frowned and thought hard for a moment. He had hoped the Fuerconese commander would take a more cautious approach. Even so, the enemy had yet to bring their weapons or active shields online. Sending the three ships forward might simply be their commanding officer's attempt to get a better reading on the ships at the edge of their system. That was the only thing that made sense. No commander, certainly no competent commander, would send three ships against a taskforce. Not even the Fuerconese were that foolish.

Or were they?

He leaned back in his chair and considered the tactical display. If he were the enemy commander, his first act would have been to scan the unknown ships. Then he would have moved the bulk of his ships forward, letting the trespassers know that he neither feared them nor would he hesitate to open fire if he felt they presented a threat. If that failed, he would bring up active shields and his weapons would go hot. Experience had taught him most commanding officers tended to back down after they saw a ship or two under their command destroyed, the crews lost.

So what were the Fuerconese up to?

"Comms, message to Commanders Chakotey and Flewellen.

Their ships are to drop back and assume a position that will allow them to escape out-of-system if the Fuerconese manage to get the upper hand."

"Aye, sir." The communications officer quickly relayed the order. Then he turned to glance at Dorescu. "Message away, sir."

"Do we have an ID on the ships yet?"

"None yet, Captain. If the ships are broadcasting their ID codes, we have not been able to pick it up."

"Recommendation, Mr. Kovacz?" He looked at his first officer.

"Hold position. Increase our alert level and have LACs ready to launch," Kovacz answered. "I'd also recommend putting a single LAC up to launch secondary probes. They might be able to pick up what our sensors might be missing."

"Or it could be taken as a hostile act." Dorescu stared ahead. Kovacz was right, much as he hated to admit it. The probes, small and easy to miss if you weren't looking for them, could give them information they did not yet have. But getting them in place, that was the problem. Did he dare risk it?

Suddenly he sat up, all but snarling in frustration. Probes! What if they had missed probes the Fuerconese had in place? That could explain why their ships not only had remained in the area but why they were sending the three out to investigate. By all that was holy and unholy, had they missed something so simple?

"Go to active sensors," he snapped. "Do they have probes in the area?"

He waited, impatience turning into frustration which turned to anger. It wasn't that hard to read a screen and make a report.

"Nothing, sir," Kovacz reported from where he stood behind the ratings reviewing the data as it came in. "There was one anomaly but it has not repeated."

"Location?" He got to his feet and moved to stand in front of the tactical display. A moment later, a blinking yellow dot appeared on the display. He stared at it. It blinked once, twice and was then gone. It might be nothing or it might be everything. Too much rested on the success of this mission for him to take chances.

"Possibility it is a probe that is running a random power cycle?" He looked to his tactical officer.

"Doubtful, sir. None of our intelligence – or information from our advisor – indicates the Fuerconese have managed to perfect the tech needed for such a probe. Even if it powered down to minimal levels, we would still be able to pick them up, especially since we know where to look right now."

"Let's not run any risks. Comms, send this to all our ships." He moved back to his chair, considering how to phrase it so none of his commanders jumped the gun. "Orders. All ships to bring up active shields and take their weapons hot in 70 minutes. That is seven zero minutes. Confirm order at end of transmission.

"Orders, in 60 minutes, that is six zero minutes, all ships will increase speed by one quarter. At that time, implement Approach Plan Zeta. I say again, Approach Plan Zeta. Confirm order at end of transmission.

"Orders, radio silence in effect starting immediately. Short burst transmission only to the *Anubis*. Exceptions are as follows: appearance of new enemy ships, intercept of enemy transmission, confirmation of location of enemy probes or scans. Confirm order at end of transmission. Dorescu out." He sat back and listened as each ship confirmed his orders. "Bridge crew, send for your relief. Instruct them to gear up before reporting for duty. Once they report, you are dismissed to gear up. Report back as soon as you have."

"Your thoughts, Captain?" Kovacz asked softly as he moved to stand next to the command chair.

"We have to assume they not only know we are here but at least suspect who we are. While they haven't come straight at us, they are approaching too carefully to think we might be nothing more than merchants. All we can hope for now is that they are uncertain enough they get careless and come inside our weapons envelop before they realize their mistake." He paused and leaned back, closing his eyes in thought. Then he sat up, a demonic grin on his face. "Comms, new orders. Transmit on my command. Disregard previous orders. Maintain current status. Maintain only passive shields and scans until ordered otherwise."

"Sir!" Kovacz protested. He fell silent when Dorescu slashed a hand through the air.

"Kovacz, trust me. We're going to lure them into a trap. Thank about it. They can't know for certain who we are. They haven't seen our new ships and we certainly haven't done anything to call undue attention to ourselves. We will maintain our current status. However, once the Fuerconese ships are within weapons range, we will bring up our shields and our weapons will go hot. They will never know what hit them and, by the time the ships they are holding back realize what happened, we will be on them. Trust me, this will be a good day for the *Anubis* and our brothers."

"Devious as always, Captain, and that's why you make us rich." Kovacz chuckled as Dorescu nodded in agreement.

"And our *advisor*?" the first officer asked, once more showing his distaste for the Midlothian.

"It's going to be a fight, Kovacz. People die in battle, especially space battles. It will be with much regret that we report the loss of Commander Hughes to his Midlothian masters. At least we will be able to tell them he died bravely, fighting our common enemy."

"Kovacz, I promise when we move on the fool, you can have him first. Then I think it only fitting that the crew gets to *play* with him for a while. But I want him alive through it all. I claim the right to dispatch him from this plane."

"Agreed and many thanks, Captain."

"Then, let us see what more we can do to make sure we give these Fuerconese bastards a surprise their people won't ever forget."

18

"You look like you got some rest, Ash," Thrasher said as the Ready Room hatch slid shut behind them. "I guess I ought to ask permission to call you by your given name, seeing how you outrank me now." He grinned and motioned her to a seat.

"Nah. I remember all those nights when you emptied my pockets at poker." She grinned, relaxing some. The concern she had felt when she learned he wanted to speak with her before the briefing eased. "Although, I will admit to having a moment of concern when Connery said you wanted to see me."

"Sorry." He sat and poured a mug of coffee from the carafe in front of his place. Then he looked to her, lifting the mug to see if she wanted one. She shook her head. "I thought we might compare notes before the briefing. You probably know more about what we might be facing than I do. Besides, I received a comm from Fuercon I wanted to share with you."

Ash sat back and nodded, her concern returning.

"Let's start with what the good news. FleetCom forwarded copies of the formal pleas made by not only Sorkowski and O'Brien, but all the major players in the conspiracy surrounding what happened to you and your people. Several of the others are still trying to negotiate better deals but the JAG feels certain they will end up pleading out as well."

Ashlyn blew out a breath. "Thanks."

"A Lieutenant Liu included a message, asking me to assure you the investigation is still ongoing and he feels they are getting closer to locating the subject. He said you would know who he's referring to."

Another nod. Unless she was very wrong, he meant Moreau.

"I've forwarded the report to you. I wanted to give you the basics because I'm afraid you aren't going to have time to go over it until we deal with our *visitors*."

She sat up, alert and concerned. "I take it there's been a change in status."

"Nothing major but sensors picked up a series of comm bursts and then the ships went silent. More troubling, two ships have broken off from the main body and are moving away. My guess is they are the rearguard and are under orders to get away if we do engage."

"That and it gives them the opportunity to see if we are trying to flank them." Neither action that a harmless merchant convoy would engage in. "What has the Admiral said?"

"To trust my gut and not be stupid." He grimaced and Ash smiled. She could hear Tremayne saying just that in a private message.

"Sounds like good advice to me."

"I'm going to push up the timeline. We will be within the outer limit of our weapons range in half an hour. Once we are, Comms will hail the intruders. They are to identify themselves and allow boarding. If they are who we think, they won't respond right away. One thing we have all learned about the Callusians, they think we are weak and will try to bluff. That gives you time to get your LACs in the air as well as the attack shuttles."

"I agree we need to be proactive, Rafe, but if the rest of the Fleet doesn't arrive to back us up pretty damned quickly, things will go bad."

"The Admiral has already started the transition to our location."

Ashlyn nodded. She had expected him to tell her just that but part of her duty was to make sure Thrasher wasn't leading them straight to their deaths.

"They will get one warning. Failure to stand down will result in our taking any and all necessary action to secure their ships and protect Fuerconese space. Our primary orders are still in place. We are to engage with the reminder to do whatever it takes to secure at least one enemy vessel intact."

"Nothing difficult at all."

He looked at her and shook his head, smiling slightly. "Let us hope."

"I also received orders to make sure you remember that you are to stay onboard. Admiral Tremayne's exact words were, 'Remind her she can't coordinate all her Marines from the middle of a firefight.'"

"Rafe, I promise I will do as she says."

"As long as it suits you," he finished for her. Before she could say anything, he continued. "Ash, normally I'd hold you to it. But we both know this situation can go bad without warning. If you need to board with your people, you'll do it – in the second or third wave. Not in the leading wave. However, I would prefer you to stay onboard. Not because of the Admiral's orders, although doing so would make my life a lot easier."

He pushed away from the table and got to his feet. She watched, her brow creasing in concern, as he moved to the far end of the room. When he turned, his expression was worried.

"The reason Tremayne put me in charge of this little greeting party is because I am senior, not only in time in grade but in wartime experience. The other two commanders are good. They wouldn't have been included otherwise. But they are inexperienced when it comes to fighting the Callusians."

She waited, beginning to understand his concern.

"Then there is my XO. As you saw, he's a good man but he is not someone I want running an op, not yet at any rate."

"And that has what to do with me, Rafe? I'm a Marine, not a Naval officer."

"True, but you have been in situations like this. Hell, Ash, we saw more than a few similar to this when we were shipmates." He ran a hand over his hair and shrugged. "My crew, and not just the Marines, respect you. If things go bad and they see you standing in, doing what needs to be done – even if it is only coordinating what the Marines are doing – they will be reassured we not only can but will hold out until the rest of the Fleet arrives. That's going to be especially important if something happens to me and the XO takes command."

She might not like it but she understood his concerns. "All right."

"I assume you'll want to brief your people in person. I'd appreciate it if you were on the bridge before we issue the hail."

"Understood." She thought for a moment. "Rafe, if I may proffer a recommendation."

He inclined his head.

"With your permission, I'll work from here. Lieutenant Lashay is more than capable of making sure the platoon is prepped. It will also be easier coordinating with the LAC crews. Just let me tell Connery and send her down."

He gave her a grin that did not reach his eyes. "There was one more order from the Admiral. She was forwarding it from Brigadier General Shaw. Until you return to the *Phoenix Rising*, the lance corporal is to remain at your side."

She didn't say anything. Orders were orders, whether she liked it or not. "I understand."

"I'll be on the bridge. Join me when you can."

With that, he left the Ready Room, the door sliding shut behind him. A moment later, it opened and Connery stepped inside. She braced to attention and waited for Ash to speak.

"I assume you received additional instructions from the Master Guns," Ashlyn said.

"I did, ma'am. Also, just so the Colonel knows, I also received orders from General Shaw."

Of course, she had. It wouldn't surprise Ashlyn to discover Okafor had included her own orders as well.

"Don't look like I'm going to bite your head off, Connery. I have a feeling both of us would much rather be in the staging area, waiting to take the fight to the Callusians."

"I know I would, ma'am."

"Since that isn't going to happen, let's make sure the rest of the platoon is ready to move. Captain Thrasher has moved up the timetable. We have less than half an hour to make sure everyone is in position to move."

Not much time but enough, assuming Lashay had done as she'd ordered earlier. Damn but she wished the powers-that-be had let her bring First Platoon.

———

"SIR, WE ARE BEING HAILED." Comms bent over his console, his shoulders hunched.

"Visual?" Dorescu asked.

"Aye."

"Put it up."

He leaned back and watched as the display before him changed from the tactical display. Gone were the representations of his ships and the approaching Fuerconese vessels. Replacing it was a single image, the Fuerconese flag. His lips pulled back and bared his teeth at the sight. A few seconds later, the image of a light-haired man replaced it.

"This is Captain Rafe Thrasher, commanding the *Nagato*. You have entered Fuerconese space. Identify yourselves and prepare to be boarded. Once we have determined you are carrying no contraband, you will be free to go about your business."

Dorescu slammed his fist against his thigh and then signaled the comms officer to open transmission.

"Captain Thrasher, this is Commander Meersham, commanding the *Thomas Augustine*. We are a merchant convoy out of Halstrom's Landing. The terms of our treaty with Fuercon gives us free passage through your system."

"Not in times of war, Commander," the Fuerconese captain said.

"All ships coming in-system, especially when they are not following normal transit routes, are being stopped and searched. We require you to power down your shields and weapons systems and stand by for boarding."

"Captain Thrasher, as you just pointed out, it is a time of war. Before I agree to your terms, I need to confirm your identity. Pan out your video feed so I can identify your uniform."

"Once you do the same, Commander Meersham," Thrasher countered.

Dorescu made a sliding motion across his throat, signaling Comms to cut the feed. How dare Thrasher demand anything?

"Comms, how quickly can you bring up the overlay? I need him to see a merchant uniform."

"Thirty seconds, sir." His fingers flew across his board. Each passing second seemed to take minutes and Dorescu fought the urge to pace. Finally, Comms signaled he was ready. "Comms restored, sir."

"Captain Thrasher, my apologies," Dorescu said, risking a quick glance at his image in the lower right corner of the display. "You know how it is. Our owners would rather spend money on themselves than on the parts we need to keep our systems running." He lifted one shoulder in a half-shrug and gave a little smile. As he did, he cursed mentally. Thrasher was making no attempt to hide either the fact he was a Fuerconese Naval officer or that he and his crew were ready for battle. There was no mistaking the light armor they wore.

Damn them!

"Of course, Commander. Now, I must insist you do as instructed. If not, you will leave me with no choice but to order my ships to open fire. You have two minutes to give me your answer."

Without waiting for a response, Thrasher ended the transmission. For a moment, Dorescu stared at the Fuerconese flag that replaced the captain's image. Two minutes! Not long enough to get his LACs in the air but long enough to activate ship's defenses. It would take the guns longer to come online but that didn't matter. Thrasher was like every other Fuerconese commander he had faced. All bluster and too little action to back it up. He would soon learn how foolish he had been to challenge Anton Dorescu.

"Shields up and weapons hot," he ordered. "Get the LACs launched. As soon as weapons are online, open fire."

"Sir, they have launched their LACs!"

"Good. Let them learn how foolish they are to challenge us." Three ships against his taskforce had no hope of survival. "Let's get this done. A few prisoners, some playthings and riches to line our pockets if we do it right. Think of the praise they will shower on us when we return home."

———

"Sir, they have brought up their shields and sensors read their weapons going hot."

"I guess they aren't quite as friendly as they wanted us to believe." He studied the plot for a moment before looking up. "Colonel?"

"LACs have launched and are moving into position, sir. Shall I launch the attack shuttles?"

"Go ahead." He nodded to Comms to signal the other ships to go to battle stations.

He turned his attention back to the plot. As he did, he liked what he saw. The LACs were assuming positions that put them between the Callusian taskforce and his three ships. At Ashlyn's order, they would begin their attack run. If their luck held, the LACs would be enough to keep the enemy engaged until Admiral Tremayne the rest of Second Fleet were in position. It was their best bet to survive the battle.

While Ashlyn passed on the order for the attack shuttles to launch, Thrasher continued the plot before him. As he did, he felt the familiar tensing, the slight touch of electricity coursing through him. His counterpart might have identified himself as a merchant captain but he knew better. The moment the man's image appeared on the display, Thrasher had recognized him from the briefing materials Admiral Collins had sent. This was the Callusian commander in charge of the attack on the Cassius System. Was he now here to attempt an attack on Fuercon?

If so, he will find out we aren't nearly as easy a target.

"Shuttles away, sir," Ashlyn reported.

"The boarding parties?"

"Are ready to move once the ships either stand down or surrender. The basic plan is to send teams to Bridge, Engineering, Environmental and AuxCon once we can get onboard." She paused and he waited, guessing from the look on her face she was trying to get her thoughts in order. "Captain, my squad leaders understand that our priority is to capture at least one ship with its databanks intact. However, they will not jeopardize the overall success of the mission in order to do so. Nor will they place themselves in unnecessary danger without it looking like there is a good chance they can secure the data."

"Understood and agreed, Colonel. If at all possible, I want to bring everyone home safe from this assignment." He glanced at the plot and a frown played at the corners of his mouth. "Comms, contact CIC. I want and update on the ships. It looks to me as if we're coming up on more tonnage than we initially thought."

"Aye, sir," the communications officer replied before turning to his board to relay the message.

"All right, ladies and gentlemen," Thrasher continued. "Let's not get sloppy now. Comms, inform Admiral Tremayne of the change in status. Sound battle stations."

"Aye, sir," Comms replied.

For the next few minutes, Thrasher sat back and listened as the various stations reported in. As they did, the LACs and attack shuttles closed the distance to the enemy ships. It wouldn't be long before they were within the enemy's weapons range.

"Comms, message to *Commander Meersham*. We take their silence and the fact they have activated their shields and their weapons are going hot as an act of warfare. Unless they want our ships to open fire, they will immediately surrender and standby for boarding."

"Aye, sir."

"Colonel Shaw."

He got to his feet and moved to the far end of the bridge, motioning for her to come with him. She paused long enough to say something to the lance corporal before moving in Thrasher's direction. Watching her, Thrasher nodded slightly. She might not appreciate being ordered to remain onboard, especially since she was not on the flagship where she could coordinate the action of all the Devil Dogs, but her presence on the *Nagato* meant he had a resource most ship's captains never did.

"Captain, the bogeys have just changed formation. Their engines have powered up and they are on an approach vector that will cut behind us if we maintain current speed and course," Tactical reported without taking her eyes from her display.

"Understood. Inform the other ships to slow and execute Plan Omega. Comms, inform Admiral Tremayne."

"Aye, sir."

"Colonel, bring the LACs around to their attack vectors."

"Aye, sir."

Ashlyn quickly conveyed the order. Thrasher nodded in approval as she instructed the COLAC to begin transmitting a visual back to the *Phoenix Rising*. Once she had, she waited, the fingers of her right hand drumming a staccato tempo against her thigh. Hearing it, Thrasher smiled slightly. For some reason, it was slightly reassuring to know she wasn't as calm as she seemed.

Realizing the train of his thoughts, he turned to covertly study her. She might want personal vengeance for all she and her people had suffered – and he wouldn't blame her if she did. – but she would never let that desire put others in danger. She would do her duty, even if it meant staying onboard the *Nagato*.

"Care to share?" she asked as he smiled slightly.

"Just glad you're here, Ash." He looked around to make sure no one could overhear. "If anything happens and I'm taken out of action, you have the con until someone my rank or higher can take over. Do not let the XO assume command."

"Rafe, no can do. You know that. Wrong service track."

"Orders, Ash. Not just from me as ship's commander but from the Admiral. She said to tell you it will be nothing more than what you had to do when you assumed command of the light cruiser in docking orbit."

"Except for this little matter of a Callusian taskforce bearing down on us." She did not sound amused.

"Incoming visual, Captain," Tactical reported.

"Put it up," he replied and returned to his place in the center of the bridge.

A moment later, the holo display showed LACs pouring out of bays from the leading ships. Reports started coming in from CIC over the battle net with the number of LACs, their classification and probably armament. As soon as CIC finished, the COLAC requested orders. It didn't surprise Thrasher to hear Ashlyn giving the COLAC permission to engage.

"Sir, this doesn't feel right," Ashlyn said as they watched the distance between their LACs and the enemy's narrow. "Could they be trying to slip ships – or maybe even something else, probes maybe – past us?"

"Captain, we just picked up a transmission burst from the lead ship," Comms reported before he could respond.

"Content?" He moved to stand behind the young man, eyes narrowing as he watched him work.

"I can only guess, sir. It's going to take a while for the computers to break the encryption."

"If there had been any doubt about their intentions, notwithstanding the way they launched their LACs, there isn't now. They wouldn't be sending encrypted messages if they were innocently here,"

"Guns, fire at will."

"Fire at will, aye."

"We have incoming!" Tactical reported.

A shrill alarm shattered the silence following her announcement. Thrasher watched as the tactical display was updated. His mouth hardened to see several enemy LACs breaking through. The COLAC's voice came over the battle net, ordering several of their own LACs to pursue. At the same time, the *Nagato* prepared to open fire.

"First volley away, Captain. Implementing Fire Plan Hades."

"Enemy missiles incoming!"

"Damage control teams, stand by."

"LACs incoming! Collision course!"

Thrasher cursed and opened ship-wide comms. "Brace for impact. Brace for impact." He checked the bridge crew, relieved to see them quickly buckling in.

"Captain, get your ass into your shock frame!" Ashlyn ordered.

The *Nagato* shuddered and bucked as the first LAC hit its shields. The screens flared as the LAC tumbled, breaking apart only moments before its torpedoes exploded. she was hit. A second LAC followed the first in, somehow managing to avoid the defensive screen laid out by the *Nagato's* turrets. Thrasher turned, ordering all compartments sealed. As he did, part of him noted the almost businesslike way Ashlyn slammed her helmet into place, quickly checking the seal. Then the ship rocked violently again and he felt himself flying through the air. There was pain and then all went dark.

19

"Two LACs broke through their line, sir!"

Dorescu leaned forward, his attention focused on the tactical display. He listened as reports came in. Other than the two LACs that had managed to break through the Fuerconese line, their fighters were less than effective. The Fuerconese LACs were faster, their shields stronger. Worse, their weapons were tearing the Callusian LACs to pieces. If their lasers didn't find a target, their torpedoes did. The attrition rate was as bad, if not worse, than it had been in the last war.

And this after the Midlothians had assured them their new targeting systems would be as good, if not better, that the Fuerconese's. This battle already put the lie to that claim. Making matters worse, their countermeasures appeared to be more effective as well. The LACs, at least some of them, carried decoy missiles. Between them and chaff, his weapons system was having difficulty staying locked on target.

It would only delay the inevitable. The Fuerconese ships might have the advantage in technology but he had the numbers. The loss of the LACs would have to be explained to Command but they would overlook it when he proved not only that the Fuercon System was not as secure as they had always thought but was ripe for the taking.

"The *Nagato* is damaged, sir. It's venting atmosphere and sensor readings confirm damage to Engineering."

"Order the LACs to break away and focus their fire on the *Nagato*. Tirol Squadron is to break formation. Focus on the trailing ship, designated Gamma Target. Vandal Squadron is to focus on the second shit, designated Beta. The *Nagato* is ours."

"Aye, sir." The communications officer relayed his orders.

"Status of the rest of their ships?"

"The last report had them on an intercept course. Time to intercept sixty-seven minutes, Captain."

He started to nod and then paused. What he Kovacz meant by "the last report"? "Explain!" he snapped.

"No explanation, sir. When I queried CIC, they said that was all the information they had."

With a curse, Dorescu signaled CIC. As he did, he wondered if he had made a mistake by keeping Kovacz on the bridge. Under most circumstances, the first officer would be in CIC, a precaution in case the enemy managed to get a direct hit on the bridge. Dorescu had chosen to send the second officer to CIC this time. He had wanted to prove to Kovacz the benefits of serving with him far outweighed the danger of trying to kill him. Then there was the issue of Hughes. When the time came to deal with the Midlothian, Dorescu planned to not only let his first officer have a little *fun* with him but to make sure he had a record of it. Blackmail often convinced the reluctant not to do something they might both regret.

"Why have you not updated the information on the main Fuerconese formation?" he demanded once the assistant tactical officer answered his comm.

"Sir, there is no new information. The Fuerconese ships are somehow managing to jam our sensors. Either that or they have come to a full stop."

"Adjust your damned equipment and find out where they are!"

"Incoming!"

"Launch countermeasures!" he ordered.

Damn them!

He gripped the arms of his chair as the missiles their countermeasures missed hit the ship's shields. Reports poured in and he relaxed slightly. No major damage. The bridge crew coordinated with their counterparts in CIC and AuxCon. The gunnery crews hunched over their monitors, discussing the best way to counter the next wave of enemy fire. The Fuerconese may have gotten lucky with that first wave of fire from their LACs but Dorescu swore that was where their luck would end.

"Helm, plot a new course. Close distance with the *Nagato*. Approach from the port side. Let's take advantage of their weakened shielding."

"Aye, sir."

He sat back and watched as one by one his LACs blinked off the tactical screen. Anger burned deep within him as he realized his mistake. By ordering them to break off from the enemy LACs to focus on the *Nagato* and her sister ships, he had put them between two waves of enemy fire with little support from his own ships. Good men were dying as a result but they died for the greater glory of the cause. Their deaths kept the enemy focused on the LAC attack, giving his ships time to get into position to destroy the three Fuerconese ships. He would sing their deaths as the *Nagato* burned.

————

"CAPTAIN, get your ass into your shock frame!"

Ashlyn turned to Thrasher as the two enemy LACs broke through their defenses. She didn't need the sensor tech's report to know the LACs were accelerating. She had seen this tactic too many times in the last war. The enemy LAC pilots – Hell, who was she kidding? The Callusians had been known to do it with almost every class of ship they used – were accelerating, not away from the *Nagato* but toward it. They were suiciding into the ship in an attempt to take down their shielding and do what damage they could.

The screens flared as the LAC tumbled, skipping along them like a rock on water. Moments later, the attack craft broke apart. Almost instantly, its torpedoes exploded. The shields shimmered and Ashlyn heard someone nearby curse softly before they began issuing a series of orders to bypass the damaged circuits and route additional power to the shields where the LAC had struck.

A second LAC followed the first. Somehow, it managed to avoid the defensive screen laid out by the *Nagato's* turrets. Ashlyn frowned, knowing what was about to happen. Without waiting for confirmation, she used the battle net to order the *Nagato's* Marines, as well as the Devil Dogs still onboard, to prepare to assist all Damage Control teams. Unless Guns managed to get a lucky shot off at the last moment, there were going to be casualties.

Cursing again, Ashlyn grabbed her helmet where it she had racked it on the back of the Captain's chair and slammed it into place. Her fingers worked automatically as they checked the seal. The moment the HUD came online, she scanned the readouts. Everything read green. How long it lasted would be in the hands of the Nagato's crew, their expertise in battle, and God.

Ashlyn clung to the back of the command chair as the second LAC hit. Once again, she looked for Thrasher and another curse was torn from her lips. Instead of strapping into his shock frame as she'd ordered, he had started moving toward the Tactical station.

The idiot!

The *Nagato* rocked violently as the LAC's ordinance exploded, a small ship being tossed ruthlessly on a wild and unforgiving sea. For one moment, Thrasher seemed suspended in time between one step and another. Then flew forward like a rag doll tossed carelessly aside. There was a sickening thud as he hit the bulkhead before sliding to the decksole, unconscious.

Damage reports poured in. Calls for medics did as well. On the bridge, the lights flickered, went out momentarily before coming back on. Still clinging to the back of the command chair, Ashlyn took stock, first of herself and then of the bridge crew. Her HUD showed what she already knew. She was, so far, uninjured but her pulse and respiration were up. Battle tended to do that.

Even better, the bridge crew appeared battered but, for the most part, still able to function. Several had taken injuries but there was a reason why the Fuerconese Navy insisted on back-up crewing for all major stations. Of more concern was the damage being reported to some of the stations. Even that would not be a major issue as long as AuxCon and CIC were operational.

"Comms, send for a medic!" Lance Corporal Connery ordered from where she knelt next to Thrasher. "Colonel Shaw, I will repeat what you told the Captain. Get your ass into the shock frame before we take another hit."

"Everyone, helmet up," Ash said before doing as Connery ordered. Like it or not, until control was transferred to AuxCon and Lt. Commander Stiles, she was in command. "Get me AuxCon."

"AuxCon is off-line, Colonel," Comms reported a moment later. "Damage Control is on its way. Preliminary information is that last explosion breached the hull in that section of the ship."

"Weapon status?"

"Turret One down but the gunnery team are already working on it and says it will be back up in half an hour."

"Shields?"

"We are shunting additional power to the forward shields, ma'am. They are holding at 60 percent."

Ashlyn nodded, trying hard to remember those sims at the Academy dealing with similar situations. "Status of the other ships?"

"Minor damage."

At least that was something in their favor.

"Order them to shore up formation. Until we get our shields and Turret One back up, they have the lead positions." She studied the tactical display. Their LACs were managing to keep the enemy LACs away from them but it was only a matter of time before another broke through or, worse, the enemy opened fire. "Guns, Tactical, continue with the fire and response patterns Captain Thrasher approved. Comms, get me Admiral Tremayne."

"Aye, ma'am."

Ashlyn listened as reports continued to pour in over the comms. There was nothing she could do to help with Damage Control or repairs. Medical teams reported in, relaying orders to Sick Bay when needed. AuxCon remained off-line but reports from that part of the ship indicated it could be as simple as a comms failure. Part of Ash hoped that was all and XO would soon assume command. Then she remembered Thrasher asking her to make sure that did not happen.

Damn it, things got complicated in battle.

"Admiral Tremayne, ma'am," Comms reported.

Ashlyn thanked her and opened comms. "Admiral, the *Nagato* has taken two strikes from suicide LACs. Damage is moderate, but Captain Thrasher has been injured and, for the moment at least, AuxCon is silent. Probable explanation is a comms failure but the hull has been breached in that section of the ship."

"Maintain command until the status of AuxCon is determined, Colonel Shaw," Tremayne ordered. "We are closing in on your position. Maintain contact with the enemy."

"Understood, Admiral." She didn't grimace, at least she didn't think she did, but it was a close thing.

"Your LACs?"

"Cutting a very nice hole in the enemy defenses, ma'am."

"Keep putting the pressure on, Colonel."

"Aye, ma'am." She frowned, knowing she had to ask but not wanting to over an open channel. After switching to privacy mode, she continued. "Ma'am, there is some concern about the XO's ability to command under pressure. Captain Thrasher expressed those concerns before we engaged the enemy. He instructed me to take command should anything happen to him."

"I am aware of his concerns, Colonel, and concur. You are to maintain command until I am on-station and this battle is concluded. Then we will review the situation."

"Ma'am," she started but her protest died when Tremayne shook her head. "Aye, ma'am. I would appreciate it if you would tie me in with Tactical. I'm a Marine, ma'am, as you know, not a space jockey."

"No worries, Colonel. New order of attack coming through shortly. Until then, maintain your current status."

"Aye, ma'am." She paused as the lift door opened and a medical team appeared. "Medics are here for the captain, ma'am."

"Relay his condition to me, Colonel, as soon as you know it."

"Aye, ma'am."

"Keep comms open, Colonel. Tremayne out."

Ashlyn entered the command to end privacy mode and once more turned her attention to the bridge crew. As she did, she realized Connery had assumed the position next to the command chair she had taken before Thrasher's injury. She gave the lance corporal a nod of approval. Then she studied the tactical display.

"Comms, order to all LACs. They are to begin their run against the leading edges of the enemy fleet. Let's see if we can't get their birds to follow ours and give us some breathing room."

"Aye, ma'am."

"Tactical, status?"

"With the Colonel's permission, we will begin Attack Plan Pericles."

"Captain Thrasher approved the plan?"

"He did, ma'am. It's designed to utilize the other ships as the screen you ordered while still letting all three ships have maximum weapons effect."

"Do it."

The ship rocked again as another missile made its way through their defenses. Almost instantly came the report that the shields held. Without a word, Ashlyn punched a series of commands into her terminal and studied the results on her screen. So far, their counter-measures were dealing with incoming enemy missiles but that would not last long. The enemy had them outnumbered. Sooner or later, the *Nagato* and its sister ships would start running low on offensive and defensive ordinance. All they could do was hope the rest of the fleet arrived before the situation went critical.

"Damage Control. Lt. Commander Seaver," a woman's harried voice said in response to Ashlyn's hail a moment later.

"Commander, what's our status?" Ashlyn asked. As she did, she wanted to sigh in relief. She had served with Seaver before and trusted the woman not only to do everything she could to keep the *Nagato* up and running but to also tell her the truth.

"Auxiliary Control is still off-line, Colonel. The hull breach in that section is two compartments away. Unfortunately, it severed major system controls in the section. Preliminary readings show essential systems are running on backup, so they should have O2 but we won't know for sure until we can make entry. A crew is working its way there now.

"I also have crews working on levels 17-B, 31-A and 2-C as fire control. Your Devil Dogs are a great assistance."

"Thank you, Lt. Commander. Keep me informed." She turned to Comms. It was time to bluff and see if the enemy commander blinked. "Send this out," she said and carefully considered what to say. "This is Lt. Colonel Ashlyn Shaw, First Division First Battalion Fuerconese Marine Corps. No more games, Captain. Your ship has been positively identified as the *Anubis*, a Callusian battlecruiser. The *Anubis* and other ships in your taskforce were responsible for the invasion of the Cassius System, in violation of the cease fire in place at the time of the invasion. You are also responsible for the destruction of the *Tarrant* and the deaths of most of her crew.

"You have one chance to survive this encounter with your ships intact and your people alive. Stand down all weapons and prepare to be boarded. You have committed an act of warfare by encroaching on Fuerconese space. Failure to immediately comply will result in your destruction. Shaw clear."

"It's sent, ma'am."

"Lance Corporal Connery." She looked up at her Marine escort, glad now that she hadn't tried to convince her she didn't need a babysitter. "I need you to get down to the bay. Inform the LT that he will be leading the boarding party on the *Anubis*. I want vid on every move and I want you on the LT throughout the mission. So keep your comm linked with me."

For a moment Connery looked as if she might argue. Then she

glanced around the bridge and nodded. Ashlyn had a feeling they would discuss her decision to send Connery away from her post later, after they had dealt with the enemy.

"Aye, ma'am." Connery saluted and quickly left the bridge.

"Comms, send a message to the Flag. Let them know what's happening," Ashlyn continued, removing her helmet and racking it on the side of her chair.

"Aye, Colonel."

With that, Ashlyn leaned back and closely watched the plot before her. The feed from the LACs confirmed the enemy fighters had broken away from the *Nagato* and her sister ships. Now they were engaging the Fuerconese LACs, trying to keep them away from the Callusian ships. A slight smile touched Ashlyn's lips as she saw one and then another enemy LAC destroyed. This was the kind of fight her LAC pilots excelled at. She trusted them to do everything possible to winnow down the enemy ships and keep them from once more engaging the *Nagato*.

"Guns, target the lead elements of the Callusian taskforce. Our orders are to try to take at least one of the ships but if we have to destroy them, we will. The safety of the Home System must be maintained."

"Missile trajectories plotted, Colonel," Tactical reported. "Recommend including noisemakers along with our standard payloads."

"Do it." She leaned forward, forearms on her knees as she considered their options. There were simply too many unknowns, not the least of which was why the enemy had chosen to attack here, of all places. It didn't make sense. "Guns, confirm the fire plan with the other ships. Once you have confirmation, open fire."

"Aye, ma'am," he said as the *Nagato* was once again rocked.

"Comms, order all ships to open fire," she commed when the *Nagato* was once more rocked. "Take them out."

"With pleasure, ma'am."

"Ladies and gentlemen, let's keep these sons-of-bitches busy until the Admiral and the rest of the fleet arrive."

———

"THIS IS Lt. Colonel Ashlyn Shaw, First Division First Battalion Fuerconese Marine Corps. No more games, Captain. Your ship has been positively identified as the *Anubis*, a Callusian battlecruiser. The *Anubis* and other ships in your taskforce were responsible for the invasion of the Cassius System, in violation of the cease fire in place at the time of the invasion. You are also responsible for the destruction of the *Tarrant* and the deaths of most of her crew.

"You have one chance to survive this encounter with your ships intact and your people alive. Stand down all weapons and prepare to be boarded. You have committed an act of warfare by encroaching on Fuerconese space. Failure to immediately comply will result in your destruction. Shaw clear."

Damn them!

Dorescu could no longer sit still. How had they identified his ship, much less the others in the taskforce? More importantly, how had they tied them to the invasion of the Cassius System? One possibility came to mind and he snarled angrily. Had their Midlothian allies betrayed them as they had Fuercon?

He'd put that very question to Hughes as soon as they dealt with the Fuerconese ships. Shaw must think him a fool if she believed he would surrender a taskforce to her three ships.

"Sir, their LACs are breaking off!"

He turned to the tactical display. Why would they call their LACs off after issuing their ultimatum? It didn't make sense. None of it made sense. That meant one thing. They had something up their sleeves and thought they could catch him unawares.

"Missiles incoming!" the scanner tech barked.

Dorescu waited, barely daring to breathe, as the missiles closed in on the taskforce. One part of his brain noted when their countermeasures were launched. The first wave was always the most dangerous. Neither the computers nor the crew had a firing pattern to analyze. All he could do was hope their greater firepower – and greater number of available countermeasures – did the job of protecting their ships.

"Enemy missiles deploying active countermeasures. We can't lock onto their missiles."

"Go to manual targeting," he ordered. "Reroute all unnecessary power to the shields."

"Aye, sir. Rerouting to shields."

"XO, analysis?"

"Two things, Captain. Why is Shaw in command? The Fuerconese have never let Marine officers command warships. Also, why were they in this sector? It is almost as if they were expecting us."

He nodded, his expression grim. The first question posed by Kovacz was not nearly as important as the second. It also went hand-in-hand with how the Fuerconese knew about the *Anubis* and its role in what happened in the Cassius System. Even if they had managed to recover the data his ships had downloaded to the servers planetside on Cassius Prime, they should not have been able to break the encryption. That meant someone had to have leaked the information to them. No matter how he looked at it, he kept coming back to the same explanation.

The Midlothians had played his superiors for the same sort of fool they had played the Fuerconese.

Little good that knowledge did him right them.

"Order all ships to open fire. Press the attack and let's deal with these fools once and for all." He returned to the command chair and sat, thinking hard.

Alarms screamed, threatening to pierce his skull, as other missiles made it through their defenses. Damage reports choked the ship's comms. They were venting atmosphere from several areas. It didn't matter. The essential areas of the ship remained untouched and all turrets and tubes were undamaged.

Let the Fuerconese score their hits. It didn't matter. They were only prolonging the inevitable.

"Sir, bogies approaching!"

He watched as one after another red light appeared on the

tactical display, each one representing an enemy ship. That answered the question of where the rest of the Fuerconese ships had gone. Somehow they had cloaked their position as they closed in on Shaw's ships. That was their bad luck. He would deal with them just as he would deal with the *Nagato* and her sister ships.

"IDs?" he snapped.

"Tentatively identified as Second Fleet. Flagship is the *Phoenix Rising* commanded by Admiral Miranda Tremayne."

It had been a trap and he had led his taskforce straight into it. The last intel he had on Second Fleet, provided by the Midlothians, had it leaving the system almost two weeks earlier. That had been the deciding factor in moving this part of the operation up. He never would have attempted the mission had he known Tremayne's command was still in-system along with First Fleet.

Now he had no choice. To flee without scoring at least one kill would be to lose face. Worse, it would be all the opening Kovacz needed to try to take the ship. Should that happen, Dorescu knew his superiors would look the other way. They suffered failure even worse than did he.

"Order the taskforce to shore up the formation. They want a fight, we will give them one. Focus all fire on the *Nagato*. Secondary target to be determined momentarily." If the gods were with him, Tremayne's flagship would be the next to die.

An almost insane gleam in his eyes, Dorescu listened as his orders were relayed to the rest of the taskforce. The fire teams kept up a running report as they fired on the approaching enemy ships. Unfortunately, their LACs would be caught in the crossfire. It didn't matter. They knew the risks and they knew their duties. They either did whatever was necessary to damage the enemy ships or they died a coward's death. This was his battle to win and he would not let anyone, no matter who they were, rob him of it.

———

"COLONEL, A TEAM HAS REACHED AUXCOM," Lt. Commander Seaver reported.

"Status?"

"We have indications that the crew inside are still alive but the hatch is jammed. The damage from the LAC caused the bulkhead to warp. We're going to have to cut through the door and that's going to take time."

"Keep on it, Seaver, and keep me informed." She turned her attention to Comms. "Inform the Admiral."

"Aye, Colonel." A moment later, she turned to Ashlyn, a relieved smile on her face. "The Admiral sends her regards and reports that Second Fleet is on station and will be uncloaking momentarily. She asked me to pass on that the betting pool is up to five to one that the enemy commander will need a new pair of pants very shortly."

Ash grinned, hoping Tremayne was right. The cynic in her warned not to get overconfident. From what she knew of Dorescu, he would not give up, at least not easily. Even faced with the firepower of Second Fleet, he would try to deal as much damage as possible before ordering his ships to withdraw. The latter had to be prevented, no matter what the cost. They needed to capture at least one ship, preferably the *Anubis*. More than that, they had to do so before the ship's databanks could be scrubbed.

"Let's make sure we give the Admiral an appropriate greeting, everyone. Tell the LACs to resume their run on the enemy ships. Focus on the *Anubis*. Keep Dorescu and his people focused on the LACs until the fleet is in place."

20

Captain Bernard Hughes cursed long and hard, partly in pain but mostly in frustration. Calls for help with damage control filled the air, alternating with alarms signaling another incoming attack. Dorescu had lost his mind. There could be no other explanation. Why else move into Fuerconese space without adequate intel or force? While he would never shed a tear over the man's death, he would prefer his not accompany it.

From what he could tell, and that wasn't much now that Dorescu had cut his link to the bridge cameras, the Anubis had managed to deal damage first. But, like so much the Callusians did, it had not been enough to incapacitate the enemy. Instead, the attack served to strengthen the Fuerconese resolve to not only hold this sector of the system but to defeat the invaders.

Not that he could warn Dorescu of the consequences of his actions. Nor could he fulfill his duties as an advisor. When the first alarm sounded, he had considered his options. He knew the likelihood of Dorescu, or one of his crew, using the battle as cover for killing him. It was a risk Hughes was willing to take in order to try to talk some sense into Dorescu. If he could persuade the man to withdraw from Fuerconese space, they had a chance to not only survive but to complete their original mission.

So he had changed into his light armor. Then he tried to leave his quarters, only to find them secured from the outside. Now he paced the outer room like a caged animal, wondering how long it would be before the Anubis took a fatal hit or Dorescu sent someone for him. Death awaited with either option.

He moved back to his desk. Working carefully, he opened the comms panel. The ship rocked yet again as he studied panel. Then he went to work. Dorescu might have cut his official link to the bridge but Hughes had certain talents that had not been included in the Callusian's briefing packet, including the ability to reprogram almost any comm system.

Half an hour later, he carefully replaced the cover for the comms panel. If he hadn't managed to short something out one of the times the ship had been rocked by enemy fire, he should be able to not only tie into the bridge feed but the tactical display as well. That should let him know what was going on.

He watched in growing concern as Dorescu paced the bridge. Reports poured in from not only the *Anubis'* damage control teams but from the rest of the taskforce. Almost every ship had taken damage. Several of their smaller, lesser armored ships had been forced to fall back, using the rest of the taskforce as a screen between them and Second Fleet.

Had they walked into a trap?

Hughes swallowed hard. Second Fleet should not have been there. If there had been anything to indicate its presence, he would have done everything possible to force Dorescu to turn back. The Callusian might think himself invincible but Hughes knew better. He had taken part in campaigns during the last war that had included not only Ashlyn Shaw but Miranda Tremayne as well. Between the two of them, they had not only the experience but the determination to do whatever was necessary to not only stop Dorescu's ships but destroy them if forced to.

For more than an hour, he watched as the battle continued. Could

Dorescu not see that it was turning to Second Fleet's advantage? Their countermeasures were much more effective than the Callusian's. For every missile that penetrated Second Fleet's defenses, at least five of their missiles made it through Dorescu's defenses. The Callusian taskforce was being torn apart.

Worse were the enemy LACs. If he didn't know better, Hughes would swear their pilots were the Devil's disciples. With the addition of Second Fleet's LACs, they had all but destroyed their Callusian counterparts. Now they engaged the taskforce, moving faster than their weapons crews could adapt. There did not seem to be rhyme or reason to their attacks. Hughes guessed the LAC commander had ordered his pilots not to rely on the usual one or two lines of attack but to have their navigation computers use a random attack pattern, changing not only their approach vectors but the timing of their attacks. If so, that meant Dorescu's crews had little hope for their own targeting computers to find the pattern for the next attack run.

Why didn't Dorescu realize the mission was lost? If he wanted to survive to fight another day, he had to call the retreat. If he didn't, they would all die. The problem was the Callusians saw death in battle as something to be desired. Hughes doubted Dorescu would consider for even the briefest of moments retreating, much less surrendering.

That meant he had to act if he wanted to live. The first order of business was to find a way out of his quarters. It might take time to hack through the locking system but he could do it. The real challenge would be maneuvering through the corridors of the ship to the escape pods. If he managed that, he could use one of the pods and be off the ship before Dorescu knew.

Then all he would have to worry about was being targeted by either side. Long odds, to be sure, but they beat waiting for death to come.

Damn it, he wished he had never agreed to take this assignment.

———

THE LIGHTS DIMMED AGAIN but this time did not return to normal levels. Dust drifted from overhead, a reminder — not that he needed one – that the *Anubis* had taken yet another hit. The bridge was filled with the odors of blood and bowels thanks to the comms tech who had failed to duck when part of the inner bulkhead buckled and then broke free. It had sliced the man almost in half. The comms officer had simply kicked the tech out of the chair to his right before continuing to try to restore comms with the other ships of the taskforce.

"Captain, we can't take much more of this," Kovacz said, clinging to the arms of his shock frame as the *Anubis* rocked under another round of fire from Second Fleet. "We have lost another two ships."

"We will complete the mission," he growled. "Helm, lay in a course to take us down the starboard side of Target Alpha."

"Sir, that means we will open our portside to them and our shields are still compromised and weapons down fifty-five percent on that side."

"Are you disobeying orders, Helm?" He pushed to his feet. Without giving the man time to respond, he pulled his sidearm and shoved the muzzle against the back of his head. The helmsman's head exploded. Blood and grey matter splattered across his board. Dorescu grabbed the back of the man's uniform tunic and hauled him out of his chair. Then, using his side arm, he motioned Kovacz to take the helm.

"Sir, we can't keep this up. We are running low on torpedoes. Most of our turrets are no longer functional. Our bays, with one exception, are no longer useable. Damage Control reports it can't keep up with the demand. We are venting atmosphere and risk losing all shielding if we take another hit." Kovacz spoke softly, calmly, his eyes never leaving Dorescu's face.

"You have your orders." Dorescu lifted his side arm for emphasis. Then he stalked back to his chair. "It would do all of you – especially you, Mr. Kovacz – to remember that I am in command. You will follow my orders or meet the same fate as your former shipmate." He nodded to the assistant helmsman's body. "We will complete our mission before leaving the system. Anyone who doubts our ability to do so is a coward and a traitor. You will be dealt with now or later, the decision is yours. This is your chance to prove you are true warriors, worthy of calling yourselves Callusians."

The *Anubis* shuddered again. Alarms sounded throughout the ship. As more sections of the ship vented atmosphere, calls for help, for rescue came across the comms. Dorescu ordered them silenced. The trapped would either be saved or not but not now. Not until the battle was won.

"LACs incoming!"

All he could do was watch helplessly as his nearly crippled turrets tried to lock onto the LACs. He heard himself order their remaining counter-measure torpedoes launched. Sweat pricked out on his forehead as too few, far too few LACs were stopped. The others continued to plow through the debris, bearing down on the *Anubis*.

"Shields down," Kovacz reported as the LACs fired.

"Engineering reports system critical. I repeat, system critical," Comms added.

Dorescu threw his head back and snarled like a wild animal. How had it gone so wrong? If he wanted to survive, he had to order his ships to fallback. He also had to trust the other commanders to shield the *Anubis* from subsequent attack. A bitter laugh escaped his lips at that thought. He had no doubt what would happen. The moment one of them saw the opportunity, they would destroy the *Anubis*. That would be the penalty for not successfully completing the mission. Part of him approved but that other part, the part that had no intention of accepting death, swore not to let that happen.

By the gods, he couldn't believe it. He clung to the arms of his chair and rode out what he knew was far from the last hit *Anubis* would take before the fight was over. All around him, the bridge crew clung to their seats and worked diligently to counter the enemy fire. At least they had stopped pleading to withdraw. What happened to the crew he had been so proud of? That crew would have enjoyed the battle, their first real fight in much too long. Death might come to any or all of them but it would be a death with honor and no one could hope for better.

But these cowards wanted not honor but life. Each and every one of them who had begged him to retreat would die. If the gods were just, they would die by his hand.

A hand touched his shoulder and he started nervously. Looking up, Dorescu cursed softly. This truly was a nightmare. Standing at his side, anger and something else, something that turned Dorescu's bones to jelly, was the Midlothian. His hand moved once more to his side arm. Before he could bring it to bear, Hughes twisted it from his grasp and leveled it at him.

"You!"

How dare this *coward* interfere? Wasn't it bad enough he had refused to let them loot Cassius Prime as was their right as conquerors? He had also demanded they abide by the Accords as much as possible in dealing with prisoners. That had been almost harder to accept than anything else he had done. No bounty and no slaves. He had done his best to turn them into the enemy they fought to defeat.

Now he stood there, so smug and confident, as if convinced he was about to witness Dorescu's ultimate humiliation. The fool. Did he think that side arm was the only weapon Dorescu had on him? The Callusian looked forward to seeing him beg for mercy just before he slit his throat.

But he had to play this carefully. The enemy was in those ships attacking his taskforce. It was also on the bridge. Any doubts he might have had disappeared the moment Hughes entered the bridge. If the cowards had been loyal, they would have stopped the Midlothian before he took two steps. They knew he had been confined to his quarters. Dorescu swore he would make each of them, as well as whoever helped Hughes escape his quarters, pay with their lives.

"What do you want?" He bit back a laugh as Hughes stumbled when the ship was once again rocked by enemy fire.

"Captain, it is time to leave the battle," Hughes said firmly. "We can't risk any of your ships falling into their hands."

"I'll decide when it's time to leave the field," Dorescu said coldly.

"This isn't your fight any longer, Midlothian. You aren't giving the orders."

"Captain, I suggest you think again." He gestured with Dorescu's side arm. "You have this ship because of my government. Your task-force exists because of the money and technology we shared with your people. Do you really believe they won't take action against you and those you care for if you allow these ships to fall into the hands of the enemy?"

"I have this ship because I command it and my people crew it," Dorescu countered. "Your government won't say anything about what happened because they won't know."

———

HUGHES TIGHTENED his grip on the pulsar and glanced around the bridge. As he did, he angled his body so he could keep the crew, as well as Dorescu, in sight. Most of them continued to man their stations, doing all they could to keep the Fueronese ships from breaking through the last of their defenses. A few, however, had stopped to watch the confrontation between him and their commanding officer.

Interesting. He had fully expected them to try to stop him as soon as the lift arrived on the bridge. Instead, they had ignored him as he moved in Dorescu's direction. No, that wasn't quite right. Kovacz had watched, anticipation reflected on his expression.

"Your government won't say anything about what might happened because they won't know."

Dorescu's words confirmed his suspicions. The Callusian had no intention of letting him live. He would never return home, not as a hero, nor even as a fool. If he was lucky, there might come a time when his family would be told what happened and why. He doubted it. Watchman tended to bury those, including any mention of them, who failed him. The most he could hope for was to be listed as MIA in the annals and that would be that.

It wouldn't bother him except it was so bloody unnecessary.

Dorescu was a madman. Worse, he was the product of those his superiors wanted to deal with. From what he had learned while onboard the *Anubis*, most Callusians were like Dorescu. They didn't care about anything as much as they did defeating an enemy, even if there was no way to do so. Death to them was eagerly anticipated. That attitude reminded Hughes of something he had read about some ancient religious sect. Their "true believers" believed all the infidels had to be killed and if they died in the process, they would be rewarded in the life beyond.

Except there was no life beyond and certainly no reward except the eternal sleep of death.

Like it or not, he was about to meet that so-called reward.

Well, he could still fulfill one part of his mission. He would make sure there was no evidence of his involvement in the mission. Hopefully that would be enough to keep suspicion from his homeworld.

"You're not a fool, Dorescu. You know I've been reporting regularly to my superiors. If I fail to check in on time now, they will begin asking questions I promise you don't want brought to the attention of your superiors."

As he spoke, Hughes saw the almost imperceptible signal that passed between Kovacz and one of the other members of the bridge crew. He waited, wondering if this was when they would make their move against him. Possible but there was another possibility he had to consider. They could wait, knowing their captain would sooner or later lose patience and try to rush him. Even if Dorescu managed to get the pulsar from him, Hughes knew neither of them would live. Kovacz had the look of a man who was about to mutiny and take command.

Gods help them all.

At least he wouldn't die alone. A smile touched his lips. Seeing it, Dorescu blanched. Then the Callusian's eyes narrowed as he studied Hughes. The Midlothian had no doubt Dorescu was trying to figure out why he smiled. Little did the Anubis' commander know that his people weren't the only ones who valued honor and bravery. He would deal with Dorescu, making sure he could never again go against orders from Midlothian, before taking down as many of the crew as he could before they killed him.

"Consider this the revocation of your authorization to use any and all Midlothian tech, Dorescu."

He whipped the pulsar into position and fired. Dorescu's cry of disbelief died before it formed. He slumped in his chair, the top of his head gone. Before the life drained from the captain's eyes, Hughes turned, taking aim at Kovacz. As he did, other members of the bridge crew acted. Some dove for cover. Others looked as if they were considering attacking. He used their moment of indecision to fell two more. Then he swung in Kovacz's direction.

"Thank you, Mr. Hughes, for removing a problem for me." Kovacz grinned. A moment later, his fist caught Hughes on the point of his chin.

I should have told Watchman to go to hell.

21

———

"Colonel, incoming message from the flagship."

Ashlyn moved to stand behind the comms station and placed a hand on the young ensign's shoulder. As she did, she looked around the wreckage of what was left of the *Nagato*'s bridge. Its bulkheads hadn't been breached but that was about all she could say. Most of the stations had sustained damage and had been forced to go to backup systems. Damage Control had been too busy elsewhere in the ship to send more than a skeleton team up. At least the Anubis and its two sister ships had been able to fall back to the rear, letting the rest of Second Fleet continue the battle against the Callusian taskforce.

"Put it on, Ensign."

A moment later the screen filled with the image of the flag bridge. Miranda Tremayne stepped into the picture and Ash touched a finger to her forehead in what had to pass for a salute just then.

"Admiral."

"Colonel Shaw, what's your status?"

"Engines down to twenty percent. Our chief engineer was injured in the fighting but his assistant assures me his people can get us back up to forty percent in a day or two, assuming we can cadge some parts from the fleet."

"Anything we have you need is yours."

"Thank you, ma'am." She bent and softly told Comms to pass the message on. "Damage control teams are still working to free members of the crew that were trapped in the fighting. The CMO and his people are hard pressed right now to keep ahead of the injuries coming in."

"We will get you help there as soon as we can. Your Marines?"

"Our LAC numbers have been cut almost in half, ma'am. Most of our crews have been rescued, fortunately. I will be able to get you a full report once the COLAC and I have a few minutes to confer. As for shipboard Marines, those originally assigned to the *Nagato* have proven to be invaluable. They worked with both Damage Control and the medical teams as well as filling in where they could, according to their specialties. The Devil Dogs have helped with Damage Control and Lieutenant Lashay reports they have cleared the staging area bay so the attack shuttles can launch if necessary."

"Excellent, Colonel. I had hoped that might be the case." Now Tremayne grinned.

Seeing it, Ashlyn hoped the Admiral had good news.

"We have received a hail from the *Anubis*, Colonel, and I thought you might want to listen in."

"I most definitely would, ma'am."

"We'll tie you into the feed. I'm letting Captain Vilhjalmsson take the lead on this."

Ashlyn thought for a moment. "Ma'am, I have one request. Captain Thrasher has regained consciousness and is in his quarters. The CMO sent him there with orders not to get out of bed. I would like him linked in as well."

"Of course." Tremayne nodded in approval. "One thing before I signal Captain Vilhjalmsson to respond to the hail. It comes not from Dorescu but from a Pyotyr Kovacz who identifies himself as the *Anubis*' captain."

"That is very interesting, Admiral."

"I thought so." Tremayne turned away as someone out of sight said something. Then she stepped out of the picture.

As she waited for Tremayne to return, Ashlyn told the ensign to send someone to Thrasher's quarters to prepare for the incoming transmission. Then she moved back to the command chair. As she sat, she felt every minute of the last eight hours. She also knew that, given the choice, she would never be tied to a bridge during battle again. She was a Marine and did not want nor enjoy filling in for her Naval counterpart.

"Colonel."

Ash turned to the speaker and nodded to see Lance Corporal Connery. Then she noticed the mug of coffee and sandwich the woman carried. Before she could say anything, Connery passed them to her, telling her to eat. "The Mess isn't up and running yet but they did manage to get coffee and tea going and they're making sandwiches as quickly as they can," she explained.

"Make sure everyone up here gets something ASAP," Ashlyn said between bites.

"Already done, ma'am. They'll have something here shortly."

Ashlyn thanked her and continued eating. Finally, after more than eight hours, the fighting was finally dying down. Dying being the operative word. Both sides had lost people and ships. Second Fleet's losses weren't as bad as they could have been and Ashlyn knew that was because the *Nagato* and her sister ships had done everything possible to hold the Callusian taskforce in place until the rest of Second Fleet could arrive. Now that they were no longer in the middle of the battle, Ash knew the *Nagato* had been lucky. It would not have been able to hold out much longer if the rest of the fleet hadn't arrived when it did. Even so, all it, as well as its sister ships, would require extensive time in the Yard before they would see battle again.

"Do we know anything about this Kovacz?" she asked when Tremayne reappeared on her screen a short time later.

"Not much, Colonel," Tremayne's Intelligence officer, Lieutenant Brendan McCrary, replied. "He has been assigned to the *Anubis* for at least the last year. Like most Callusian officers, he worked his way up the ranks through a combination of ability and blackmail and convenient accidents to those immediately above him in rank."

"Speculation?"

"Either Dorescu has been injured or killed in the fighting or he met one of those unfortunate accidents, ma'am."

It couldn't have happened to a nicer man, as her mother used to say.

"If you're ready, Ash, Captain Vilhjalmsson will accept the hail."

"We're ready here, ma'am. I'd be lying if I didn't say I wanted to hear what this Kovacz has to say."

"I think it safe to say we all want to hear it, Ash." Tremayne turned to her chief of staff and told him to let Vilhjalmsson know they were ready to proceed. "I'll want your impressions after the contact ends."

"Aye, ma'am."

"One minute, Admiral," someone off-camera said.

"Comms, contact the COLAC and tell them to standby. Weapons to remain hot and all pilots on alert," Ashlyn ordered as she waited for the connection with the *Anubis* to be established. "Let's see if this Kovacz has more sense than Dorescu."

"Aye, Colonel. COLAC to standby."

Ashlyn sipped her coffee and waited. A few moments later, her display split into two screens. To the right was the tactical display. To the left was Captain Vilhjalmsson's image. He said something off-screen before turning to face her. "Admiral, ready when you are."

"Let's see what he wants, Lars," Tremayne's voice said.

"Aye, ma'am. Switching transmission so you see what I do." The image changed to his screensaver. A moment later, it changed and Vilhjalmsson spoke. "Captain Kovacz, this is Captain Lars Vilhjalmsson, commanding officer of the *Phoenix Rising*."

"Captain Vilhjalmsson." The image on the screen showed a man who looked as if he had aged years in the last few hours. Exhaustion grayed his complexion. He held himself as thought his ribs had been injured. But it was his expression that drew Ashlyn's attention. He reminded her of some of the few Callusian prisoners they had taken during the last war. Angry to have been captured, to know they had been bested by someone they knew was beneath them, but resigned to the fact that there was no other option left to them.

"Captain Kovacz, you and your taskforce have violated Fuerconese space and fired upon ships of our Navy. You either surrender now and let us board your ships or we will destroy those of your ships that still survive." Vilhjalmsson tone sent shivers down Ashlyn's spine. She most definitely did not want to get on his bad side.

"What are your terms?"

"There are no terms, Captain. You will take your weapons and engines off-line. You will instruct your personnel to offer no resistance when our forces board your ships. You will make no attempt to scrub your computers. You will make no attempt to hide or space any cargo, no matter what it might be. If you violate any of these, we will open fire."

Kovacz's mouth worked angrily but he said nothing. Finally, he gave a single curt nod.

"You will acquiesce on the record, Captain."

"Agreed," he all but spat.

Ashlyn touched the control stud to signal Tremayne. Almost instantly, the Admiral responded on a private channel.

"Ma'am, have Captain Vilhjalmsson tell him that we know he has a Midlothian advisor onboard and we expect him to be turned over to us, in good condition, or they will face the consequences."

For a moment Tremayne said nothing. Then she chuckled. "You're evil, Ash. By putting it that way, we plant the seed of doubt in Kovacz that the Midlothians have betrayed them, just as they betrayed us."

"Yes, ma'am. It might loosen both their tongues when the Intel folks get hold of them."

"Consider it done."

"One last thing, Captain Kovacz," Vilhjalmsson continued a moment later. "We know you have a Midlothian *advisor* onboard. We expect you to turn Commander Hughes over to us and he had best be in good condition."

If possible, Kovacz paled even more. "All right," he all but spat.

"Excellent. Issue the order to your ships to power down all but essential life support systems. Our LACs will remain on patrol. Once we have confirmed your compliance, we will begin sending over boarding parties. Vilhjalmsson, out."

The screen changed momentarily to the Fuerconese flag. Then Tremayne's image once more appeared. "What do you think, Colonel?"

"He'll do as Vilhjalmsson said but I would expect a few surprises from his people." She studied the tactical display for a moment. The size of the taskforce had been cut by at least two-thirds. "This is the first time we've managed to capture more than a ship or two. We have to expect at least some of those onboard the surviving ships to try to choose suicide over becoming a POW. If they can take some of us with them, all the better."

"Recommendation on boarding?"

For a moment, she considered the question. "Acting on the assumption that Dorescu was as paranoid as most of the other Callusian commanders we've encountered, I recommend boarding the *Anubis* first. If I'm right about him, there is a very good chance the *Anubis* had the ability to take command of any or all of the other ships in the taskforce. Besides, I have a feeling that the longer we wait to take Hughes into custody, the shorter his life expectancy."

"This is your call, Colonel. Draw up a plan for your Marines, supplemented by the other Marines in Second Fleet, to board and clear the ships. Once they are under Marine control, we will send over Navy crews to strip out their databases and determine if the ships are capable of making it to the Yard where they can be examined by the Intel folks as well as R&D."

"Understood, Admiral. Give me an hour. In the meantime, I'd recommend letting my LACs return to refuel. There should be enough LACs from the rest of the fleet to cover in their absence."

"Forward your immediate needs for the ship as well, Colonel."

"Yes, ma'am."

"Tremayne out."

Ashlyn blew out a breath and closed her eyes. Exhaustion pulled at her. Pushing it down, she opened her eyes and glanced around the bridge. Injured, exhausted, they crew continued to work. They coordinated with their teams elsewhere in the ship. Pride filled her as they did. If they had thought it odd to have a Marine take over when Captain Thrasher went down, they never let it show, Instead, they had worked as hard for her and she had seen them work for him. If she had anything to say about it, she would make sure each of them received commendations. They had earned them.

"Lt. Caldwell, you have the com. I'll be in the Ready Room." She stood and moved to where the navigator sat. He looked startled as she held out her hand. Then he grinned and got to his feet. His grip was firm as he shook her hand.

"Colonel, I know I speak for everyone onboard when I say it would be an honor to serve with you any time and any place."

"The honor has been mine, LT." She jerked her head toward the captain's chair. "You have the com."

"Aye, ma'am. I have the com."

With Connery on her heels, she made her way to the Ready Room. As soon as the hatch slid shut behind them, she sagged and reached for the table. Leaning her weight on her left hand, she drew a long, shuddering breath. Instantly, Connery was there, helping her to a chair.

"Ma'am, were you injured?" Concern filled the lance corporal's voice.

"No." Not really, not when compared to what some of the rest of the crew had suffered and certainly nothing she couldn't handle. "It's just the letdown. I'd much rather be fighting dirtside than do a repeat of the last eight hours."

"I hear you, ma'am." Connery grinned in understanding. "And with all due respect, Colonel, you did better given the circumstances than some of the Navy types I've been around."

"Thanks, but let's hope I never have to repeat it." She blew out a breath and stretched. "Contact Lashay and tell him I want the attack shuttles ready to launch in an hour. If I know the Admiral – and I do – she won't waste any time once I get the boarding plan to her."

"Yes, ma'am."

"Then see if you can't rustle up a pot of coffee and whoever is now senior among the Marine's assigned to the ship. We may need to use some of them to fill in any holes in Lashay's force."

With that, Ashlyn activated the workstation at the end of the table. As she did, Connery contacted Lashay and then the Mess. Once finished, she activated the holo over the table, programming it to show not only the tactical display but what was happening on the bridge. Ashlyn looked up once, nodded in approval and then returned to work.

Forty-five minutes later, Ashlyn sent her proposed boarding plan to Tremayne. As she did, she knew it was far from optimal. The Devil Dogs onboard the *Nagato*, as well as the Marines assigned there, had suffered more casualties than she first realized. Anger flared, as did guilt. She had no doubt if she had been in command of the Devil Dog contingent, the casualties would have been fewer. Her head told her she couldn't have done anything. She had been needed on the bridge. Her heart, however, wouldn't accept it. At least not yet.

As a result, she had to plug some of the holes in the boarding party for the *Anubis* with Marines she didn't know. Worse, they had not trained with the Devil Dogs. The cohesion that came from knowing your squadmates and training with them would be missing. The potential for something going wrong increased because of it. Knowing that, she knew she was going to have to convince the Admiral to let her do something she knew Tremayne would be against.

Not to mention Talbot.

"Comms, get me Master Gunnery Sergeant Talbot onboard the flagship," she ordered. "Lance Corporal, are you ready to do some real work now?" she asked as she got to her feet.

"What does the Colonel have in mind, ma'am?"

"Let's see how the Admiral reacts first."

Fifteen minutes later, they entered the staging area. As they did, Ash was glad she kept in shape. The lifts in this part of the ship were out of order and she and Connery had done more than a bit of back-tracking to avoid corridors jammed with Damage Control teams. As they moved from deck to deck, Ashlyn's amazement that there hadn't been more deaths grew. So did her respect for Thrasher. She knew one of the main reasons those numbers were as low as they were was because the captain made sure his people were well-trained. That was something else she planned to discuss with Tremayne when she had the chance.

"Stand easy," she said before the Marines already gathered could brace to attention. "Where's the LT?" she asked when she looked around and didn't see him.

"Here, Colonel." He appeared from one of the attack shuttles.

"How long until we're ready to launch?"

"Flight crews are finishing their pre-flights, ma'am If everything reads green, we can launch in fifteen. It will take that long to finish loading."

Before she could answer, her comm signaled an incoming message. "Shaw."

"Colonel, I thought I made it clear you were to stay out of trouble," Talbot said, a faint trace of humor in his voice.

"I know, Master Guns, but I've always wanted to try my hand at commanding a ship in battle."

"You do know the Devil Dogs won't let you abandon us for the Navy, don't you, ma'am?"

"Well, if that's the case, then give me an update. What's the status of the rest of the battalion?" She started off in the direction of the office Thrasher had assigned her, motioning for Lashay to follow.

Ten minutes later, she slid her comm back into its place at her left thigh. Talbot's report eased much of her concern. As expected, their LACs had taken a major hit and she would have to discuss replacement equipment and personnel with not only her mother but General Okafor as well. That would wait until they returned to Fuercon. For the moment, she needed to focus on the task at hand.

"LT, any questions?" she asked. As she did, she moved to her foot-locker and unlocked it. There were a few things she wanted from it before the shuttles departed.

"Negative, ma'am."

"Then join your men. I'll be there shortly."

He threw a quick salute and left the office. Connery stepped inside, her expression serious.

"Colonel, what are you doing?" she asked seriously as Ashlyn continued to pull things from her footlocker.

"Lance Corporal, unless you took a hit to the head during the battle and forgot what it means to be a Devil Dog, you know very well what I'm doing." Realizing her words were harsher than she'd meant, she sat back on her heels and looked up. "Sorry. I didn't mean to snap."

"Not a problem, ma'am, but my question stands."

She cast a look at the closed door. "The LT is a good officer but I've had to supplement the ranks with non-Devil Dogs. I can't risk some of them mistaking the lieutenant for a wet behind the ears officer fresh out of the Academy. So you and I are going along to make sure there are no problems."

"The Master Guns won't be happy but I think it's a good call, ma'am."

"Then add any gear you need for the mission, Lance Corporal. I want to launch as soon as I hear from the Admiral."

———

COMMANDER BERNARD HUGHES groaned and rolled to his side. His head pounded and his jaw felt as though it was broken. He swallowed and then ran his tongue carefully over his teeth, wincing to find several of them broken. The last thing he remembered was being on the bridge. He had done what he should have long ago. He had killed Dorescu. Then Kovacz and at least one other attacked. In that moment, he'd know he was dead. So why was he still alive?

What if he wasn't alive? What if this was the afterlife he had never really believed in?

No, it couldn't be. He hurt too badly. It was too loud with alarms blaring and people moaning and crying for help. The distant sound of small arms fire reached him, a bare whisper over the sound of the alarms. But he recognized it and wondered whether it was the enemy or if the crew had mutinied.

Neither of which helped him any.

Opening his eyes a slit, he looked around. He lay on the deck. Where, he wasn't sure. All he knew for certain was that he wasn't alone. Others lay on the deck around him. Most appeared to be injured. The smell of death filled the area. Had they brought him here to die?

Gods above and below, he needed to know what had happened since he lost consciousness. Did he dare risk letting the Callusians know he had regained consciousness?

Gathering his strength, he slowly rolled onto his side. Nausea washed over him, taking him under once again.

"Secure the area!" someone ordered as he once again regained consciousness. "And someone silence that damned alarm."

Almost instantly the noise level lowered. Booted feet moved through the area. Hughes lay still. The accent of the speaker told him all he needed to know. The *Anubis* had been boarded. His fate suddenly went from bad to worse. The Fuerconese would recognize his uniform and want to know why he was there. He had no doubt the Callusians would betray him at the first opportunity. His only hope was to find a way to force one of the boarding party to kill him. He could not let them take him alive.

The sound of boots on the decksole neared. Once again, he prepared to move. It would have to be quick, no matter how badly he hurt. If he succeeded, the pain would end. More importantly, his death would protect his homeworld. Nothing else mattered.

Through slitted eyes, he saw a pair of black boots stop next to him. Canting his eyes upward, he knew his guess had been right. He recognized the black battle armor of the Devil Dogs. Part of him wanted to laugh aloud. Dorescu had earned death. Not only had he put all of Watchman's careful plans in danger, he had been foolish enough to go up against the best SpecOps unit of the Fuerconese Marines. At least when he forced one of them to kill him, he would have the satisfaction his death had come at the hands of a worthy opponent.

He tensed, readying to move. Instantly, as if he had been waiting for Hughes to move, the Devil Dog planted his foot firmly in the man's back. Hughes' breath hissed out between clenched teeth. Before he could recover, his arms were wrenched behind his back and secured. Then he was rolled onto his back and he found himself looking up into the faces of two Marines.

"Jaeger, send for Angel. Tell her we have the package." He grinned down at his prisoner. "Then finish securing the area."

"Aye, Corporal."

"Commander Hughes, consider yourself a guest of the Fuerconese Marine Corps."

Hughes moaned softly, an almost overwhelming sense of failure washing over him.

———————

"ANGEL, Jaeger just reported in. Says they have found the package," Connery reported.

A smile lifted one corner of Ashlyn's mouth and she turned to look at the lance corporal. The Devil Dogs had been onboard the *Anubis* for almost three hours. Much to her surprise, they had met with little resistance. Kovacz and the ship's surviving officers had met the attack shuttles as they landed. Unarmed and unarmored, they had submitted to thorough searches before they had been taken into custody.

After securing the landing bay, the Devil Dogs had broken into fire teams. Ashlyn led the team to the bridge. Once there, she had discovered what happened to Dorescu. His body, along with those of several others, lay against the far bulkhead. One look was all she needed to know they had not died of battle-related injuries. They had been executed and she wondered if that way why Kovacz had been so willing to surrender.

"Excellent." She motioned to Lashay. "Falconer, signal the flag that the ship is secure. My recommendation is that we transfer the surviving crew off-ship and put a skeleton crew onboard. I have a feeling the spooks would love to get their hands it. Make sure she understands we'll need an engineering team to stabilize the engines."

"Roger than, Angel." He signaled to one of the two Devil Dogs guarding the lift. "Ranger, accompany Angel and Brigit."

"Sir!"

"Where is Jaeger holding the package?" Ashlyn asked as the Ranger's partner sent for the lift.

"Deck Three near the Sick Bay, Angel."

"No lifts," she said and moved toward the service ladder.

The last thing she wanted was to get stuck between decks. Just because they had not encountered any real resistance since coming onboard, she wasn't going to take any chances. It was too easy to sabotage a lift tube, not to mention the fact power was still intermittent to parts of the ship. That meant climbing and that took time. Then there were corridors made inaccessible due to battle damage. But it gave her a better idea of the shape of the ship and it explained why they have found fewer survivors than expected. Though she hated the loss of life, she couldn't help feeling pride that the LACs under her command, as well as the *Nagato* and her sister ships, had managed to keep the *Anubis* and the rest of the taskforce from overrunning them.

"Angel." Jaeger and his partner braced to attention as she entered what looked to be enlisted quarters.

She nodded and looked past him to the man seated on the edge of the bottom bunk. Face swollen, the front of his uniform covered in blood, he showed all the signs of having been beaten. Remembering the dead on the bridge, she wondered if there was a connection. Not that it mattered just then.

Frowning at the man, she glanced at Jaeger and jerked her head in Hughes' direction. Instantly, the Devil Dog stepped forward. One hand closed around the Midlothian's upper arm. Hughes hissed in pain as he was roughly hauled to his feet. Ashlyn nodded once and stepped forward, Connery at her side.

"Name?" she snapped.

"Kieran Hardisty."

She shook her head, doing her best to look disappointed. "Let me help you. Your name is Commander Bernard Hughes, Midlothian Space Navy. You were a decorated officer in the last war and dropped off the scene in the last year or so. You have also been acting as an advisor to the Callusians, taking part in the invasion of the Cassius System and other hostile actions by the *Anubis* and her crew."

He continued to stand silent, as she expected. Well, she had a way to end that – she hoped.

She entered a code on her comm and waited. A few minutes later, two more Devil Dogs appeared, Kovacz between them.

"Since you two know one another, I won't bother with introductions," she said coldly. "However, your answers to my questions very well may determine how long you live."

Unlike Hughes who continued to stand so still he might as well have been a statue, Kovacz struggled against the iron hold of the Marines on either side of him. Ashlyn saw it and knew who the weak link was.

"Where are his quarters?" She jerked her head in Hughes' direction.

Kovacz couldn't answer quickly enough. The moment he fell silent, she motioned for him to be removed. Then she turned her attention back to Hughes and the Marines guarding him.

"Has he been searched?"

"He has."

After making sure his partner had Hughes well in hand, Jaeger stepped forward. Ashlyn followed him to the small table against the bulkhead. On it rested several items, none of which were of much interest until she came to the last one. Cylindrical about half the size of her hand, it looked similar to some of the detonators she had seen.

But there was something different about this one. What needed to be answered and quickly.

She carefully picked it up and turned back to Hughes. She knew the moment he saw what she held. His reaction was small but she had been looking for it. A quick intake of breath, a slight narrowing of his eyes. Good. She could work with that.

"Mr. Hughes, I'll make this simple. As a member of the Midlothian Space Navy, you are bound by the treaties between our worlds. The fact that you have been willfully assisting our enemy makes you an enemy combatant at best, a spy at worst. I could make a case right now for spacing you. However, I have a feeling that is exactly what you want me to do. Dead, no one can compel you to reveal what you know about the collusion taking place between your government and the Callusians."

She didn't wait to see if he would respond. "So let me tell you what my recommendation to Admiral Tremayne will be. When news of what happened here is released to the media, so will the news that we have had a spy in the Midlothian Space Navy. It was something we did not initiate. He came to us when he discovered that his superiors, and his government, were betraying Fuercon and its allies. A man of honor, Commander Bernard Hughes risked everything to make sure that betrayal cost no more lives than it already had. Because of him, we were able to retake the Cassius System when he got word to us that the bulk of the Callusian force had moved on and we were able to turn back the invasion of our own system after he warned us of the upcoming attack. You will be hailed as a hero among our allies and be a traitor to your own people. How will your government react to this betrayal? From what I've learned over the years, they will take their anger with you out on your family and friends since you are outside of their reach."

As she spoke, she closely watched for his reaction. His breath quickened and sweat dotted his upper lip and forehead. For the first time since she entered the cabin, he looked away. He would break, hopefully sooner rather than later.

"No," he croaked. "You can't."

"I can and will," she countered. Even as she did, she knew she wouldn't. It was one thing to use an enemy's weakness against them but something else to sacrifice innocents who did not have to die. "But I might reconsider if you start cooperating."

"I can't. They'll kill my family."

"Not if you are presented as a POW, one we are going to try as an enemy combatant."

"Your word?"

"Your cooperation?" She waited until he nodded. "If you cooperate, you have my word." Now she extended the cylinder so he could see it. "What is this?"

He closed his eye and she waited. When he finally looked at her, she knew she was not going to like what he had to say. "It's a kill-switch tied into the ship's engines and computer systems. Once activated, the databanks will be wiped and the engines will go critical."

"Did you activate it?"

"No." He shook his head.

She turned and very carefully set the device down on the table. "Send for Boomer. I want that thing secured."

"Right away." Connery pulled her comm and issued the order.

"Now, Mr. Hughes, you are going to be transported to the flagship. My people have orders to keep you alive. But that doesn't mean they won't hurt you if you force their hand. Do you understand?"

"I do." His shoulders sagged and she knew he had given up, at least for the moment. "Answer me one question. Who are you?"

"Colonel Ashlyn Shaw, CO of the Devil Dogs." With that, she turned on her heel and left the cabin. Time to check in with Tremayne and brief her on what had happened.

22

"Welcome back, Ash," Tremayne said as Ashlyn was shown in.

"Thanks. I have to admit it's good to be back onboard."

Tremayne nodded and handed her a glass of whiskey. Then she motioned for her to be seated. For a moment, Ashlyn hesitated. Understanding, Tremayne smiled and moved to sit at the far end of the divan. She waited, knowing the young woman would move when she was ready.

"Is this an official or unofficial meeting, ma'am?" Ashlyn asked, still standing.

"Unofficial. I figured you needed an evening off-duty after all you've been through the last few days. But I also needed to hear the main points of what you learned. FleetCom is having a fit back home, trying to figure out how to respond to what happened."

Ashlyn nodded and moved to sit on the opposite end of the sofa. Tremayne watched as she stretched her long legs out in front of her before sipping her whiskey. As she did, the Admiral could see her tension ease. She wished the exhaustion reflected in Ashlyn's eyes did as well.

"You know most of it, Miranda." She lifted her right shoulder in a shrug. "What I didn't put in my official report was what Hughes told me on the flight over from the *Nagato*. He still hasn't given us all that much information about the Midlothian connection and he probably won't until the powers-that-be give him the reassurances he needs to know we won't reveal that he has been cooperating. Frankly, he's terrified word will get out and his family will pay the price."

"I've already alerted SecDef."

"Good." Ash sipped again. "Anyway, the short version is he knew his days were numbered. Dorescu had already killed the other advisors who had come on board with him. He believes the only reason they kept him alive as long as they did was so they could get as much out of the Midlothians as they could.

"Things came to a head when he realized Dorescu had deviated from their orders, orders supposedly given by the Midlothians. Our intelligence had been right. They were supposed to attack the Drakkana System. What Hughes didn't know is that Dorescu and his superiors had decided to test our defenses in preparation of a full-scale invasion." She leaned forward and placed her glass on the low table in front of the sofa. "I don't think he's told me the entire story yet and I'll leave it to Intel to winnow the rest of it out. However, after you brought the bulk of the fleet up, he confronted Dorescu on the bridge and demanded he withdraw. When he refused, Hughes killed him. That's when he was jumped by Kovacz and the other members of the bridge crew. He lost consciousness in the fight and didn't regain it until we had boarded."

"What's your feel for him?"

"Honestly?"

Tremayne nodded.

"I think he's an honorable man who found himself in an untenable position."

For a moment, Tremayne studied her companion. There had been something in Ashlyn's voice that worried her and she wondered if the young woman identified with their prisoner. Before she could ask, Ashlyn reclaimed her glass and downed the rest of her whiskey.

"Miranda, don't look at me like that. I don't condone what he did." She once more set the glass on the table. "But I do understand. If I knew that day the Capital was attacked what I do now, I would have slipped away and done my best to kill Sorkowski and O'Brien. It wouldn't have been right but it might have helped put my ghosts to rest sooner."

"I understand." And she did. There were times when she fantasied about killing the men and all those who had conspired with them. "But enough of that. When you leave here, you are ordered to get a solid eight hours sleep. Come morning, we're heading back to Fuercon. I'm leaving several elements to patrol the area until reinforcements from First Fleet arrive."

"Sounds good to me. My people, especially Second Platoon, need to heal up and you know the state of my LACs."

"Major Laboe will be ready to brief you on the rest of the battalion after you've slept. I will say he did admirably as your new XO. I'm going to miss having him as my Marine CO."

"You always manage to find excellent CO's, Miranda. Of course, being good friends with the Commandant and the CO of FirstDiv might have something to do with it." Ashlyn grinned, her first real grin since her arrival. Then she yawned.

"True. Now let's get some food in you. Then you are to get some rest. When you wake, you are to report to Sick Bay and let the CMO have a look at you. Once he's cleared you for duty, report in."

"I'd argue but food and sleep sound too good right now."

Tremayne smiled and made a mental note to talk with both Talbot and Connery to make sure she made her way to Sick Bay. She knew from past experience that Ashlyn would do her best to avoid it if she could.

———

"READY, GUNS?" Tremayne commed.

"Aye, Admiral."

"Issue the order."

All eyes focused on the holo display over the briefing table. The image showed all but three of the remaining ships from the Callusian taskforce. The three, crewed by officers and ratings from Second Fleet, had started their slow translation to Fuercon an hour earlier. Most of Second had gone with them. The *Phoenix Rising* and its escort had remained to oversee this one last duty.

Missiles raced across the distance separating the Phoenix from the damaged ships. Over the comm, the countdown to impact sounded. No one spoke. Ashlyn wasn't sure anyone breathed. When the first missiles found their target, those gathered in the Admiral's Ready Room seemed to relax.

"Ships destroyed, Admiral."

"Confirmed. Helm, let's go home."

As the holo display ended, the hatch slid open and several enlisted entered. They quickly served coffee and tea to those who wanted it before leaving. Once the hatch closed behind them, Tremayne rapped her knuckles on the tabletop, calling for order.

"Ladies and gentlemen, let me start by conveying the congratulations and appreciation of FleetCom, SecDef and the President. Luck was on our side this time. We managed to not only confirm that the Midlothians are involved with the Callusians but we have managed to do something no one has done in recent history. Not only did we basically destroy the invading taskforce, but we captured half a dozen of their ships. We have prisoners, some of whom I'm confident will cooperate with Fleet Intel.

"First Fleet will be reinforcing the picket we established while those ships damaged in the fighting put in for repairs. Ship's commanders, coordinate with Captain Montgomery on what repairs are needed. Also, I expect your after-action reports by end of day.

"When we arrive home, set up rotating schedules. Those not on duty are to be given leave. Get me your recommendations for awards and commendations before we arrive home." Tremayne paused and looked around the table. "Questions?"

When there were none, she dismissed everyone. Then she leaned back and sighed heavily. They had been lucky this time. Next time, they might not be.

23

———————

"Do you realize how lucky we were this time?"

President Derek Harper stood before the bay window, looking outside. His hands were clasped behind his back. He spoke softly but there could be no mistaking his anger and concern. The fact he was right only drove it home all the more.

"Don't answer." He turned and waved a hand, dismissing the question. "I know you do. Luck was on our side and we have to take advantage of it."

"I think I speak for us all when I say we agree, Mr. President," General Helen Okafor said.

"No formalities tonight, Helen. We have a lot to discuss before Second Fleet returns." A soft knock sounded at the door. Harper called out and a moment later the door opened. Several servers entered, carrying drinks and light snacks. "What do we know so far?"

"Miranda has been careful with what she's transmitted," Richard Collins said as the doors closed behind the retreating servers. "But reading between the lines, it sounds like she is bringing us a great deal of intel and more for Rico's people to work their magic on."

"And we are sure they have confirmation of Midlothian involvement?"

"We are," Okafor answered. "If Miranda has been tight lipped, Ashlyn has been down right silent. But she did sent word that they had a very special package for us. That means only one thing. Not only did they get the confirmation we were hoping for but they have taken Hughes into custody."

Harper sank onto a chair and shook his head, a slight smile on his lips. "You're sure?"

"I am. We had agreed on that code phrase before she shipped out."

"Then we may have been luckier than I thought." He lifted his glass in a toast. "How bad were Second Fleet's losses?"

"As you said, sir, we were lucky. Their ship losses were minimal. They will need some time in the Yard but they should be able to get back in action in a month or so. FleetCom will have to evaluate Second's personnel needs once they have received the casualty list and reviewed the treatment plans for the injured," Collins said.

Harper turned to Okafor next. "And the Devil Dogs?"

"No deaths for the main force but a number of injuries." She pulled out her datapad and consulted it before continuing. "The LACs, on the other hand, were hit harder. I don't have the final casualty report but the preliminary lists a dozen deaths and many more injuries. The biggest issue is the loss of equipment."

"All right." He ran a hand through his hair, his expression serious. "I believe it is clear that our so-called allies have turned against us. The fact we now have an officer in the Midlothian Space Navy in custody and he was captured onboard a Callusian warship leaves little doubt, at least in my mind. So how do we proceed?"

For a moment, no one spoke. Then Okafor looked at Collins. He nodded and she drew a deep breath.

"Without more detailed information, I see three courses of action available to us, sir," Okafor began. "We can proceed as though nothing has changed and we don't know the Midlothians are conspiring against us. We can hold the line where it is, building up our forces and consulting with our other allies to make sure none of them are involved. The last option is to fall back to the Home System and see how things shake out."

Harper leaned forward, elbows on knees, his expression serious. "Richard?"

"I agree with Helen. However, I would urge you not to make any decision until we've had a chance to debrief both Miranda and Ash. They have information we don't, information necessary to making an informed decision."

"Agreed, but I still want to hear the arguments for each of the options."

Instead of answering right away, Okafor got to her feet and moved to stare out the window, much as Harper had earlier. She didn't speak until she turned back to the room a few moments later.

"The first option would be the best in many ways but it will also be the most difficult, if not impossible, to pull off. If we could keep Midlothian in the dark, we can start feeding them false information. That, in turn, can help us pinpoint exactly where the leaks are happening. However, doing so will also make it difficult to continue our investigation without raising their suspicion. It would mean keeping them out of certain briefings they would normally have been included in. Then there is the possibility of them learning we have Hughes in custody. It could all blow up in our faces."

"Agreed, although I wouldn't mind stringing them along for a bit longer."

"None of us would, Mr. President," Collins said. "As for the second option Helen laid out, it and the third option carry much the same dangers. While they both allow us to build up our numbers, it also lets the Callusians continue unchecked. Such an approach could also turn our remaining allies against us. Worse, it would play into Midlothian's hands. We would come across as weak and tentative, just as we did during the last war. Our biggest advantage this time, at least as far as our allies are concerned, is they know you will keep your word about doing everything possible to defeat the Callusians once and for all."

"I note neither of you recommend confronting the Midlothian

ambassador with what we know and sending a message to Midlothian through him that we will not put up with their treachery."

"It very well may come to that, sir," Okafor said. "But, for the moment, we don't have enough information. We may not have it even after Second Fleet arrives and Fleet Intel has had the opportunity to interrogate Hughes."

"What information?"

"We still don't know if the Midlothian government is officially behind this treachery or if there is someone else behind it. Are we ready to declare war against an ally?"

Harper didn't answer right away. Instead, he stared into the fireplace, his expression thoughtful. "All right. Until we have a chance to debrief Miranda and Ashlyn, we will continue with our plan of battle as it's currently laid out. I don't want any discussion or communication about what Second Fleet discovered until I give the go-ahead. Understood?"

"Understood," they replied.

Harper sat up and shook his head. He had not been happy when he learned Second Fleet had delayed its transit to the Drakkana System. It hadn't made sense to him for the fleet to stay in-system while it waited for the two Devil Dog companies to meet up with it. Now he saw that delay as providential. If Second Fleet hadn't been waiting on the outer edges of the system, who knew how badly things could have gone for Fuercon. He still had a hard time wrapping his head around the fact the Callusians had actually sent a taskforce into the system.

"There is another factor to add to the equation before I make a final decision about how to react to this betrayal," Harper continued. "I received confirmation just before your arrival that Martyn Baudin was found dead earlier today. The investigators said there is no doubt he was murdered. This was the second murder associated with the Midlothian embassy in the last few weeks. The first was Kael Paulus. Paulus was found in an alley. He had been stabbed. Blood found at the scene belonged to one Evan Moreau."

"Moreau?" Okafor demanded. "You're sure?"

"I am and I take it you know the name, Helen."

"I do, sir. It has been linked with the conspiracy against Ashlyn Shaw."

"And the circle grows ever larger – or perhaps smaller," the President mused. "The investigation also revealed evidence of a third person there and it appeared that after Paulus was killed, Moreau and the other party fought. Blood was found near the opening of the alley that also belonged to Moreau."

"The two deaths can't be a coincidence." Collins' expression turned thoughtful.

"Agreed, Richard, especially since Baudin is not unfamiliar to the Intel people. He is Alexander Watchman's right hand and where he goes, bodies either show up or people disappear."

For several long moments, no one spoke. Then Okafor blew out a breath. Harper understood. He had known about the connection between the murders and the Midlothian embassy for some time. But knowing about Moreau's connection with the conspiracy against Shaw added another dimension to everything. How many plots were they going to uncover before this was over?

"I think that is at the least preliminary confirmation that the Midlothians have been working against Fuercon for some time now." He climbed to his feet and began to pace. "I want to meet with Miranda and Ashlyn as soon as they are on-planet. Brigadier General Shaw and Secretary Klingsbury, as well as Colonel Santiago, will be included in the meeting."

"Aye, sir," Collins and Okafor answered as they, too, stood.

"Richard, I'm relying on you to make sure the system is secure."

"I understand, sir. I've already ordered my division COs to increase patrols."

"Helen, I want you to re-evaluate how your Marines are being used and where we have them stationed. I want the system, and especially Fuercon, protected."

"Understood, Mr. President."

His comm beeped softly. "My apologies, but I have a meeting with the Secretary of Education in a few minutes."

As they left, he wondered if they knew more than they had told him. It wouldn't surprise him if they did. They wouldn't talk to him about something if they felt they needed more confirmation of the information or if they thought he needed to have plausible deniability.

And that was what made them not only excellent officers but two of his most trusted advisors. Hopefully, between them and a few others, Fuercon would not only weather the war but prevail.

———

WATCHMAN READ the report a second time and then a third. With each time, his anger grew. How had it gone so wrong so quickly?

Stupid question. The answer was simple: Dorescu. He, like so many of his kind, cared for nothing but killing the enemy. It didn't matter if they most or all of their own people died in the process. The Callusians had a warped sense of honor and believed nothing was more glorious than to die in battle.

From the beginning, from that first meeting when working with the Callusians had been brought up, he had been against it. Playing Devil's Advocate, he had warned the others that no good could come from trusting the Callusians. They had ignored him. Greed drove them, blinding them to the potential disaster that lay ahead.

Now it looked like his predictions might be coming true.

But it hadn't happened yet. All he knew for sure was that the Fuerconese had managed to intercept Dorescu's taskforce and defeat it. What worried him was the lack of information coming from Fuercon. In the past, the media would have been alive with the news. So far, there had been no mention of it. Nor had there been any mention about when, or if, Second Fleet was returning to Fuercon.

Worse, there had been no word from Fuercon itself to confirm the report. Under the terms of too many treaties to count, they should have notified Midlothian and their other allies to share information about the encounter. Instead of information there had been silence and he had no way to find out why.

That was another source of concern. Baudin's last report had relayed news of the death of Kael Paulus. What the report had not included was information about Moreau. Worse, Baudin had not made contact since then. He hadn't known why until that morning when he received word from the embassy on Fuercon that Baudin had been killed. No, there were no suspects. The capital police were investigating but had no leads. Their working theory was Baudin had been a tourist who happened to find himself in the wrong place at the wrong time and paid the ultimate price.

Watchman knew better. Somehow, Moreau had discovered the reason Baudin was on Fuercon. She had killed him. Of that, Watchman had no doubt. That was bad enough. Worse, if Moreau thought he had written her off, she became more than a loose end. She became a loose cannon and might decide to come after him.

Damn the gods, he hated loose ends. There was only one way to protect himself until he could deal with Moreau, something he now looked forward to doing himself. Like it or not, he needed to shut down all operations on Fuercon except for those run out of the embassy, at least for the near future.

In the meantime, he needed to find an operative he could trust and who would not be known to Moreau to locate the woman. Nothing more, just locate her. Once they had, he would act. She wasn't his first operative to outlive her usefulness, nor would she be the last. He had recognized the attempts in her reports to cover her ass and to put the blame for anything that went wrong on others. Now she had left a string of dead bodies that could all too easily be tied back to her and, in turn, to him. She had signed her own death warrant. All he had to do was make sure she died in such a way that it never came back on him.

Until then, there was no shame in doing a strategic withdrawal to reconsider battle plans. Let the others continue their disastrous relationship with the Callusians. They might even get lucky. If they did, he had more than enough dirt on them to prevent them from moving against him. It would only be a matter of time before they either fell into the fold or suffered some tragic accident.

No one got the better of Alexander Watchman and he had no intention of letting that change.

"Sir, your aircar is here. You are due at the theater in half an hour," his secretary said over the comm.

"Thank you, Sylva. Tell the drive I will be there shortly."

He checked his appearance in the mirror and smiled. The world might be crumbling around him, at least metaphorically speaking, but he would not let that stop him. He knew what real power was and when to use it. That time wasn't there – yet. When it came, no one would be safe.

———

THE MOMENT the door closed behind her, Evan Moreau leaned against it wearily and closed her eyes. Never before had she been so exhausted. She stayed on the move, changing her appearance as well as where she stayed. No two nights were spent in the same location.

Damn her luck!

And damn Alexander Watchman and Ashlyn Shaw and everyone else who stood in her way.

Pushing away from the door, she reached up and began stripping off her clothes. As she did, she kicked them away in distaste. She would kill for a designer suit and shoes. Instead, she wore off the rack work clothes. They helped her blend in instead of stand out. They fit the cheap rooms she had been renting. God, what she would give to go back to the life she had known just a month before.

The day would come when she could return to it. All she had to do was play it smart and keep her eyes open. Completing the job for Watchman – and killing Shaw – would take the heat off. Watchman might never again trust her to work for him, but he would leave her alone.

"Just keep you head and follow the plan," she said softly as she moved into the small bathroom. "It will be over soon enough."

That didn't make waiting any easier.

Padding across the thin carpet of the bedroom a few minutes later, Moreau wondered if the authorities had tied Paulus' murder to that of Baudin. Did they suspect the level of treachery where their Midlothian "allies' were concerned? It didn't matter if they knew or not. By the time the Midlothians moved against Fuercon, she planned to be far away.

As she slipped into a silken robe that cost more than most people made in a month, her one luxury in this latest hellhole, Moreau smiled as she thought of Baudin's death. She had taken her time with him, needing to make him pay for hurting her. The drugs she'd paid the bartender to slip into his drink had worked as expected. Unable to resist her "in" they go for a walk, he had followed her out of the bar. As she had him take her to his waiting aircar, she had laughed to see the fight in his eyes, a fight that could not escape his mind. Once at the aircar, she had him buckle into the passenger seat and she had taken them to a park near the downtown district, knowing it would be closed and she would have plenty of time to play with him.

Everything would work out. She would make sure of it.

24

"Everyone is here, Mister President."

Derek Harper nodded without turning. How long he had stood before her office window, staring unseeing into the distance, he couldn't say. But it hadn't been long enough – or maybe it had been too long – to erase the trouble that lay ahead. Trouble Fuercon hadn't looked for and certainly hadn't asked for or wanted. But there it lay, ready to destroy all Harper held dear if he wasn't up to the task of dealing with it.

Closing his eyes, he drew a deep, calming breath. This wasn't the time to give in to emotion or to engage in "what if's." Time for that would come later. Now duty called and he couldn't turn away from it, no matter how much he might want to.

With a decisive nod, he turned from the window and moved across the office toward the door. As he passed his desk, his right hand closed over the small, black jeweler's box. Almost absently, he dropped it into his jacket pocket. Then he continued on his way down the path he had chosen but had never expected to take this particular turn.

In the four weeks since the first word of the Callusian taskforce's entry into Fuerconese space, Harper and his closest advisors had worked almost non-stop in an effort to determine how deep the cancer of Midlothian's betrayal ran. He had no idea how many hours intelligence officers had spent interrogating not only Commander Hughes but the Callusian prisoners of war. Despite the information they have offered, as well as that retrieved from the databanks of the captured Callusian ships, there were still questions about how deep the conspiracy ran.

Now, waiting just down the hall, were his closest advisors. They were to meet briefly before he addressed the joint Houses of Congress. He was well aware of what most everyone expected of the session. They would get it and more, much more. He prayed they were ready to face the consequences because there was no alternative acceptable to the action he was about to take.

Five men and women quickly climbed to their feet as he entered the library. Three, resplendent in Mess Dress uniforms, snapped to attention. The others unconsciously came to a modified form of attention, betraying their own military backgrounds. The President quickly put all but two at their ease.

As he approached Miranda Tremayne, the woman watched him closely. Her blue eyes reflected her curiosity even though nothing else betrayed her thoughts. Smiling slightly in approval, the President paused before her. Without a word, he extended his hand to Linden Klingsbury. Her Secretary of Defense placed an old-fashioned leather portfolio in his hand and then stepped back.

"We'll do this a bit more formally shortly," the President began, a hint of a smile playing at his lips. "With the reality of declaring war against a supposed ally, it has been decided that the Navy needs a slight realignment. Effective immediately, you will be the new commanding officer of First Fleet, designated as Home Fleet, Admiral Tremayne. Admiral Collins will assume command of Second Fleet. Don't worry that he will see this as a demotion. He didn't and, when I told him what sort of new toys he would get to play with, he asked me to tell you he was more than glad to turn the defense of the Home System over to you."

As he spoke, he pressed the 'folio into Tremayne's hand. Inside was a hard copy of her new orders. She tucked the leather 'folio under her left arm and braced to attention once more. With a smile, Harper motioned for her to step back.

Then he turned his attention to Ashlyn Shaw who looked back at him in undisguised suspicion.

"As for you, Ash, you've done everything was asked and more," the President continued. "Despite the way the previous Administration turned its back on you and your people, you put duty ahead of vengeance. You have lived up to everything a Marine, much less a Devil Dog, should be." He stopped and grinned, enjoying himself. "You even proved that a Marine is more than capable of commanding a ship larger than an attack shuttle in battle. I hope you realize there are some in FleetCom considering changing things to allow permanent assignment of Marines as ship XOs and COs. I do believe there's been some discussion of using you as the test subject."

She didn't say anything. She didn't need to when her expression said it all. He laughed for a moment before deciding to let her off the hook.

"Don't worry. Not only have I told them I wouldn't allow them to take you away from the Devil Dogs but General Okafor said she would turn the Devil Dogs lose on anyone who tried to take you from them.

"As much as I wanted to promote you to full bird colonel, General Okafor convinced me that you aren't ready to accept another promotion. All that means is you are at the top of the promotions list for the next round of reviews So I'll have to settle with pinning another medal on you and in telling you that you have the thanks of everyone in the System for your actions onboard the *Nagato*.

"Now," he continued seriously. "For the moment, the Devil Dogs will be assigned to the Home System. This is a temporary assignment until your LAC elements are back up to full strength and your people have had a chance to heal up from their injuries. Once they have, you have one assignment. Take the battle to the enemy and don't stop until the war is won and won decisively. Destroy the Callusians, Ashlyn, and then we will deal with the Midlothians."

"Aye, sir." She crisply saluted, her expression serious but her eyes gleaming with the hunt.

"Now, in less than an hour, I will be addressing Congress. I will inform them of the evidence against Midlothian and asking them vote to negate all treaties we have with them. I will then close all transit routes to Midlothian traffic unless the vessel has been boarded and inspected by our people. Secretary Klingsbury will issue a full briefing packet come morning."

Harper paused, looking each of his guests in the eye. Almost two years ago to the day, he had agreed to run for office. He had pledged then to defeat the Callusians. Little had he known it would turn into a war with Midlothian.

"I want each of you to be with me as I address Congress. Let the members of both Houses, as well as the public, see we mean business," he continued and they each nodded in understanding and agreement. "We had best be on our way."

With that, he led them out of the library. No one seeing the small procession could doubt their determination. But would it be enough to rally their allies the coming weeks, months, perhaps even years, as this new battle played out against Midlothian and their Callusian allies?

Dear God, please give us the strength to see this through, Harper prayed as they stepped into the lift that would carry them to the basement garage and the aircar waiting to whisk them to the Capital and a destiny none of them had ever wanted.

AUTHOR'S NOTE

When I started *Vengeance from Ashes*, the first book in the *Honor and Duty* series, I had envisioned the series consisting of three books. By the time I got to the second book, *Duty from Ashes*, I realized Ashlyn Shaw's story arc could not be finished in just three books. Well, it could but the last book would turn out to be 200,000 words and probably much more. That doesn't seem like much in an e-book but in print it could be used as part of your weight training.

Honor from Ashes represents the middle of the current story arc. But don't worry. Once the arc is finished there will be more stories in the *Honor and Duty* universe. I love these characters too much to say goodbye to them yet